THE UNFINISHED Man

THE UNFINISHED Man

Jim Wayne

Fleur-de-Lis Press
Louisville, Kentucky

Cover art: Michelangelo Buonarroti, Studies for the Libyan Sibyl, 1508–1512,
    © The Metropolitan Museum of Art
Book design by Jonathan Weinert

Printed in the United States of America
First Edition

Library of Congress Cataloging-in-Publication Data
Wayne, Jim
The Unfinished Man.
I. Title
Library of Congress Control Number: 2016934534

ISBN 10: 0-9960120-0-1
ISBN 13: 978-0-9960120-03

Fleur-de-Lis Press of *The Louisville Review*
Spalding University
851 S. Fourth Street
Louisville, KY 40203
502.873.4398
louisvillereview@spalding.edu
www.louisvillereview.org

For all the victims

What matter if I live it all once more?
Endure that toil of growing up;
The ignominy of boyhood; the distress
Of boyhood changing into man;
The unfinished man and his pain
Brought face to face with his own clumsiness . . .

William Butler Yeats
"A Dialogue of Self and Soul"

CHAPTER 1

FATHER JUSTIN MATHIAS ZAPP, at forty-six, did not want his small world disturbed. Years before, with bricks they fired themselves and limestone they quarried across the creek, German and Irish immigrants had built St. Peter's Hill church, rectory, and school. Between the creek and the parish buildings, which sat atop the highest knob in the county, lay the lush farmland that fed the parishioners and, through their tithing, Justin.

By Canon Law of the Catholic Church, Justin held complete command of the complex of sturdy structures and the management concerns in his parish—not that he longed for power or domination over anyone. All he wanted was for his people to leave him to his books, scholarly writing, and quiet. He, in turn, would make sure he administered the sacraments so each one could attain salvation.

It was shortly before noon on a hot day in June 1958, and Justin was so absorbed in the latest Yves Moinet article in the journal *Theological Studies* that he failed to hear the doorbell. Wearing rimless reading glasses, he sat hunched over his desk, surrounded by four walls of perfectly organized books and periodicals. In the corner a small fan tried to stir the thick humid air in the pastor's office with a mild hum.

Mrs. Bernice Mayer, the rotund rectory housekeeper, escorted the guest to Justin's door.

"Top of the morning!" Monsignor Mark O'Connell was nearly six feet tall and possessed hierarchical dignity in his gait and voice. The sunlight streaming through the office window intensified the whiteness of his Vitalis-oiled hair, combed to precision and trimmed close to his pink neck and ears. His head appeared perfectly proportioned to his height and frame. His metal-frame glasses failed to filter the deep blue of what looked like caring eyes. In the monsignor's presence, Justin sensed the weight of clerical power.

"Here again to nudge me to some important event, monsignor?" To maintain distance, Justin was careful never to address his deanery superior by his first name.

"Yes, ever the solicitous pastor to my pastors. I'm on my way north for a closing of Forty Hours tonight and thought you might join me for lunch in town." His voice held a mild starchiness. Justin noticed the monsignor stood several feet from the desk, perhaps to avoid glancing at the reading material that occupied the younger priest. His superior's ruddy cheeks gave hint of the joy he found in good wine.

"A rain check?"

"The rain check of my last invitation was never used. And the one before that. I'm beginning to think you may not be interested." The over-sweet smell of his aftershave permeated the room and mixed with the aromas of bacon frying and coffee brewing in the kitchen.

"Oh, I don't mean to be ignoring your invitations—I mean—I guess I just prefer to eat lunch here at the rectory."

The senior priest moved to a straight back chair across from the large, oak work desk. His tailored coal black suit set off the bleached Roman collar, tight around his wide neck. "Is that an invitation?" Deftly the monsignor maneuvered closer to the longer meeting he wanted.

Justin felt cornered.

"No . . . I mean, yes, sure, I think we can arrange that," he said. He leaned back in his chair. His armpits were damp against the pale blue buttoned shirt with an open collar.

"Sounds delightful," the monsignor said.

With the push of the intercom button, Mrs. Mayer was directed to set two places at the dining room table. Justin turned from the papers and open volumes on his desk and, with a forced smile, suggested they proceed to the dining room. The best Justin could hope for now was to endure this necessary ritual, diplomatically reject him again, and send him north.

Justin led the way across the hall and flipped on the overhead chandelier in the large room with ornate white crown molding and ivy and white peony wallpaper. The simple mission-style oak furniture had been bought by one of his predecessors a half century before and was in showroom condition; Justin ate his meals alone at the kitchen table. Eucalyptus stems, which Mrs. Mayer had put in a tall vase on the polished, long table, gave a welcoming smell. Seated across from one another at one end, the priests prepared for the confrontation Justin had wanted to avoid.

"Registration for the conference is available now." Without hesitation Mark went straight to the real purpose of his visit. For weeks he had been urging Justin to attend the North American Liturgical Conference in Cincinnati in August. The annual meeting had never been held this close to southern Indiana, so it was a rare opportunity to hear some of the most respected scholars in the worldwide liturgical reform movement. Justin noticed how baby smooth his superior's face appeared and wondered if he'd ever done physical labor.

"I suspect you know more about the topics than the experts lecturing, but I think it'll do you some good." For the last dozen years the mon-signor had relied on Justin to draft deanery pastoral statements because he was an astute observer of theological trends. Justin had been assigned advanced studies at Catholic University in Washington after his ordination and had since published dozens of articles, primarily on the emerging topic of Jewish-Catholic relations, in prestigious journals.

Mrs. Mayer set before each priest a pale yellow Melmac plate with a bacon, lettuce, and tomato sandwich, sliced with precision into four wedges.

"These are the first tomatoes of the year," she said. "Elmer starts them from seeds in January in milk cartons he saves from the school cafeteria."

"My thanks to your green-thumbed husband," the monsignor said. "What a special treat."

The housekeeper beamed.

Justin lowered his eyes to try to let his guest know that conversation must pause when Ms. Mayer was within earshot. How much of his life she spread about the countryside he never knew. Once she left the room, Justin attempted to explain his position.

"I really prefer to tend to my duties here." Smiling, Justin focused on the sandwich.

"What duties? This is the smallest parish in the archdiocese." Mark was crisp and forceful in between bites. "You spend your life as a hermit on this knob. Sure, you write some heady articles for journals, but you could make time for this conference if you really wanted to." Then, shifting to an engaging tone, he said, "Besides, I'd like to introduce you to some influential bishops and abbots to let them know what a scholar I have among my priests."

Mrs. Mayer returned to discreetly serve coffee; she pretended to ignore the monsignor's words. Her pink cotton dress, covered with a flower-patterned apron, had been starched and pressed as smooth and clean as the altar linens she hand laundered every Monday morning. Momentarily forgetting her presence, Justin responded again with his mild counterproposal. "With due respect, I'm sure your meeting in Cincinnati will be informative and you'll see many of your old friends, but I feel duty bound to tend to the responsibilities here."

In fact the parish pretty much ran itself with three Benedictine sisters, who managed the small school; Mr. Mayer, the sexton, who tended to the buildings and grave digging; and Jimmy Schultz, who ran the feed mill in town and oversaw the financial and business decisions.

With just under a hundred undemanding families, most faithful in their Sunday obligation and tithing, the parish was an ideal place for scholarly, introverted Justin to focus on his passion for theology.

"Let me put it to you this way. As your local superior, I want you to attend this conference. And I want you to give the priests of the deanery a full report at the priests' meeting in September."

Mrs. Mayer returned to the kitchen.

"Are you requiring me to attend?"

"Yes." Crossing his arms, the monsignor sat back and beamed.

"Very well. I'll send the registration in today."

From the vestibule in the church next to the rectory, Mr. Mayer rang the steeple's lone bell to announce the Angelus. The two priests paused from lunch as the older one began the universal noon prayer of the church, "The angel of the Lord declared unto Mary. . . ."

Throughout the intercessions, Justin's thoughts wandered. He worried how much Mrs. Mayer had heard and who would soon know of the tension between Justin and the monsignor. By the time the tolling and prayer ended, he was sure obedience to his superior would lead to the usual intense physical disruptions.

CHAPTER 2

A T THREE THE FOLLOWING morning Justin sat at the desk in his upstairs bedroom, reading the Latin words of the first hour of Matins from his worn, leather-covered breviary. The Divine Office is a worldwide ritual of the church, a daily requirement of every priest, consisting of psalms and readings parceled into eight group-ings, recited at various periods from dawn until dark. His blurry mind tried to concentrate on the words before him, especially Psalm 50, which he translated, "God's word to the wicked man is this: what right have you to recite my laws and make so free with the words of my covenant, you who hate correction and turn your back when I am speaking?" His index finger fanned the upper right corners of the thin pages, worn with years of use.

Justin closed his eyes and thought how he hated correction from the monsignor, who inexorably wanted to shoe horn him into roles that never fit. It was a constant battle to maintain the space Jus-tin needed to study and write in solitude. Mark would gladly have Justin flitting about the deanery and archdiocese to meetings and giving lectures rather than doing the required intense research to make even a small mark in theological circles. Repeatedly Justin turned his back on his superior's invitations. And each time Justin said no, guilt rushed over him. How could he be so consistently self-righteous and proud? He'd ask forgiveness. He'd go to confession in town the next day.

He looked up at the wooden-framed picture of the Sacred Heart hanging above his single bed, which was outfitted with a pale green cotton spread and puffy down pillow. His grandparents had brought the picture from Germany in 1836. The rest of his bedroom was modestly furnished with a simple veneered dresser, the small desk, and wooden chair, as well as a lounge chair upholstered in heavy navy fabric. Above the desk, on the cream-colored wall next to a two-foot crucifix, was an equal-sized black and white photo in an oval metal frame. The picture was taken on his first birthday on the pillared front porch of the weathered frame farmhouse several miles from the village of St. Boniface. His expressionless parents held a boy with a grin identical to Justin's on his good days.

The Trappist monks are up at this hour for Matins each morning, he thought to himself. He returned to whispering the psalms. Distracted, he thought how his insomnia, not a monastic schedule, occasioned his prayer at this darkest hour of night, the period when Satan was supposed to be at full strength. Since retiring at ten-thirty, he'd wrestled with the directive of Monsignor O'Connell to attend a conference that he knew would be filled with confident clergy, many younger than he, who were on ascending career escalators.

He thought, too, of the man ordering him to the meeting, to whom he promised obedience as the representative of the archbishop and God. Justin suspected Mark wanted Justin to be what he felt he would never be: one of those easy, holy, self-assured priests who savored the status of the Roman collar and who would cooperate in making the monsignor stand out among his peers for having a noted scholar within his army of submissive clerics.

After he finished Matins, he moved to the overstuffed chair at his open window, staring at a full June moon now west of mid sky. The vastness of the universe had always captured his imagination, enabling him to lose himself momentarily in the transcendent. Where does it begin? Where does it end? With the Soviet Union's launching last month of its third Sputnik and America's three satellites now rotating earth, Justin realized he was living in a period of history when humans believed any goal could be achieved. Yet, within his personal space, the opposite was true. As much as he savored time alone with his books and abstract thoughts and musings on God, he sensed he would forever be locked within the borders of his own flawed psyche. No prayer—and he was a man of deep piety—seemed strong enough to muster the grace he needed to enjoy life the way others seemed to do.

The Cincinnati conference would require going through the motions of gracious etiquette with his peers and small talk about church matters. But for Mark O'Connell to think such a gathering would break open Justin's personal prison showed how little his superior understood Justin. In fact, with time, his isolation had grown. His anxious reaction on this night made him realize how much harder it was to mingle with his peers than it had been just a few years before.

By four-thirty he'd fallen asleep in his pajamas, robe, and slippers next to the window as the coolness of the June night washed over him. The Mayers' rooster jarred him awake an hour and a half later, marking the start of another long summer day. He reached for his breviary, this time turning to Lauds and Prime. He praised the coming of this day and its Creator—a Creator capable of liberating the Hebrew people from the grip of Pharaoh but unable to free Justin from himself. He watched the morning light, beyond the rectory, in the wide meadow, create long shadows from the nearby stand of locust trees, flush with creamy, dangling blossoms. He wondered how he was able to master intricate arguments in scholarly journals yet fail to master his own sleep patterns and relieve the tightened stomach and pulsing pain across his brow whenever distress possessed him.

The next six weeks were Justin's purgatory. He lost nearly twenty pounds and felt as if he had aged nearly as many years. His body was as bound in knots as his feelings and thoughts. He tried to focus on his research and writing, but the energy for the tasks seemed lost, dissipated, or, perhaps, spent on the worry and fear of being forced into a formal gathering of his peers that he wanted with all his being to shun.

Yet, from the day of the lunch with the monsignor to the departure for Cincinnati, Justin was faithful to daily office and mass, Saturday confessions, two weddings that had been scheduled months before, and a funeral for a sixteen-year-old boy killed as his grandfather's tractor flipped when he drove it up a steep hill. In a manner that had gained Justin the reputation among his parishioners as being holy, he performed his priestly duties with solemnity and focus and without fanfare or drama. Despite his depth of theological knowledge, his sermons were refreshingly simple and appropriate for the farmers, workers, homemakers, and young Catholics of St. Peter's Hill. Going from the rectory to the sanctuary and back, like a man on a mission to himself, he didn't socialize before or after church services. He received civil respect and appreciation from the souls under his care, who had little idea of his growing reputation in the world of scholars, or, more significantly, his downhill emotional and physical toboggan ride.

On the August morning Monsignor Mark O'Connell arrived to take Justin to Cincinnati, Justin correctly anticipated the monsignor would notice Justin's weight loss since it was the first time he had seen Justin in two months.

"Jesus, Mary, and Joseph! What's happened? You look like death warmed over!" The monsignor stood with a blank stare next to the open trunk of his car, a heavy, chrome-adorned 1955 Oldsmobile 88.

"I'm fine. Just lost a few pounds, that's all," Justin said.

He wrestled his suitcase out the front door and down the rectory's four front steps. If he looked thin to Mark, Justin suspected he might embarrass his dean at the conference because, for all Justin knew, he was going to Cincinnati primarily as the monsignor's enhancing prop. But as much as Justin might have wished, his superior gave no hint of cancelling Justin's participation in the meeting out of embarrassment. They loaded the suitcase in the wide trunk, flanked by rocket shaped tail lights, and left for Cincinnati.

Driving over and around hills and curves on U.S. 50 toward the Queen City, the monsignor held his eyes on the road and asked, "When was the last time you saw your doctor?"

"I'm fine. Really. I typically loose a little weight in the summer months and pick them up again in the winter."

Justin stared out the side window at rolling pastures with grazing Holsteins standing like sculptures, their heads lost in thick clover and fescue. Between these fields were deep forests, dense with undergrowth of blossoming honeysuckle and sumac beginning its late summer transition to brazen reds. Whiffs of the honeysuckle reminded Justin of life on his family's farm where the wild blooming vine tangled the perimeters of the creek bed. On one late summer day a very young Justin and his father hunted crawdads in the clear water where the sweet smell of the gentle cream and yellow flowers filled the air at dusk.

For the trip, Mark wore a short-sleeved, pressed white cotton dress shirt with an open collar. Even before leaving St. Peter's Hill, perspiration seeped under his arms and across his back. The side window vents blew in not just rural smells of dried grasses and manure, but also August's heat. As they traveled through tasseled fields of corn and ripening soybeans, the landscape changed along the two lane road: fewer hills, the highway straight. Heavy humidity compounded their discomfort; the air was so thick with moisture their chests seemed compressed and weighted down, as if sacks of grain sat on their lungs. Justin noticed a growing wind ruffle the leaves of the crops and silver maples. He turned to see through the rear window dark clouds, moving from the west, promising relief with a heavy shower before they reached Cincinnati.

With patience the older priest asked again, "And when did you last see your doctor for a physical?"

"It's been awhile."

He looked over at Mark who cleared his throat and turned his eyes from the road long enough to give a paternal wink to Justin. He spiced authority with charm.

"Am I sensing another ecclesiastical requirement about to be imposed on this country pastor?"

Justin smiled to himself then turned again to glance out the back at a black Monon Railroad diesel engine passing along the tracks they had just crossed. It pulled a long line of box cars; its roar and whistle rose, then faded.

"The requirement is in writing by an even higher authority."

"What?" Justin looked again at the monsignor.

"St. Paul, I am sure you remember, tells us our bodies are temples of the Holy Ghost. I don't think God wants his temple to crumble from neglect." Both hands on the wheel, he focused on the gray highway while he lectured the younger priest.

"I understand. I'll make an appointment after the conference."

Monsignor O'Connell grinned. Justin noticed the pastures, cattle, and forests had diminished; the land was flat and filled with more growing grains. Tall, deep-green elms, poplars, oaks, and sycamores bordered the manicured fields. The tree leaves' underbellies turned upward, like Can-Can girls' skirts, a sure sign of a pending, welcome rain.

Within minutes, in a heavy downpour, Justin asked to stop at a Texaco station to relieve himself. The sky had darkened to a deep gray; the winds bent limbs and leaves and threatened the Burma Shave signs along a fence row. Like a camera's flash, lightning lit up the broad horizon as thunder interrupted the priests' conversation. Before arriving at St. Paul's Seminary that evening, the monsignor had pulled into four gas stations for Justin's relief: two Texaco, one Gulf, and one Sinclair. The storm brought with it cooler air; cloudless, piercing blue skies at twilight; and calm.

CHAPTER 3

L IKE MOST AMERICAN CATHOLIC seminaries in the mid-twentieth
century, St. Paul's was a set of imposing structures on a properly
landscaped campus, closed to the surrounding world. The original building was constructed, during the economically prosperous
1920s, of yellow brick and limestone in a Romanesque style. To
accommodate the anticipated number of seminarians with the post-
World War II surge in births, the diocesan-run institution under-
went an expansion so it could house a thousand students. Along
the small incline to the main building, mature linden trees lined
the long drive, creating a tunneled entry way into an isolated milieu
for the training of America's priests. The conference here in August
1958 promised a forum for major thinkers versed in the enhance-
ment of the universal rituals of the church—rituals designed to lift
the souls of the faithful to the transcendent.

Exclusive invitations had gone out to clergy, although more than
a hundred laymen and religious sisters and brothers, as if pioneers of
a church yet to be, were on hand as well. The sight of priests and seminarians in their black flowing cassocks and birettas and the sisters
in their stiff linen headwear and ankle-length dark dresses with dan-

gling rosaries at their sides, gave evidence of the uniquely Catholic enclave Justin and his superior entered as they passed the gatehouse.

"May I help you, monsignor?" young Tom Gentry said. He stood next to Monsignor Mark O'Connell's black-and-white luxury car in the parking area near the covered entrance to Murphy Hall wearing a freshly ironed cassock and collar. One of two dozen seminarians assigned to assist participants, he carried himself like the accomplished athlete he was.

"Thomas! What a surprise! I am glad you're able to attend the conference."

Justin correctly surmised Mark recognized the young man as one of his deanery's seminarians who was in his diaconate year, the last year, at Presentation Seminary in Indiana. On track to be ordained the following May at age twenty-six, he easily pushed the weighty luggage in a cart the short distance across the parking lot to the foyer. The two priests walked behind him.

Once settled into his Spartan room, with a sink, plain wooden desk, and chair, Justin stretched out on the single bed to calm his throbbing head and tense stomach. After thirty minutes, with no easing of pain, he joined his traveling companion at the entrance to the massive reception hall on the first floor, with its tall arched ceilings, lined with ornately-framed, life-size portraits of Cincinnati's bishops and archbishops over the last century. The room smelled of floor wax and fresh brewed coffee.

As the monsignor greeted Justin, Justin rushed to excuse himself. From his first year in the seminary Justin learned to recognize his gastric upset, which, like his headaches, accompanied times of fret and social demand. On this first day of the conference for nearly 700 people, Justin feared the monsignor would abandon him in the social chaos in favor of a conversation with one of his superior's many influential acquaintances. But what distressed Justin even more was the idea that he'd fail to get to a men's room on time, thus embarrassing himself.

Upon re-entering the reception, Mark introduced Justin to an important abbot from Pennsylvania, describing Justin as, ". . . one of my most scholarly priests." Justin's forehead pounded, especially the right side.

Such flattery, which the monsignor used frequently, jarred Justin. He felt it enhanced the monsignor's image in church circles more than it accurately described Justin's scholarship.

The pleasantries continued as Justin followed Mark through the maze of clergy who sipped whiskey, gulped bottles of beer, or nursed steaming mugs of coffee. Most smoked cigarettes, pipes, or cigars. Some munched nuts and small sandwiches, which dozens of seminarians, in their roles as aproned waiters, served. The alcohol's smell washed over Justin, causing him to recoil in disgust. The socially bubbling scene, in contrast, seemed to energize his superior. The monsignor was a polished church glad-hander. Jovial and confident, Justin thought, as he shadowed his superior with each step. An esteemed clergyman on the move, the older priest was complimentary with everyone. Could Justin ever master such behavior even if he exorcised his personal demons? But more importantly, did he even want to?

At exactly six-thirty the casual and serious conversations were interrupted with a deafening electric bell, calling the guests to the nearby refectory. Every priest and nun in the room was familiar with the mores of seminaries and convents, where days are divided by abrasive bells ending one event and announcing another, from the morning wake up to the great silence of night. The lay participants, on the other hand, stayed alert for clues to their next moves in this nearly foreign culture. Then, like a pack of hungry black lemmings, the clergy and nuns shuffled toward the refectory; the laypeople followed. Justin hoped he wouldn't stand out if he detoured to the men's room, should the urge require it. The urge never came.

With ten other priests, he and the monsignor sat at a long table.

The walls of the dining room were pale yellow, the windows curtain-less. At one end stood the Virgin Mary in life-size plaster on an ornately carved wooden pedestal. With a lowered, tilted head and open hands at her waist, she appeared to be offering help as needed. At the other end of the room, a six-by-eight-foot framed print of DaVinci's "Last Supper" graced the wall. White tablecloths and napkins, as well as late summer bouquets of mixed-color zinnias, gave the refectory limited softness in this all male institution. A rotund seminarian served prepared plates of pot roast, potatoes, and green beans while another poured coffee. Justin watched the monsignor to determine his actions.

Breaking all conversations, the raspy voice of Carl Malter, the Archbishop of Cincinnati, blurted from speakers on the walls, "Let us pray." Everyone stood, chairs rudely screeching on the hard floor, and listened to the prelate.

"Before we begin eating, I have a sad announcement," the archbishop said. The room fell into complete silence.

"This afternoon we received word that Father Basil Epperman died in an auto accident in rural Iowa. Some of you may remember him as a respected teacher and spiritual director at Presentation Seminary some years ago."

Before the archbishop finished praising the priest and offering a prayer for his soul, Justin drowned him out with a prolonged scream. All heads turned from the archbishop to Justin, his body shaking. He collapsed on the floor, taking his supper plate with him.

The chaos that followed, with hundreds of the clerics and nuns shocked, curious and confused, demanded the immediate care of Justin.

∴

The concerned dean, dressed now in a much-wrinkled cassock, followed the Cadillac station wagon ambulance in his Olds to University Hospital's emergency room. While the attendants, dressed in whites, rushed the patient into an examination room, the monsignor, Justin later learned from O'Connell himself, met with the nursing staff. As he gave pertinent information about Justin, in an instant, as if pierced with an arrow, the monsignor realized the extent of Justin's isolation. When asked to give the names of immediate family members, the monsignor paused and said, "He has no family."

CHAPTER 4

JUSTIN ZAPP ONCE HAD a family. A small, sheltering family. After his father died when he was seven, the surviving women—his mother, grandmother, and great aunt—moved into the village of St. Boniface in a rural area within thirty-five miles of Presentation Seminary. The institution for the training of the clergy sat, like St. Boniface and the Zapp farm, isolated among the rolling hills and creek bottom grain fields that characterize Southern Indiana. Justin would enroll at Presentation six years later.

The women knew their seventeen hundred acre farm, which had been cultivated for decades by Justin's immigrant grandparents and his parents, had to be sold to provide for the diminished family. The 1918 auction of the land, barns, house, and machinery brought enough to provide for the four of them the rest of their lives. For the two oldest, this time was short. When, at age eight, he began the fourth grade at the parish grade school, his aunt and grandmother died, leaving him to be raised by his now financially secure mother.

"Have you ever thought about going to Presentation, Justin?" asked Father Schindler after mass one Sunday in 1922. A young eighth grader, Justin knew he'd been eyed by his pastor as priestly timber even before the frail man broached the issue. The pastor had called on him to serve as altar boy at masses on special feasts—Christmas, Easter, Pentecost—and at the funerals of several prominent parishioners. The kindly man was in his late sixties, though he looked much older. He made sure the nuns who taught the smart boy placed him on the honor roll during his seventh and eighth grade school years to boost his chances of admission to the seminary.

"My mother asks me the same question, Father. I don't know."

Indeed, years later, Justin realized his mother looked to sequester her son from the sins of the threatening world any way she could. Justin's father had been an ambitious man who inflicted repeated miseries with his infidelities and drunken spells that were endemic to many Klein County marriages. Despite the inconsistent kindnesses to Justin, the depressed drinker cast a dark shadow over the Zapp home that never lifted, even years after his death by stroke at the age of fifty-two in 1917. As if to defy such dark forces, Mildred Zapp determined to raise Justin by strict rules, regulating his playmates, radio programs, and books, and doing everything conceivable to shape her son to be the opposite of his father. To cope in this constricted world, the boy retreated into a limited sphere of controlled curiosity, safety, and callowness.

"Keep your soul pure for God," she told him one night before he climbed the stairs for bed. At twelve he understood he was to keep the commandments, including "Honor thy father (he had none) and mother." Years later he would understand that what was implied by the maternal admonition was control of sexual urges that erupted within him once he entered Presentation. Sins of the flesh were the most lethal in the mind of Mildred Zapp. From "Thou shall not commit adultery," the sixth commandment, a host of sins were extrapolated but never spoken. Justin graduated the eighth grade at thirteen from the tiny rural Catholic school with nothing but unanswered questions about sex.

For his mother, who bore him at the late age of thirty-nine, the thought of guiding her son through his passage into manhood must have terrified her. Sending him to the seminary after grade school seemed an ideal solution. There, without ever speaking it, perhaps she hoped his sexual stirrings could be controlled by strict rules, and Justin could be guided by spiritual men who would protect him from the threatening world in ways she could not.

By the time Justin was ordained in the archdiocesan cathedral in the spring of 1935, his mother had been dead two years, leaving him no family, but with a substantial inheritance. The frugal woman had kept her money safe from the bank collapses of the Depression years; Justin was independently wealthy.

∴

"Can you tell me what brought you here?" The petite woman had introduced herself as Miss Aaronheim, a social worker at the teaching hospital's psychiatric unit. At fifty-nine, known by her writings and lectures for in-depth understanding of psychoanalysis, her reputation was solid. She was a gifted teacher to the young residents as well as the best psychotherapist in the region.

"They tell me I collapsed in the refectory at St. Paul's. I don't know what happened." Justin's mind was in a fog from sedatives. He sat facing her on an upright cushioned chair with an end table next to him—Kleenex ready, if needed. He wore an open collar white dress shirt and black slacks

The office was open and uncluttered. She sat in an identical chair next to a small steel desk which was clear except for a phone, fountain pen, and thin leather-covered calendar. The curtains framing the tall hospital window next to Justin were light green and pulled back by tasseled gold ropes, letting in light from the lush courtyard one story below. The curtains, along with a large simply framed floral print on the light gray wall behind her, struggled to give gentleness to the institutional, cold room. There were no family photos or personal mementos to give clues about the slight woman's life outside this small space.

"Do you remember anything that preceded your collapse?" She sat with a legal pad on her lap shifting her eyes from Justin to the paper as she penciled notes on her new patient.

"Barely. I recall someone saying Father Basil had been killed." He squinted in curiosity, sizing her up.

"Anything else?"

"No."

Indeed, Justin's initial visit with Miss Aaronheim was difficult for both of them. She seemed frustrated in her attempts to piece together why he had such a strong emotional and physical response in the dining room surrounded by his peers. Unaware of what caused the scene two days before, he wanted to forget the entire event and return as soon as he could to St. Peter's Hill.

The staff had other plans. They assigned him to individual therapy with Miss Aaronheim three times a week. The first week produced little progress as he dismissed the need for his hospitalization. By their fourth session, on Monday of his second week in the hospital, she pursued her information with more directness.

"I am curious to know about your relationship with this Father Basil who died?" She was gentle in style and voice, but firm. The deep green leaves of a large maple in the courtyard looked limp as the late August heat gripped Cincinnati. An open window and oscillating floor fan, strategically placed in a corner, whirling as fast as it could, did little to cool the sultry room.

Justin tightened his fists when he heard the name of the dead priest and shut out his feelings like a scared turtle shuts out the world. He stared at her with contempt. She wore her short, graying hair in curls and dressed professionally in a modest, conservative, navy skirt and floral, short-sleeved blouse. Her makeup was conservative as well, with mild cheek blush, muted lipstick but no eye shadow or enhanced lashes. When she read in silence from her notes, she used the half-framed glasses that otherwise dangled from a silver string below her small breasts. A petite, jeweled, floral brooch graced her left collar. At a little above five feet tall, she seemed trim and healthy, both physically and mentally.

"What about him?"

"Did you know him?" She sat straight.

After a long pause he looked from his lap out the window at the maple's leaves, now slightly swaying and loosened. "Yes, I'd known him since I was thirteen." He did not want to remember.

"In what setting did you know him?" She mined for more.

"What does he have to do with anything?" Justin gripped the soft fabric of the armrests and looked, without blinking, into her eyes. His voice was firm, as if insisting the door to his private space stay locked.

She persisted. "I'm curious about him. Monsignor O'Connell reported to the psychiatrist that you collapsed at St. Paul's after the announcement was made of Father Basil's death in a car accident."

"I guess I wasn't feeling well," he snapped. "And I was weak and the news of his death made me . . . I . . . I . . . I really don't think this has anything to do with Father Basil. I was having intestinal issues and headaches and was not well when I came to the conference. I hadn't been sleeping much. I fainted. That's all. I wish you and the doctors would understand this and dismiss me. I'm fine."

"I realize you want to get back to your parish work, but I think our team would like to spend a little more time with you to make sure we're not missing something important." She was caring, like the woman who raised him, but unlike his mother, Miss Aaronheim's voice was strong and confident. A loud ambulance siren blurted through the window then stopped.

Justin closed his eyes. He wondered if he could trust her. His mother, simple as she was, loved him, and he learned trust from her. Was Miss Aaronheim worthy of similar trust?

"Will you let me explore with you some things about your life that may be burdens?" She leaned toward him.

"We all have our crosses." He turned his head again toward the window. A quick rain tapped on the open window and screen, leaving quarter size drops on the wide marble sill.

"Yes, we do. But we don't have to carry them alone."

CHAPTER 5

B Y THE THIRD WEEK at University Hospital, Justin remained circumspect with Miss Aaronheim. Early in the relationship she
established herself as an available confidante and guide, if Justin
chose to use her as such. But deep within him something strong
continued to restrain him. He was intent on just going through the
required rituals to comply with the medical staff and return to St.
Peter's Hill as soon as possible.

Having spent twelve years of his youth in a regulated institution
of the seminary, Justin adjusted to the expectations and routines of
the hospital better than most patients. He had a separate room and
bath and spent little time with the other men in the unit lounge. A
variety of ages and educational levels marked the group of patients
being treated with him. Ever cautious about closeness, Justin was
careful to avoid conversation about his personal life with anyone.

But with time he realized the expectations of the staff, especially Miss Aaronheim, were curiously different than anything he'd
ever encountered. His years in church institutions did not allow for
looking at life experiences through any lens but faith. If he felt troubled, prayer would lead him to an answer. The sacraments, espe-

cially Holy Communion and confession, would provide the graces to endure life's crosses. No priest ever asked about his private life, as if such inquiry would cross some invisible boundary established to protect the entire clerical structure handed down over the centuries. The single priest who had crossed a line with Justin did so with an evil heart.

Under Miss Aaronheim he was learning that psychiatry's intention was to rid him of suffering by exploring the root causes of his sadness and anxiety. Her warmth and care reminded him of vivid images from his childhood when his mother caressed him after he'd rushed to her bed during a thunderstorm or awoke from a nightmare. With an embrace, comforting whispers, and kiss atop his head, she would sit with him until he calmed. He knew he was safe and loved.

In the presence of Miss Aaronheim he felt a similar security and care. Yet he remained cautious about her intentions. Could a complete stranger care for his welfare in ways that he'd experienced with his own mother? And was she attempting to void his personal understanding of the Christian ideal of carrying one's cross by turning over decades-old traumas like scattered pieces of a jigsaw puzzle?

∵

On an early September Sunday afternoon, Mark paid Justin a visit in the hospital's shaded courtyard. The waning summer's burgundy-and-white crepe myrtles across the lawn were beginning to shed, creating circular carpets at the shrubs' bases that contrasted with the Kelly green lawn, kept lush with regular watering. A cool breeze had replaced the oppressive midday heat and humidity.

"I trust you're getting better?" the monsignor asked. He wore a stiff pressed black suit and starched Roman collar, as well as a concerned smile.

"I am more relaxed, yes." Justin was glad to see a familiar face, but cautious as ever of the superior, who was eleven years his senior.

"You look better. Put your pounds back on, and yes, you look rested." He was his jovial self, as if his cheerfulness could minimize the seriousness of Justin's mental state.

But Justin was eager to minimize as well. "So I think I am ready to get back to St. Peter's Hill."

"When the doctors say you return, you return."

Justin wondered if Mark was concerned that a premature discharge would allow a repeat of Justin's refectory behavior in a public place, confusing people and diminishing the status of all clergy, to say nothing of embarrassing the dean.

"And what have my parishioners been told?" He leaned forward on a bench across from the monsignor. A blue jay called from a low limb of the maple.

"That you're sick in the hospital and that you'll be back soon."

"And the priests at the conference?"

"Justin, I've protected you. I always will. Ideally I'd pull you from this place and put you in a Catholic mental facility. I'm a little concerned about secular influences in this public facility, you know, with Freud and all that." He leaned back on the wooden bench and crossed his arms over his chest, exposing a gold cuff link from under his coat sleeve.

Justin kept quiet.

The monsignor cleared his throat and continued. "But there is a plus having you in a general hospital. Who back home will ever know that you are in the psychiatric ward within the hospital? The priests of the archdiocese and others who saw what happened all know what I've told them: you had a seizure and are here to stabilize your medication." He was like a self-assured parent speaking to a naïve child.

"But I didn't have a seizure." Justin sat erect and raised his voice and looked directly at the monsignor.

"Do you want me to protect you or not? We priests protect one another from anything that may scandalize people. People must look to us as spiritual giants who have no weaknesses. You have a great future ahead of you, Justin. You're brilliant. I plan to recommend you for higher studies, perhaps Rome, if you are interested."

"Rome?" His eyes widened.

"At the Pontifical Immaculate Conception College, maybe. With advanced studies, the doors will fly open for you to teach, write, research, publish, lecture, and move wherever you want in the hierarchy of the church."

Justin looked up at the blue jay, which, as if prompted, took flight. In Rome, Justin knew he could study under the world's most renowned theologians. He could devote his energies to what he loved most. Moving up in the hierarchy had no appeal, but scholarship excited him in ways others are excited by business, sports, or the arts.

Before his imagination totally seized him, he returned to the truth about his illness.

"But I don't have neurological problems." He wondered whether his own honesty would nudge the senior cleric toward truth. Justin suspected the monsignor to be one of many shining pieces of a clerical mosaic that had weathered centuries of assaults by honest people.

"If you think the archbishop would approve your advanced studies knowing you've had a nervous breakdown, you're mistaken. And your colleagues would pigeon hole you as an untouchable if they knew you'd been in a psych ward. What do you want me to do?" When he shifted on the bench the sun hit a cuff link, casting a quick beam into Justin's eyes.

Justin returned to his room more confused than consoled by the monsignor's words.

∴

On Monday morning he met again with Miss Aaronheim.

"Monsignor O'Connell is telling a lie about me." Justin's anger did not overtake his measured words.

"A lie?" The morning light settled on her lap where she placed her small hands, one over the other. He noticed she did not have a wedding band. And after the first several sessions she no longer took notes, instead focusing total attention on him.

"Yes, he's telling the archbishop and the other priests that I am in the hospital being treated for a seizure. It's a lie." He had slowly grown more comfortable in her presence, knowing, with her assurance, what he said would never get back to the monsignor.

"Why would he do that?"

The more he talked the more he realized she had no experience of the world of Catholic priests and its unique set of mores.

"It's what priests do, he says. Priests cover for each other." Even as he spoke the words he grew aware of the oddness of such clerical ways.

"And what do you want to do?" The morning sunlight shifted slightly from her, onto the polished floor.

"I don't want to participate. I was taught never to lie."

"Do you lie?"

He felt she was not judging but rather helping to clarifying his thoughts. "No."

"And Father Basil?"

Justin fell into an extended silence and kept his palms over his eyes as if to keep her out.

He took in a deep breath, lowered his hands, and took a long pause. Finally, turning to the window, he said, "He hurt me."

"Hurt you?" Her voice was low and tender.

Justin filled with tears. He heaved in and out, his narrow shoulders shaking.

Miss Aaronheim said nothing.

"Father Basil was my spiritual director when I was a freshman at Presentation," he whispered, sniffling and pulling a tissue from the box on the side table.

"And he hurt you?" She waited for more.

"Yes. Over and over. I didn't know what was happening. I should have, but I didn't."

"How did he hurt you?" Her voice was steady and professional, yet warm.

He shut his eyes, as if to stem the flow of liquid pain.

"Can you tell me what he did to you?" Her words were nearly inaudible.

"I . . . I . . . I can't." His breath quickened and a slow sob continued. Again he stared out at the strong maple, bold in the center of the courtyard.

After several moments of quiet, Miss Aaronheim tried again. "It will help if I understand what you experienced with Father Basil. Please."

"No. No. I can't say it. No one knows."

Miss Aaronheim was still during the remaining ten minutes of the session. So was Justin.

∴

That afternoon, before supper, he sat on a limestone bench under the same maple praying his breviary, this time the Vesper hour. As he routinely read the Magnificat, he was struck by words from Luke's gospel that had usually washed over him with no impact: "He will bring down the mighty from their thrones and rise up the lowly . . ." He put the prayer book at his side and fell into a stupor, pondering the meaning of those words in the context of the day's session with Miss Aaronheim. Basil Epperman was the mighty one indeed and Justin was the lowly boy-seminarian. In his fiery death in that car, God brought him down. Now, in this artificial world of the psychiatric unit, the gentle, persistent Miss Aaronheim wanted to crack open a decades-old seal, exposing his deepest wound. Was this the preordained occasion for him, the lowly one, to be raised up?

He sat in the shade and stared beyond the walls enclosing the courtyard into the late afternoon sky. Breathing in and out he pleaded, "Guide me, Holy Ghost, guide me."

That night he rested with the hope he'd be directed how to purge the real-life incubus he'd sequestered for over thirty years.

At their next meeting Justin said nothing for over fifteen minutes, as if to collect his courage. After this lengthy pause he inhaled and began in a low voice.

"The first time was right after I arrived. Each of us had private meetings with our assigned spiritual directors. I knocked on his door, and he yelled, 'Laudator Jesus Christus, young man! Come in!' I didn't know what he was talking about. He yelled, 'You're supposed to say, "Laudator Jesus Christus" and I respond "Nunc et in aeternum, amen" and then you walk in. It's Latin for "Praise be to Jesus Christ" and I answer "Now and forever, amen."' Another odd church ritual I thought. So I walked in and sat in a narrow wooden chair next to his cluttered desk. He had all the lights out except for a dim lamp over his papers and books on his work space. The yellowed window shade was drawn, shutting out the world. The small room with creaky wooden floors smelled of cigarette smoke and whiskey."

Justin burst into uncontrollable tears. He bent over with his face in his lap, his muscles constricted.

After several minutes of sobbing, Miss Aaronheim said, "You are safe. You're safe here."

Justin sat erect and looked up at her, startled. "Okay, okay! I want to finish. I've never told anyone this before. I have to finish!" It was as if the prayer the previous afternoon had loosened decades-old moorings. A strong, mysterious power took charge, perhaps the Holy Ghost.

"Very well. Tell me what you want to tell me."

"He asked me about my family . . . my mother. I told him I had no brothers or sisters or father. Then he said, 'Seems I have to teach you a few things about life if you are going to be a good priest for the Lord.' Then he told me I had to learn how to drink and smoke so I could feel comfortable with my future parishioners. He'd teach me some things my father should have taught me. That evening he kept making highballs for me with Coke and whiskey. That's all I remember."

"And that's how he hurt you?"

"No, no. That was just the beginning. He was also the infirmarian. That's how he'd gotten the whiskey during Prohibition . . . for medicinal purposes. When students were sick and needed to be separated from the others, he decided who would sleep in the infirmary, which was in an isolated wing across the hall from his room. There were five beds in one big room and the sick ones would have their meals and Communion brought to them."

He paused and looked out the window. He felt heavy tears drip from his high cheeks. Miss Aaronheim waited while Justin collected his memories.

"I hate him!" he yelled. "I hate him and hope he's burning in hell." Then he immediately contradicted himself. "No, I don't. No, I don't. I've got to forgive him, don't I?"

Miss Aaronheim remained expressionless.

"He did evil things. He got me so drunk I passed out and he had his way with me in the empty infirmary, after the others were all in their beds in the dorms. I woke up the next morning with dried blood on my rectum and sheets and wondered what had happened. I didn't remember anything."

He stared into space, seeing nothing but the chalky infirmary walls of over three decades before. At the edge of the bed with a heavy hangover, he again seemed suspended in confusion, feeling intense burning pain in his rectum.

"Father Zapp? Father Zapp? Can you hear me?"

Justin turned to her, "Yes, Miss Aaronheim, I hear you. I haven't thought of these things in a long time. No one knows about what happened."

After another long pause she asked, "Is there a reason you've never talked about any of this before now?"

"Lies. No one wants to know the truth, and people would lie about it all if I talked about it. So I just kept quiet. But I don't want anymore whitewashing. I don't want to be part of it anymore. The woman who raised me taught me right from wrong. That's all stuck with me. That's what God wants me to do."

"And is someone lying now?"

"I am lying if I let Monsignor O'Connell tell people I am in the hospital for health reasons so I can go to Rome. He is creating something false. A lie. I am here because of what I did thirty-four years ago."

"Something you did?"

"Yeah, I did it. It happened twelve times that first semester at Presentation. I know because I still have my calendar of 1923 and marked with an X each time it happened in September, October, November, and early December. When I came back after Christmas break, Basil was gone. No one explained why he went or where he went. But I knew I'd done something terribly sinful."

Miss Aaronheim seemed to let him sit with the feelings of his own guilt until the session's fifty minutes were up.

∴

That afternoon, he retreated to the silence of his room and again reflected on the words of the Magnificat, this time reversing his thinking, wondering if he was the haughty one now being brought low. He was the guilty one, he felt, the proud seminarian and now high and mighty priest, who could have stopped Basil Epperman from hurting boys in other settings. His ego was bigger than he wanted to admit. An overwhelming shame smothered him. Shaking with guilt, he knelt at his bed and wept.

Collecting himself, he closed his eyes and tilted his head to the ceiling, as if seeing his God within his own imagination. "O God, I am sorry. Have mercy, have mercy." Tears continued to flow.

Was this emotional tempest God's punishment for failing to report the dangerous Basil Epperman? And why didn't he just walk out of the room when he was first offered alcohol? How could he be such a coward, so spineless?

When he composed himself, he resolved to lock the entire issue back into its vault forever. God, he figured, would exact judgment as he saw fit; Justin was at his mercy.

∵

At the next session Justin announced, "I don't want to discuss Father Basil anymore." His voice was firm.

"Something's changed?"

"I'll return to the parish and get on with my life."

"And continue to ignore the deep hurt you experienced?" She steered the discussion where Justin refused to go.

He felt attacked. "I'm not ignoring anything, ma'am. I just don't think it's necessary to rummage through the past. It's upsetting, so why dwell on it? It's over."

"No, it's not over. It's alive in you and it's taking tremendous energy to keep it hidden, making believe it's not alive." Her gentle persistence was evident in her tender, yet strong tone.

"Don't you understand? The more I talk about it the more upsetting it is." He leaned toward her as if to leverage his firm words.

She didn't alter her erect sitting position. "Yes, I understand it's very difficult to discuss. But putting the trauma in words helps us examine it as adults. It helps us understand truth, with no distortions. This is how we humans heal."

The gospel quote flashed in his mind: "What is truth?" Pilate asked Jesus. Then the thought evaporated. "Look, I've managed all these years without telling anyone what I did, until now. But talking about it here has only made it worse, don't you see?"

"Yes, I understand how difficult this is. But as we continue the pain will lessen and the healing happens. In some ways it's like re-breaking a broken bone that wasn't properly set."

Justin slumped in his chair and remained silent for the balance of the session.

For the next two sessions Justin made no mention of Basil. Miss Aaronheim was patient and made no comment, letting Justin sort the nightmare experiences at his pace.

Then for a late September session he arrived tense.

"I think I am finished with therapy." He looked out the window. The maple leaves were beginning to ease into gold and orange in the late morning breeze.

"Oh?" She waited for him.

"There's nothing more to discuss. We've gone two whole sessions talking about trivia. I'm ready to go home."

"Trivia?"

"Yes. You know all you need to about me. I'm feeling fine. My weight is back up and I'm rested."

A male cardinal chirped on the window sill, looking at the clear blue Ohio sky.

"Until the next trigger?"

"I'll handle it better next time."

"It's impossible to carry heavy guilt and pain every day and not eventually have another break." He imagined her standing outside the fortress he'd constructed around his inner self pleading to enter.

"Guilt?" Even as he said the word he knew he could not sustain the pretense. She sat in silence and looked at him expressionless.

"Okay. Yes. I am guilty. Remember, I didn't stop him. I participated. I'll carry the burden the rest of my life." He felt his face turn red as he closed his eyes.

Within seconds he wept.

After a long pause she asked in a soft tone, "Help me understand. What is your sin?"

"I didn't stop him!" He raised his voice to convince her of what was so obvious to him.

"How could you?"

"I don't know, but I should have. Don't you see that?" His entire body felt on fire with rage.

"No, I don't. It seems from what you're telling me that you were a boy and this was a grown man with authority over you." She was calm and deliberate. "As spiritual director didn't he have a say over whether you were qualified to stay in the seminary and become a priest?"

"Yes, yes." He calmed at her caring tone more than her words and tried to gather his thoughts. "He had to give a report every three months to the rector, telling him whether I was making progress in my spiritual development, and if not, he could recommend I be expelled." He slipped into a clarity that characterized his scholarly argument of a theological point.

"So what were your options? To go to the rector and tell him your spiritual director just got you drunk and raped you?"

"Stop! Stop it!" Justin put his hands over his ears and shut his eyes.

Miss Aaronheim said nothing and waited.

"Is our time up?" Justin stared at her and lowered his hands.

"If you want it to be."

"That's what I want."

∵

That night Justin tossed in his bed with thoughts of Basil Epperman, the middle-aged alcoholic with the bourbon blush face, graying, thick, curly hair, and deep demanding voice. He recalled how, as Miss Aaronheim surmised, he threatened to find a reason to dismiss Justin if he dare tell anyone of the actions between them. Justin remembered how proud his widowed mother back home was to have him at Presentation. He was to be the first priest in the family's one hundred year history in America, and his nascent clerical status lent her a certain small town status in St. Boniface beyond the wealth accumulated from the sale of the land holdings. His expulsion from the seminary would have devastated her. And he would return to his hometown clothed in shame.

Now remorse engulfed him. All these years later he felt he was at fault for what happened. He hadn't stop it, and he should have. But how? What could he have done?

∴

In the next therapy session, he sat across from Miss Aaronheim in a daze. He had not slept for two nights and was in no mood to stir up the horrors of Basil again.

CHAPTER 6

A T THE SUGGESTION OF Miss Aaronheim, Justin was prescribed sleep medication. By the time he returned for his Friday session, he was rested, if a bit fuzzy headed from the sedative.

"Where did we leave off Monday?" Justin asked her. The morning rush hour traffic noise came through the open office window.

"I think you're the one doing the work here." She was skilled from years of clinical practice and the sound training she received at the social work school at Smith College. In fact, she technically could not provide psychotherapy to the patients in this medical setting, but the psychiatrists in charge knew she was the most gifted of the staff, and ignored the traditional established medical guidelines to take advantage of her abilities.

"Yeah, well, I can't get the guilt out of my mind."

"Help me understand again, what is this guilt all about?"

His stomach churned and the throbs began again along his right forehead. He crossed his arms. A honk from a car on the street interrupted a silence between them.

Miss Aaronheim waited. The intensity of her eyes made him feel nothing distracted her from her mission of full empathy.

After several minutes the priest said, "I was a boy, voice like a girl's and didn't even know what a wet dream was. But I was scared. I had to report to him once a week. The same time, eight o'clock, every Monday night during study hall. At four minutes before the hour I'd leave my classmates all hunched over their desks memorizing Latin conjugations or working algebra problems. All alone I'd march down the long hall of the far off wing of the building and pull open the metal fire door that connected the minor seminary to the priests' rooms. I remember my palms sweated well before eight, and I'd keep rubbing them on my cassock so they'd stay dry and no one would know I was nervous. In the priests' quarters the old wooden floors creaked so I'm sure he knew when I was approaching his room. 'Laudetor Jesus Christus,' I'd say in my high pitch as I pushed his door buzzer. He'd yell back in his gravel voice through the open transom window, 'In aeternum, amen.' As soon as I entered the bleak chamber, my 'lesson' would begin again. The same routine. A little chatter, given one then two then three drinks. I don't remember how many. I'd get foggy. He'd guide me, staggering, across the hall to the infirmary and, sometimes, I remember, he'd fondle my arms and shoulders and thighs. Then I don't remember anything else until morning. He drank with me, so he always smelled like whiskey and smoke . . . and that Vitalis hair tonic."

"You were so young and vulnerable."

Care wrapped her words, words that spoke the truth of who Justin was thirty-four years before, almost to the day. He heard her compassion, though, more than her words, and he wept with his head bent.

"I didn't stop him. Even though I was drunk, I didn't stop him." He pulled a tissue from the box on the table next to him.

"And?" She waited for more.

"And what? What more do you want? Don't you understand? I am a Catholic priest who didn't stop another priest from making a sex partner out of me, and he kept on using little boys after he left Presentation. I know he did even though I have no evidence. I should have stopped him then, or I should have reported him after he left. Think how many men are probably living with what I'm living with? How many other lives did Basil ruin? How many could I have saved, if I had had the guts? I am a fraud and a liar. I am not worthy of being a priest, of changing bread and wine into Christ's body and blood with the same hands that touched Basil and did nothing to stop him." He sat numb at his own words, rubbing his knees with his moist palms at a nervous pace.

Miss Aaronheim gave him the time he needed for his flood of feelings to slow before she said, "I don't think you could have acted responsibly. A thirteen-year-old naïve boy walking into the private room of a mentally ill man who had total control over his destiny could not possibly have acted on his own behalf to stop the powerful man's advances."

"But I should have. I should have done the right thing, even if it meant being expelled and no one believing my story, don't you understand?"

"No. No, I do not." Her voice was now one of authority and control. She would not tolerate his attempts to cast himself as the perpetrator and willing sex partner.

"Let's be clear about what you are telling me. You were a boy, an immature, innocent boy. An aggressive, manipulative, charming man used you to satisfy his distorted sexual urges. He was the authority who controlled your fate. To whom could you turn? One of the other priests? Didn't you already tell me how they cover for each other? Who would believe a thirteen-year-old minor seminarian just weeks into his training? And what about the loving Mother you left at home? She trusted those same priests at Presentation to protect you. Would she believe you or them?"

Justin listened. Now, for the first time he felt he had put into words what he'd long ago harbored inside. The way he explained it to her was exactly as he had explained it to himself for all these years, over and over in his mind, each time stirring guilt he could never admit even in the confessional and each time trying to bury it deeper and deeper. Sin had compounded sin in a cover. But now he understood the story from someone else's point of view, someone who knew how the mind works, someone who knew what was real and what was illusion, someone who appeared to authentically care about him.

Seated upright, with her hands over her lap, her professional voice intoned, "You were a victim of a sick man's desires. You are guilty of nothing." She took a deep breath and repeated, "Nothing."

Justin put his face in his hands so he could piece together the words. Then he looked directly at her, his eyes stinging and flooded with tears. He exhaled and said, "I know you're right. I just don't feel it yet."

"There's no rush. You've never heard this kind of response to your story because you've never shared it. I don't have a church agenda. You are my only concern here. Take time to feel my observations and see if they ring true in your heart."

∵

Over the next few weeks Justin's sessions with Miss Aaronheim continued three times a week. In between the meetings, Justin spent long hours alone in his room in silence, no longer absorbed with journals and books about theology. He prayed and poured what energy he had into his emotional healing, even if he knew he had no power to force his mental health any more than a diseased man forces his physical health.

One warm night in October he sat on the porch of the hospital, overlooking the manicured courtyard. A brick wall, partly covered with deep green ivy, bounded one side of the rectangle; bright yellow mums and a Kelly green lawn, divided with meandering cobblestone paths, were shaded by the center piece, the old maple. The hospital's covered porches enclosed the three other sides of the quiet space.

It reminded Justin of a monastery, a place that is supposed to be a sacred, placid oasis. He listened to the cicadas and tree frogs and the small lily pond's bullfrogs all making their rhythmic music. Every one of them had a mission, he thought, even if they were not aware of it. We poor humans had to sort through all of our life experiences and impulses and curiosities to figure out what God wants of us. Even with hours of reflection, prayer, therapy, and guidance from wise men and women, we still don't ever know for sure if our actions line up with God's will for our brief lives.

"Guide me, Holy Ghost, guide me," he whispered. Calmness enveloped him. He heard the soft, slow beat of his heart among the encircling creatures' soothing sounds.

His thoughts then shifted. He knew the monsignor would disapprove of the work of Miss Aaronheim. His heart sped up. The superiors in the church considered Freud an atheist, one outside the communion of the saints. But those guidelines didn't match Justin's experience of therapy. She is a kind, skilled professional, he thought. After nearly twenty meetings with her, he was beginning to deal with the most emotionally jarring experience of his life. How could that be sinful? Didn't Jesus himself spend much of his mission healing people and casting out demons? Couldn't God be using the gifts of Miss Aaronheim to heal me, Justin reflected.

And then he prayed further: "Help me understand what you want, what my life mission is. Heal me. Let me forgive Basil in my heart. Seven times seventy times. Don't let me blame myself for the evil done to me. Amen."

What he prayed for he wanted to do, but his feelings spoke the opposite. Still, with the gentle pleas and steady breathing, his heartbeat again slowed.

∴

On the morning of October 9, 1958, the day he was to be discharged, Justin met with Miss Aaronheim a final time. With the office curtains tied back, the morning light filled the room, creating a sense of openness that reflected how Justin felt about the next step in his healing.

"What can I say? You've helped me. Thank you." He had regained most of his weight and his face wore a healthy sheen, the dark half circles under his eyes mostly gone. In the safety of the hospital setting the intestinal irritations and headaches had gone too. Returning to daily tensions of his life in Indiana loomed, a world outside the safe, cocoon-like hospital. But at this moment the excitement of going home overshadowed all else.

"It's been an honor working with you. But as I've mentioned in the last few sessions, I am concerned that your work is just beginning. I know you're assigned to a rural parish and don't have access to a therapist, but if you can arrange for therapy in Louisville or Indianapolis, I think you'd be able to continue the work we've just started."

"It's impossible under the circumstance. I'll manage on my own. If I need you, I'll make the trip back here for a session, even if it means taking a couple of days off at St. Peter's."

She reiterated her point. "Just talking about hurt does not heal hurt. It takes time for you to explore your deepest parts, to turn them over and over with someone skilled, whom you trust. This may take several years; it can't be rushed. We started the process, but you're far from finished."

"I'll pray about it." Despite incursions into the private territory of his pain and guilt, he still just wanted it all to go away so he could return to the quiet of his study at the country rectory.

Miss Aaronheim escorted him to the foyer of the hospital where they exchanged goodbyes. His bags had been placed next to the reception desk. As arranged, Monsignor O'Connell waited in his big Oldsmobile under the limestone arched portico to drive him home.

"Justin, you look like a changed man!" The monsignor was his positive out-going self. But Justin surmised the monsignor masked his likely unease about what had happened to his priest during the previous sixty days. If there were demons to be wrestled, Justin thought, the monsignor surely would prefer Justin at a priests' retreat under the guidance of a qualified spiritual director rather than a Jewish woman in a psychiatric ward of a secular hospital. He recalled their last conversation about the cover-up plotted by the monsignor. Staying at the teaching hospital played into that scheme, even as it compromised the monsignor's judgment about secular facilities. Justin speculated the good monsignor was probably curious to know what dangerous lies the hospital staff had put into Justin's head.

Justin wasn't about to tell.

CHAPTER 7

DESPITE HIS USUAL LOW grade distress in the monsignor's presence, the four-and-a-half-hour car trip home gave Justin time to catch up on news in the archdiocese. The steady perspiration under his arms and on his palms and mild throb across his forehead reminded him to be cautious in the presence of his strong willed superior. Thus Justin avoided discussing anything about the hospital stay, sensing that most of his experiences there would be suspect to his driver. For whatever reason, the monsignor asked nothing about the subject.

"The archbishop's been diagnosed with stomach cancer, but it's not public knowledge. It's always best not to burden the laity with unpleasant news when we don't have to." With ease the monsignor steered the tail-finned, oversized car around sharp twists and over gentle knolls, past fields of tan-dried corn stalks and low rows of soybeans of the same hue. On several farms, tractors churned through harvests, filling wagons with grains. The maples were a mix of scarlet and deep orange and yellow; the dogwoods and sassafras were burgundy and golden, the sumac fire-engine red. The most colorful time of year in southern Indiana had arrived.

"I'll pray for him," was all Justin said. Inside more was stirring, however. He wanted to say he didn't think it was good to keep anything from laypeople. If their spiritual leader had stomach cancer, why not tell them? What image are we trying to maintain by withholding facts, he wondered? And why treat the laity like ignorant children?

The feelings and questions were new to him. Since the meetings with Miss Aaronheim he noticed a bubbling of thoughts and emotions that surprised him, yet in a curious way also excited him.

The priests stopped at Jones Café in downtown Seymour just before noon. The very Catholic Jones family included eleven children, each assigned a job in the diner as soon as they were old enough to go to school. The tiny bell over the door jingled when the priests walked into the smells of fried onions and grilled burgers in the crowded, smoky room. They settled into a booth to study the menu. But within seconds of scanning the blue plate specials, the black and white Admiral television behind the counter announced an interruption in programming. "This is a CBS News special report from our correspondent Winston Burdette in Rome." Silence enveloped the diners and waitresses. "Pope Pius XII died of acute heart failure this morning at his summer retreat outside of Rome." The news bulletin gave few details.

After a brief hush, the patrons resumed eating and talking, perhaps moved by the news, but more likely correctly sensing their small lives in small-town Indiana would change not a whit by the passing of an old Italian pontiff thousands of miles away.

The son of Roman business aristocracy, Eugenio Pacelli was elected pope in 1939, as the Second World War was beginning in Europe. Cautious, austere, and outwardly devout, he shunned close friendships, favoring his pet canary over any confidant. Many had questioned his reluctance to condemn Hitler's atrocities, suspecting him of cowardice. Others judged his actions as necessary to avoid the slaughter of even more Jews, Catholics, and homosexuals.

Regardless, the intelligent diplomat-pope was now dead and with him his thousands of secret actions and motives of the last nineteen years.

The two men in black suits and Roman collars put down their menus and stared at one another in mutual disbelief. The dozens of non-clerics around them may not have been shaken by the news, but to the monsignor and Justin, soldiers in the pope's army, the passing of their general held unknown ramifications.

Recognizing the clergy in their presence, three customers in the next booth eyed the priests' reactions. Without a word, they, Catholic or not, perhaps knew a major era had just ended for the worldwide church. And with the archbishop's illness the local church's pastors braced for a new chapter in the Hoosier archdiocese as well.

"I have to take time for all this to settle," Justin said in a near whisper. It was as if a force had passed over him that he wanted to esteem. In the background the bell above the front door tinkled several times as customers came and went. A daytime soap opera resumed on the television with melodramatic organ sounds enhancing its tension.

∴

The return to Indiana held no familiar routines for either man as change seemed to chase change. The next day the Apostolic Delegate to the United States, Cardinal A.G. Calabrese, telephoned the monsignor with news that the one of the pope's last official acts was the appointment of Mark O'Connell as the auxiliary bishop of the archdiocese.

While never saying it, Justin had long wondered if this is what the monsignor had wished for years. Perhaps his superior felt himself episcopal timber and was just waiting for Rome to recognize it.

The years of diplomacy and social functions to enhance his reputation, the millions of dollars raised for new churches and schools, the countless actions to protect his fraternity of clerics, and his long tally of favors for the rich and powerful in the church had all paid off. His polished name reached the elite corridors in the Vatican: he was to be ordained a bishop and, if all went as Justin anticipated, the next archbishop. Who knows after that? The monsignor was still young enough at fifty-eight to be a cardinal, a member of the privileged princes chosen to lead major cities or help run the Vatican, and of course to choose among their own ranks who is pope.

Justin returned to St. Peter's Hill with a mixture of relief, verve, and trepidation, knowing the swift changes in Rome and the chancery could quickly bring shifts in his life at any moment. He longed to just get back to his books and journals, but he didn't know what his parishioners had been told about his absence and how their understanding of him might upset his longed for tranquility. Whatever they had been told, he assumed it was not the truth.

After weeks of institutional living in the hospital, he welcomed the cooking of Mrs. Mayer. Within days she'd spread the word that Father Zapp had returned with curious new pastoral enthusiasm. People noticed he smiled more and even chatted with parishioners at the bingos on the steps of the school. Justin felt the fresh vitality within himself, despite clouds of change converging.

This curious new found energy spread. Gathering half dozen leaders in the parish, he asked them to consider being an advisory board.

"This is your parish," he explained. "You should have a say in how it is run."

"But you're the pastor. You know what's right for us," Mrs. Conroy, a young nurse, said at the first meeting.

"Not true. We're pastors to each other. I don't have all the answers. No priest or bishop or pope has all the answers. We all are baptized and all have received the gifts of the Holy Ghost. We'll work together just like we all pray together."

He still savored every minute of private space for scholarly work, but he surprised himself by venturing into the lives of parishioners in small ways that also astonished them during his first weeks at home. He lingered amid the smells of rubbing alcohol and soiled sheets at hospital beds after giving Communion or Extreme Unction to sick parishioners. A family's invitation to Sunday dinner meant a casual chat about crops, the weather, and children's school work over tables filled with steaming fried chicken, kale greens, and buttered sweet potatoes. Surrounded by sprays of gladioli, roses, and chrysanthemums giving a mixture of sweetness to the listless funeral home air before an open casket, Justin listened to the bereaved. True, he wasn't at ease in any of these settings, extending himself to people who wanted to enjoy or be consoled by his company. But he willed himself to do the uncomfortable just to test his own reactions, which turned out satisfying in unforeseen ways. He felt these simple, sincere people—children, teens, and multi-age adults—seemed to really want to be with him; he felt valued.

∵

His new found openness was cut short with the October 27 phone call from Bishop-elect O'Connell. Justin was typing the final sentences for an article for *Commonweal* magazine on Catholic-Jewish relations and had not wanted distractions.

"Justin, my episcopal ordination is scheduled for the feast of St. Francis Xavier, December 3. I'd like you to be the master of ceremonies and my chief advisor in the chancery." With a pause to absorb the words, his body tensed, flushed with fear. He knew by instinct that the same overwhelming distress of the weeks before the liturgical conference might reappear, a distress that he feared impotent to manage or contain.

"Do I have a choice?" Holding the weighty black corded phone to his ear, he swiveled his seat from the typing table to the desk and put his other hand across his forehead, as if anticipating the recurrence of painful throbs.

"What possible reason would cause you to hesitate, my friend?"

"I, I, I'm just not sure." He gazed at the large crucifix next to the window.

"Not sure of what? I'm giving you a chance to be a star at my ordination ceremony and moving you to a high profile position in the archdiocese. Don't you see? Your theological writings have made you a celebrity. People everywhere tell me how lucky I am to have such a famous scholar among my priests."

"I'm not interested in being a star or celebrity. Those things better suit you than me." He closed his eyes and prayed the right words would come.

"What are you implying?"

"I, I guess I'm not comfortable being as high profile as you are, that's all." Justin felt his effort to keep the bishop-elect's strong will at bay failing.

"So I'll have to make the decision for you." Straightaway the senior cleric again moved to snare his prey.

"I get the picture. I'll be at the ordination and do what you ask." He stared again at the crucifix.

"And the move to the chancery?"

"Yes, yes. I'll take on any task you assign." He felt deflated. The freshness toward life's possibilities with a manageable life at St. Peter's Hill, which grew during the brief days following his discharge from the hospital, ended in a flash.

"I knew you'd put the needs of the church before your personal concerns. You are a good man."

The country priest felt certain this was yet another cross he would carry. His forehead tightened; his stomach rumbled.

∵

That night the insomnia returned in a rerun of the weeks before the August conference. At dawn, during his hour of prayer, he asked for wisdom from the Holy Ghost. The late autumn sun rose over the valley, ready to burn off the soft gray mist hovering above the meandering creek. When Mr. Mayer's rooster shouted a litany of crows, Justin rose from his cushioned chair to open his bedroom window to breathe the crisp cool air. Standing before the morning he prayed for inner peace to carry him through the events the newly appointed bishop had scripted for him. His mind widened, and he imagined Miss Aaronheim sitting in her office with him, comforting him, yet challenging him too. Perhaps the Holy Ghost was leading him through her in ways he couldn't readily understand.

After the eight o'clock mass Justin sat down to breakfast prepared by Mrs. Mayer.

"Did you hear the morning news, Father?" She leaned to pour the freshly perked A&P coffee into the china cup with its pastel floral trim. The starched and pressed white linen cloth gave elegance to the small kitchen table next to a tall window that opened to the meadow and woods behind the rectory. The trees' mixture of fall colors peaked the week before. Now bare, the poplars, walnuts, and sycamores stood like black chalky skeletons against a graying sky. Brown-green cedars interspersed them like swollen cucumbers.

"Another sputnik launched?" He reached for the newspaper next to his juice glass.

"Not exactly. A new pope!" She was almost giddy.

"Oh?" Justin understood the process of selecting the successors to Peter: behind sealed doors at the Sistine Chapel, the powerful cardinals mysteriously debating who among their ranks would carry the onerous office.

"Another Italian." She lingered at his side steadying the shiny pot with both hands. "He's old . . . seventy-eight. And why don't they ever choose an American?"

"We Americans are considered untamed, I suspect." He put down the paper and looked up at the matronly woman of German stock. "And the cardinals probably didn't know who to pick so they settled for an old timer who won't do anything." With patience he offered commentary; inside he felt whoever led the church was secondary to his own internal turmoil with the forced move to the chancery.

"What do you mean?"

Justin refocused. "It's just that Pius XII had been around awhile so maybe he made people weary. If they'd chosen a younger man now, he could be pope for another generation. So they probably played it safe and voted for one who won't live long and won't upset things." He unfolded the newspaper. The news of the new pontiff's election hadn't made deadline, so the stale headline below the fold stated, "Cardinals Still Undecided."

Apparently not satisfied with his explanation, she huffed and returned to the kitchen. When she reappeared with a breakfast plate of over-easy eggs, bacon, and toast, she added, "Well, anyway, he has a nice smile. They showed him on the Today show at the big window blessing the crowd. He's also looks like he's not missed any meals."

"We'll live with what God sends us." He buttered the toast. He wanted to resign himself to what had just happened in Rome and, by osmosis, wished Mrs. Mayer would do likewise. He didn't have much interest in the details of the papal election. He needed all his strength for dealing with his new bishop.

With the front page of the paper strategically placed before him, he sipped the black coffee and felt an immediate soothing. Forces beyond his control, in the Vatican and more importantly in the local chancery, would find him with no willful resistance. His body, on the other hand, with its familiar physical symptoms, let him know it would not easily capitulate.

CHAPTER 8

THE ROTUND POPE JOHN XXIII, the 278th pontiff of the Catholic Church, had been a church diplomat in Paris and Istanbul before being named the Cardinal Archbishop of Venice in 1956. During World War II, he had successfully arranged for hundreds of Jews to secretly escape extermination by the Nazis. Commentators speculated his reputation as an easy-going, non-controversial bureaucrat and diplomat led the cardinals to elect him with the belief he would be a caretaker for a few years. Justin's analysis, as explained to Mrs. Mayer at breakfast, was correct. The power brokers wanted time to screen younger candidates who could set a future conservative course for the worldwide church.

Within days of the new pope's election, Bishop-elect O'Connell was asked to represent the archdiocese at the coronation on November 15. He was a stand in for the terminally ill archbishop.

"Why not accompany me to Rome?" He'd dropped by the rectory ostensibly to give Justin a bag of fresh Winesap apples, which he'd bought at a roadside stand.

"You keep pushing me, don't you?" The smell of slow burning leaves in front of the school, left unattended by Mr. Mayer, permeated the inside of the rectory. Justin smoldered as well.

"I'm not pushing. I think you should see Rome, and this is a way to get the trip paid for." He sat across from Justin in the office with the late afternoon sun pouring on several books laid out for research on the desktop.

"And who's the generous benefactor?" Justin noticed the bishop-elect eyeing the book titles with a tilted head.

"Oh, the archdiocese will foot the bill. You'll be my chief advisor on the trip."

"Thank you for the offer. But if I go to Rome I can well afford to pay my way. So, unless you really need an advisor to go to a papal coronation, I think I'll pass." His words surprised him.

"It's just an invitation. That's all."

Justin speculated, again, that the bishop-elect would enhance his standing with the power elite if Justin was at his side. Justin possessed enough self-awareness to realize some leaders in the Curia, the church's power center, may have considered Justin to be a measured, balanced theological mind. He had written in international journals for over fifteen years.

By resisting the bishop-elect on the coronation invitation, Justin thought he might get a short term win in their strained relationship. He speculated his superior did not want to jeopardize his long term plans for the O'Connell-Zapp team by forcing the Rome trip. The bishop-elect dropped the coronation invitation.

∙∙

The insomnia, intense headaches, and gastric upset had not abated. After long periods of prayer, he decided another visit with Miss Aaronheim might help. So, while the Bishop-elect O'Connell was out of the country, Justin took off several days from work to drive to Cincinnati. She agreed to see him for two extended sessions to accommodate his limited time in the city.

Walking into the hospital again was like walking into a sanctuary. He calmed with the smells of familiar floor wax and pine scented disinfectant and the sight of sunrays beaming through the towering windows along the shiny terrazzo corridor leading to Miss Aaronheim's office.

"Welcome." She stood at the doorway to the reception room. Her gentle half smile with the single word immediately comforted him.

Nothing had changed in the office. The chairs, the curtains, the pictures, even the fountain pen and leather covered calendar on her desk were exactly as he remembered.

Awaiting his lead in the conversation, she sat serenely across from him. It was as if he'd returned to an oasis of peace after weeks on a battlefield.

"He's at it again," Justin began. Most of the leaves of the friendly maple outside the window had fallen. Those that remained, brown, orange, and deep red, fluttered in the chilly November wind.

"He?" She had the writing pad on her lap and looked at him above rimless reading glasses sitting on her small nose.

"Monsignor, soon to be Bishop, O'Connell. He tries to charm me by telling me how brilliant I am."

"Tell me more." It was a soft request. She jotted items with a yellow pencil.

"He's more ambitious than I realized. He's been named auxiliary bishop of the archdiocese, so he'll be my new archbishop soon."

"Ambitious?"

The question interrupted his narrative. She'd not changed in appearance, still neatly dressed and coiffed, her consistency reassuring to him.

"Well, yes. He's moving up fast and he seems to want me to tag along to make him look good."

"How?"

Justin missed having her to listen to him; his daily conversations with God in prayer, his only recourse when alone in pain, were not the same as having Miss Aaronheim focus entirely on him during these special moments in therapy.

"He wants me to leave St. Peter's Hill and my settled life and move to the chancery with him." The wind outside the window picked up, and weighty dense clouds moved across the pewter sky. Leaves, ripped from the maple, flew southward.

"And you feel like this is tagging along?"

"Yeah, yeah I do. I feel . . . I don't know. I feel used somehow. Like I don't matter." The words jarred him. He'd ruminated over such thoughts, especially in the dark of the night when sleep refused him, but he'd never spoken them to another person; he wanted to take the words back.

"You don't matter?" She sought more with a slight lean toward him.

"No, no, I matter. But it's my duty to do what my bishop tells me. I don't need to question it. I just need to accept my cross and move on. What I want really doesn't matter, I guess. I mean, doing God's will means being obedient, even if I suffer from it. After all, as a Catholic, I know Christ died on the cross, and that wasn't what he wanted."

"What you want really doesn't matter?"

"Yes, I mean no. Gosh, I don't know. I'm just so confused. Does God really want me to be so miserable?" He put his palms into his eyes and shook his head back and forth in a long pause.

"I suspect our earlier discussions about your need for longer therapy were correct."

"I don't need more therapy. I just need to pray more and focus on the work my bishop assigns me and not get so upset when he orders me to do what he wants. I need to be a better, more humble priest."

He closed his eyes, tightening his grip on his formula for serenity.

He coldly concluded, not looking directly at her, as if shunning any alternative she might offer, "Now that I think about it, I'm not sure I needed to see you. I can manage on my own. I just have to make up my mind to do it."

"And keep having headaches, gastric troubles, and insomnia?" He noticed she was wearing a different broach on her dress, a simple light green oval trimmed in silver.

"How do you know?"

"I don't know. But if these symptoms aren't still with you then I'm suspecting some others may have taken their place." She spoke with calm insight, yet deep care.

"You're correct." He nodded in agreement. "They are all three worse than ever."

"You may want to consider what kind of God would want you to suffer this way, using energy and time that could be spent on your scholarship and pastoral care of others."

"But suffering has merit in God's eyes too." He immediately recognized the slip into a theological debate that was a cul-de-sac.

Communicating in a loud silence, she looked at him with compassion.

"I'll pray over it," he said after several minutes.

∵

That night he stayed downtown on the ninth floor of the Netherland Plaza Hotel, the art deco skyscraper overlooking the Ohio River and Northern Kentucky. He prayed his breviary—vespers and compline—then closed the worn black leather book and sat watching the barges plying the glassy water upstream toward Pittsburgh and downstream in the direction of Louisville. The tall stacks of the coal generating plant spewed thick smoke, creating a haze over the twinkling lights of the Kentucky city of Covington and the silhouette of the noble twin towers of Mother of God Church, which was surrounded by seedy sites of notorious gambling and prostitution. Complicated thoughts raced through his mind, which was as murky as the air over the river. His forehead pounded with pain and his thin belly rumbled.

What did his God want? He wrestled with the correct response to his superior who kept intruding into Justin's world, a world that could never quite be managed and controlled the way Justin wanted. Did Basil have anything to do with all the baffling notions in his mind?

He prayed in words that felt angry. "Where are you? I'm giving my life to you! Help me!" Tears welled in his eyes making the streetlights below sparkle like fat diamonds. He cried, and then tried to sleep.

At the start of the next day's therapy session Justin felt compelled to use the time efficiently, to rush to resolution so he'd be less miserable and return to Indiana refreshed and at least partially healed.

"I feel like I can be a better negotiator with him. I need to work at this. Maybe he'll compromise with me."

"Tell me more." She sat back in her chair and looked relaxed. He wondered if she was disengaging.

"I want to get this resolved and you strike me as not interested." He surprised himself with his bluntness.

"I don't think we can resolve anything quickly. Therapy takes time."

"But don't you understand? I don't have time."

"You're quite right. We don't have the luxury of meeting several times a week the way we did when you were here. But little by little you can grow in your understanding of your feelings and actions. Ideally you'll find a good therapist near you. If not, we'll meet when we can. Regardless you'll need to keep reflecting on the issues and making choices."

She seemed to talk in circles. Didn't she realize he was about to be swept up into the manipulative world of Mark O'Connell where he'd lose what little space of liberty he held for himself. Now she was telling him he could make "choices." Inside he knew the number of choices available were few.

"I don't think you appreciate my circumstances. I'm in a crisis, and you're talking about me thinking about my problems and fixing them with different decisions. But what can I do differently right now? Help me." His pleading voice didn't seem to nudge her from her complacent posture in the chair.

"It's not my role to tell you how to live your life. But I can make observations, based on what you tell me, from this side of the room."

Justin leaned forward in anticipation. Wanting her to rescue him was foremost in his mind, even as she dismissed the notion of telling him exactly what to do.

"I think your troubles with the new bishop may have something to do with your abuse, as I sense your symptoms may as well."

Disappointed, Justin pursed his lips, as if to forestall a dismissal of her insights. Part of him feared the truth of her words, but a stronger side of him insisted on getting a quick fix so he could move on. Mulling over Basil's role in his current troubles felt futile.

He sensed her eyes on his him as he stared out the window in silence. The near naked limbs of the maple bowed against the northern wind.

∴

On the lonely drive back to St. Peter's Hill he kept the radio off so he could think. Driving west, the sky was overcast, yielding a constant cold light rain. Justin pulled his rosary from his pocket and prayed the Sorrowful Mysteries, recalling the passion and death of his Christ. He fingered the beads one by one, trying to calm himself with the paced rhythm of the Hail Marys.

After lunch at a mom-and-pop truck stop outside of Bedford, that smelled of fried bacon and sauerkraut mixed with cigarette smoke, Justin's mind seemed to open up when he took the wheel again. Perhaps the stale coffee with his meal helped.

As much as he suspected a possible link, Miss Aaronheim's

words connecting Basil Epperman and the current pressures from the bishop-elect made no sense when he sat face-to-face with her. But suddenly, on the winding highway again, he questioned the motives of his entire life. Could it be distilled into an attempt to please some church authority? Perhaps there were parallels between his life at thirteen and now.

Freedom, he realized in a flash of insight, was now confined to a tiny space reserved for such things as theological inquiries and what he'd eat for supper. Church superiors, from Father Basil to Bishop-elect O'Connell, painted the larger canvas of his life. He couldn't imagine ever being his own artist.

In the Hoosier National Forest, with bare, charcoal-colored trees on both sides of the narrow highway, the session's final words popped into his mind.

"Our work is limited, Father. I do hope you can find a qualified therapist to continue what we've started."

"Or live with the insomnia, headaches, and diarrhea?"

"The holy trinity?" she asked in return.

Justin was surprised at the Jewish woman's play on Catholic theology.

Were the wounds of nights in the seminary infirmary linked to his domination by the bishop-elect and his own physical symptoms? Prayer, therapy, and reflection had produced little insight into how they were connected, and there was certainly no healing. He concluded as he drove up the hill to St. Peter's rectory that he was living the Sorrowful Mysteries.

∴

Bishop-elect Mark O'Connell returned from his first-ever visit to the Vatican enthralled by the pomp and splendor of the ancient rituals and the culture and architecture of Rome. In an extended meeting with Justin, he described with exuberance its grandeur and history. As a member of the American delegation of prelates, he had met the gentle new pontiff in a private audience. He felt honored to walk the ancient streets in his long cassock and berretta, both trimmed in crimson.

"It was amazing! Dressed as a member of the hierarchy, strangers from around the world bowed and greeted me on the streets. We clerics never wait for a table in a café and shopkeepers give us discounts."

Justin sensed the bishop-elect's determination to be part of this "divine powerhouse," as Mark O'Connell called it. A path from bishop to archbishop, which was one step away from an appointment as a cardinal, again formed in Justin's mind.

Was this the soon-to-be bishop's calculated career path to which Justin was consigned, like a show dog following the orders of his self-important trainer? Listening to the returned traveler describe his infatuation with the Vatican, Justin sank deeper into the plush upholstered chair across the desk. Fear overtook him at the thought of Mark's ecclesial advancement. Each step forward would diminish Justin's life; he knew his destiny would be nothing more than to ensure the bishop-elect shined brighter.

On December 3, 1958, Mark O'Connell was ordained auxiliary bishop of the archdiocese. Justin, with chalky complexion and hollow-cheeks, did an impeccable job as master of ceremonies, wearing the long vestments over his thin body. He assisted the new bishop in raising the host, and then the chalice, to the simultaneous ringing of the small consecration bells and the massive bells in the cathedral steeple. The smell of smoking incense filled the sanctuary. In the pews knelt more than a thousand faithful who anticipated the new bishop would soon be their archbishop. The full-color picture of the bishop and the haggard, esteemed scholar, side by side at the high white marble altar as the pontifical blessing was conferred on the attendees, graced the front page of the Indiana dailies the next morning. Bishop O'Connell got the publicity he hungered for, carrying him one step closer to what Justin felt sure were his clerical goals.

···

The second week of December, Justin arrived at the chancery with two suitcases and seven cartons of books and scholarly journals in his black 1952 Chevy Bel Air. His assigned musty room on the third floor of the downtown limestone rectory, next to the cathedral, was dark with one large curtainless window facing an office building across the narrow alley. His office was on the first floor, down the hall from Bishop O'Connell's. Across town, at St. Edward's Hospital, the archbishop lay dying, the cancer rapidly destroying his body. His ten-room suite on the second floor of the rectory, with its French provincial, professionally-designed interior, was supposed to remind guests of the first settlers in the archdiocese who originated from post-revolution France. On the day of Justin's arrival, the suite, like an abandoned Hollywood set, was dark and quiet, smelling of Johnson's wax.

The new bishop temporarily moved in down the hall from Justin. Perhaps Mark knew it was a matter of time before the lavish quarters one floor below would be his, so he may have intentionally left packed most of the boxes he'd brought from the deanery.

Justin assumed he and Mark would settle into an orderly routine of work once the archbishop was taken to the Lord. There was much to do to address the needs of the growing Catholic population in this part of Indiana. In moments of prayerful resignation, Justin decided to be faithful to the new duties.

But unimaginable events would soon unfold to alter the expectations of both clerics.

CHAPTER 9

FROM HIS FIRST DAY at the chancery the new bishop laid the groundwork, out of sight, for changes in the archdiocese that could help speed his way to getting the red hat of a cardinal, if that was in fact his career goal. What Justin had speculated to be the calculated path of advancement seemed blatant as he observed the bishop schedule meetings with select benefactors and advisors.

The aging archbishop's health problems had left the people leaderless over the last five years. Blueprints for new churches, schools, hospitals, and a retreat house rested on shelves. It was as if the entire archdiocese was asleep. Possibilities to make a mark were limitless.

"I'd like to put the new training program for clergy under your leadership," Mark said during the first staff meeting in the archbishop's conference room. "Of course this is to be planned now, but not implemented until the proper time."

Justin assumed everyone at the table understood "proper time" meant after the archbishop was dead and Mark was in full command.

He went on to assign everyone at the table a different project to enhance the Catholic Church: building the dreams that hid within stacks of blueprints, expanding the Catholic college into a "second Notre Dame," starting a archdiocesan newspaper, launching a new vocations drive and debt reduction campaign, and creating a new public relations office to make sure Bishop O'Connell received all the credit for each new initiative.

The proper time came quickly. On January 3, 1959, the archbishop passed from this world. He'd served the faithful for fifty-six years as a priest, the last thirty as archbishop. He'd left a legacy of buildings and new priests—he'd personally ordained nearly five hundred—but more significantly he created a culture of strict episcopal control over the convents, friaries, monasteries, parishes, grade schools and high schools, retreat centers, orphanages, and hospitals. He founded the Catholic college to counter the secular education of the state universities and kept a close eye on the curriculum of the seminary, Presentation, which was within the boundaries of the archdiocese, even though it drew seminarians from twelve other states.

He had been a no-nonsense man who permitted no dissension and demanded clear concentration of power in the chancery, leaving the lay people "to pray, pay, and obey," as he was fond of telling his priests. His insistence that priests never show weakness, that they wear their clerical garb in public and that scandal in their ranks be handled quietly by the archbishop himself revealed his philosophy of maintaining a clerical elite. Justin wondered if Mark planned to mirror this leadership style.

But during the years of his illness, the archbishop's repressive style declined along with his body. Although a residue of fear remained, his ability to enforce his will all but ceased. So the question before the new bishop was whether he could get back the clout, if that is what he wanted.

Within weeks of the archbishop's requiem, the new pope named Mark apostolic administrator of the archdiocese. The title did not assure him he would be the new ordinary of the archdiocese, but with calculating foresight, the new bishop moved to fill the vacuum immediately. The staff launched their assigned initiatives the day after the word of the power transfer came from Rome.

The week after the press conference announcing the appointment, another press conference was scheduled to announce new projects, starting with clearing all debt and transforming the piles of architectural drawings into brick and mortar . . . "symbols of the permanence of Christ in Indiana," as the new bishop deemed buildings.

He scheduled individual meetings with every priest and the heads of convents and chancery departments to reinforce his role as sole authority in the archdiocese.

To deliver this same message to Justin, Mark sent Justin a copy of the letter to the Papal Nuncio naming Justin vicar general, the number two man in the archdiocese, at the same hour a press release was issued with the news of the assignment. Justin anticipated the new role since he was the bishop's chief advisor. But absent the courtesy of a personal meeting on the matter, Justin's resentment swelled.

Mark's visions of growth and power were distracted, incidentally in Justin's mind, by an unforeseen announcement on January 25, 1959, twenty-two days after the archbishop went to his reward. Just three months into his reign, the new "transitional pope," who was to be a simple custodian of ecclesial government, called an Ecumenical Council for the entire church to begin in October 1962. Every bishop in the world was to report to Rome to "open the doors of the Church and let in some fresh air," in the pope's words.

The news seemed to unsettle Bishop O'Connell.

"What is the crisis? Why call a council if there's no heresy or threat?" the bishop asked Justin on the day of the announcement.

But Justin had monitored theological trends over the last twenty-five years and understood complicated issues were percolating in

Europe and elsewhere regarding changes in the role and mission of the church, attitudes toward other religions, the cry to drop the Latin liturgies in favor of vernacular languages. Justin expected the leaders would tackle these topics in due time. But to gather the bishops in a worldwide council to debate them all at once was potentially explosive. Still, Justin understood the long bow of history, so his expectations for a council were minimal.

Several days after the pope's announcement, Mark called Justin to his plush office. The new vicar general anticipated yet another archdiocesan project the bishop had contrived in the middle of the night or while scanning the newspapers.

The office was orderly, but its walls seemed cluttered by the dozens of plaques, trophies, and other awards accumulated over decades for the bishop's many causes and projects. Justin found the exhibits distracting and self-aggrandizing.

Hunched over a broad desk covered with neat stacks of papers and several books that appeared fresh off the press and unread, he kept his eyes on an open file before him. The room smelled of Sir Walter Raleigh pipe tobacco, sweet and pungent.

"I've decided to be a strong voice at this council, and I want you to make that happen." He stretched upright in his high back leather chair and looked Justin in the eyes for a response.

"What do you have in mind?" Dressed in his pressed cassock and collar, Justin too sat erect in a room reflecting the power of his superior. The bishop's coat of arms, a five-foot-by-seven-foot symbol of pride, hung behind his desk; it was framed by American and Vatican flags on brass poles, one topped with an eagle, the other with a cross.

"Go to Rome immediately to prepare to be my peritus." The words rolled out with a satisfying grin.

Each bishop was expected to bring a peritus, or well-versed theologian, to the council to serve as research staff and advisor for the deliberating prelates. It was no surprise to Justin to be asked to aid the bishop, which he'd done for years as a matter of course. But to go to Rome two and a half years ahead of time to prepare?

"What?" The one word question reflected his shock and resentment. He wanted to be cooperative, but the insufferable bishop seemed to again consciously throw him off course to maintain domination.

"Why is it necessary? Here I have access to any material I need to advise you. Why send me thousands of miles away?" Passionate reasoning would not work, but it was all he knew.

"Because I want all the scuttlebutt at the Vatican." He leaned over his desk as if to ease into a secret. "I'm going to be the best-informed American bishop there, and I want to know the players," he whispered. "Being in Rome while the agenda is drafted, you can teach me what I need to influence and who I need to influence."

Justin's heart dropped. He was again being made the bishop's compliant agent. But more than an agent, he felt Mark wanted him as his accomplice. Was his superior attuned to the movements of God, or was he making himself god-like by trying to anticipate where and how to grab power? Although in a different guise, Justin sensed he was witnessing the unfolding of a curiously familiar type of personality.

The bishop again leaned back in the chair and raised the volume. "So, get me a report by the end of the week on which school in Rome is the best. You're going there as soon as you can get it arranged." This tone was more aggressive. The higher up the hierarchy Mark went, the more heavy handed his style. He pulled a pouch of tobacco from his desk drawer and began stuffing his pipe as Justin left.

∴

Justin again did as he was told. But not without cost. His physical symptoms had not abated since he'd left St. Peter's Hill. Headaches and insomnia characterized his days and nights. He continued to lose weight, prompted by his gastric upsets, which he attempted to keep from worsening with medication and plenty of liquids. Yet a visit to a new doctor confirmed his severe dehydration, requiring a three-day stay in St. Edward's to restore his fluid levels.

"So, you need to drink more water, right?" The bishop stood next to the hospital bed, minimizing the distress of his working subordinate. A bottle of liquid hung from a steel pole at his bedside. From it a rubber tube attached to Justin's forearm dripped life-giving nourishment into the weak priest.

"Yes, that's part of the treatment," Justin said.

The room smelled of rubbing alcohol and fresh starched, bleached linens. He'd hoped his busy superior would have just sent flowers instead of visiting. But the trip to the hospital, his first since being ordained bishop, was an occasion for Justin to observe the nurses and doctors in the hallway genuflecting and kissing Mark's ring before he entered the room. Perhaps Mark justified such adulation knowing each person received an indulgence with each kiss, relieving them of fifty days in purgatory.

Once the bishop had left, the tired priest reflected on the last session he had with Miss Aaronheim and wondered what freedom he would ever have so long as he was controlled by the man more self-serving than Justin had ever imagined. With metal supper carts rattling in the hall in tandem with p.a. requests for doctor so and so to report here or there, Justin closed his eyes and prayed for guidance.

∵

The following week, while the bishop was in Washington for meetings, Justin returned to Cincinnati. His body was temporarily restored, but his psyche continued in disarray.

In the reception room he sighed as he sunk in a soft chair anticipating the sight of Miss Aaronheim at the doorway. He closed his eyes and breathed in, filling his lungs with the air of the hospital, antiseptic pine scented air of healing and comfort.

In her office he wasn't sure how to begin. Both sat in silence for several minutes. Finally, looking out the tall window at a dull silver sky slowly yielding puffy snowflakes, he began.

"How do I get out of this?" He was comfortable in the familiar room with the attentive therapist, a sanctuary from the demanding ecclesial world of the chancery.

"This?"

She was again her consistently concerned self. Justin felt safe because he totally trusted her. But, accompanying the trust, he knew her well enough to know she might provoke and challenge him in unexpected ways at any point. Part of him welcomed this because it stretched his thinking in ways he couldn't manage on his own. And he was fully aware her actions might hold the only hope of his healing.

"He wants me to go to Rome for three years to prepare for this council. It doesn't start until late '62."

"Are there any positives to going to Rome?" She fished for possibilities that eluded Justin.

"I wouldn't have to live down the hall from him?" He gave her a weak smile to go along with his weak humor.

"Am I to understand in Rome you'd have a chance to study what interests you?"

He sat up and listened, anticipating direction. His multiple, previous sessions taught him she was skilled at occasionally letting him draw upon his own judgment to set a course of action.

"Yes, I guess so. I'd like an exciting place like Rome where theologians are constantly researching and lecturing."

"And you'd have access to one of the best psychoanalysts in the world."

"What do you mean?" It was as if she departed from a script, preparing to make a direct suggestion.

"My friend, Dr. Rudolph Goldberg, is in Rome. If you choose

to continue the work we've started, you could find no better man to be your therapist."

The snow stopped and the heavy chalk clouds moved southward.

The thought of going deeper into therapy was repulsive and appealing at the same time. Justin's whole being wanted to put the Basil Epperman chapter of his life behind. He never wanted to relive the trauma of those nights with the sick priest. If only magic could be brought to bear on his deep wound to heal it in an instant. And give him courage to deal with his bishop.

CHAPTER 10

I N THE HOT SEPTEMBER of 1959, Justin flew to Rome on a Pan Am
flight from New York. The pale blue coach cabin smelled of stale
cigarette smoke and women's perfumes. Justin, dressed in a fresh
pressed black suit and wearing his Roman collar, settled into his
aisle seat in the middle of the coach section. He hoped for an easy
flight, his first to Europe. As passengers looked for their assigned
seats, he leaned back and shut his eyes, awaiting takeoff.

When the stewardess began her robotic recitation of safety pre-
cautions, Justin looked across the aisle at an elderly priest with a
thick notebook on his lap. The two smiled. Justin wanted to cocoon himself in his seat, read, work on a draft of an article for the
journal *CrossCurrents*, and then try to sleep during the long flight
across the Atlantic. He didn't want the old priest to engage him in
lengthy chatter.

In a thick Italian accent the priest said, "I am Cardinal Calabrese."

Justin recognized the name immediately as the apostolic nuncio, the pope's emissary to the United States. He tightened in the
presence of the most powerful cleric in the nation.

"I am Justin Zapp from Indiana," he responded. He rechecked his seat belt.

"I know of your work on interfaith theology, Father Zapp." His round, smooth face seemed serene, authentic.

Justin calmed a bit, but was surprised, as always, when people told him they read his theological writings or recognized his name. Indeed, in the area of ecumenism, especially Catholic-Jewish relations, Justin was emerging as an international expert. But in Justin's mind his scholarly work was a creative escape from the emotional burdens of daily life, not a significant contribution to the debates occurring within the Catholic Church in the 1950s.

He studied the Italian's face. Was the cardinal pleased with his work or not? His calmness didn't reveal an opinion, evidence of a skilled diplomat no doubt. A toddler two rows behind them began screaming at his mother. The gentle words of the mother quickly silenced the child.

"Are you going to Rome on business or a pilgrimage?" the cardinal asked.

"Bishop Mark O'Connell wants me to study for a couple of years at the Immaculate Conception to prepare for the council."

"A wise idea. You are to be his peritus?"

"Yes."

"Another wise idea."

Was this a confirmation of Justin's work?

The cardinal leaned across the aisle to ask in a choppy accent, "Would it be possible to meet you this week in Rome?"

"Yes, I guess so. If you'd like to meet, I'm sure I could arrange it. My classes don't start until next week." Justin obsessively rechecked his seat belt.

"Magnificent! I'd like to introduce you to some of my friends who you may find helpful as you prepare for the council."

A slim, young stewardess, dressed in a tailored pale blue suit with a matching pillbox hat atop her Gracie Allen-cut, caramel-colored hair, strolled from the front of the plane, slowing at each row to check the passengers.

Immediately Justin questioned the cardinal's motives. Another manipulative cleric? A sincere show of kindness? He remained apprehensive the rest of the flight, unable to sleep, read, or write, and he made frequent trips to the lavatory. To and from the bathroom he noticed the toddler asleep on his mother's lap, his mouth open, breathing evenly. Justin's forehead pounded the entire trip.

∵

The cardinal and Justin shared a cab ride from the airport. The prelate pointed out historical sites along the way. The first impressions of Rome exhilarated the jet-lagged priest from rural Indiana. Cars and buses swerved around curves and into intersections with abandon. People of all ages crowded the ancient narrow streets and broad thoroughfares. Every city block seemed to reserve gaps for a chain linked fence encased ruin or excavation site next to expansive al fresco dining patios, coffee bars, and shops. With the cab's windows open, the layered, rich smells of garlic and roasted meats mingled with exhausts fumes. Church bells clamored between blaring taxi horns and shouts of newspaper vendors on street corners. The city was alive, Justin thought, as he rode in the back seat, gawking. But his excitement mixed with tension. He was in a foreign city on someone else's mission. Time in the Eternal City was not to be a vacation.

When the cab stopped at his apartment building, he gave the cardinal a business card with his name and Roman contact information. The diplomat smiled and said he would call within a few days, and then he proceeded to Vatican City.

Overlooking a formal garden and lush park, Justin's Roman quarters were two rooms with a small kitchen and bath on the third floor. He'd arranged the lease through the Pontifical Immaculate Conception College, a ten-minute walk away. The bedroom walls were heavy beige, interrupted by two tall windows with dark gray indoor shutters. The floor, heavy oak planks fitted tightly together, squeaked like piglets with each step. These were simple quarters, befitting a simple man, he thought, where he would sequester himself during the coming months, hoping for deserved relief from the constant demanding will of his bishop thousands of miles away.

The next day he hired a guide to show him the city. Several blocks from his apartment a deep hole revealed layers of ruins from centuries of urban living, a university archeological site. Later, standing in the Forum he understood better the passion of humans for control, power, and violence through the centuries. Here Caesars ruled by any means possible. The pen of Shakespeare immortalized one of them, Julius, who was stabbed in a political struggle by a jealous ally in the senate chamber, now a roofless stone shell.

Crossing the Tiber River he saw for the first time the massive dome of St. Peter's Basilica. The guide, in broken English, gave the history of the church and the nation-state of Vatican City, a history familiar to Justin from his childhood. The last vestige of the once threatening Papal States, the tiny Vatican now claimed the most extensive intelligence network in the world, with dioceses and parishes planted in nearly every corner of the planet.

Gawking at the sixteenth- and seventeenth-centuries' architectural wonder for the first time, it struck the American priest just how strong the church mirrored the political structures of ancient Rome. He recalled a quote of Thomas Hobbes that the papacy was "not other than the ghost of the deceased Roman Empire, sitting crowned on the grave thereof." The church had imitated the state in making itself God's governing authority on earth, an authority that secured a semblance of social order for Europe during the Middle Ages, after the collapse of the political and military eras of the Caesars. The pope is the church's equivalent of emperor, Justin thought. The College of Cardinals, who, upon the death of the "emperor," meets to choose among their ranks the successor, models the Roman senate. Like local tetrarchs and regional rulers, the thousands of bishops scattered about the known world manage the vast machinery of local churches and report regularly to the central authority in Rome. Pontiffs no longer mobilize legions for violent crusades, but their power is far reaching through a world-wide diplomatic corps, and its vast information network made up of priests, nuns, and a fifth of the earth's population who fill the pews.

And these laymen and women, he wondered, were they also not like conquered peoples, to be controlled and policed, lest insurrection threaten the established order?

As he walked the long nave of St Peter's at a slow pace, his hands behind his back and his wide eyes skyward, he was both in awe and a bit amused at the work of artist Gian Lornezo Bernini inside the largest church in the world. The lingering subtle smells of burnt beeswax candles and sweet incense lingered in the vaulted, broad house of worship. Several clusters of tourists nestled like chicks to a hen around tour guides who described the building and its furnishings in several different languages. The structure is a masterpiece, intentionally built to glorify the God of all creation with the creative use of stone, glass, and natural light. But was it not also built with money extracted from the laity in exchange for indulgences, those magical IOUs meant to be redeemed at death to minimize one's time in purgatory? And wasn't the leadership of the church at that time shaken by fresh thinking of Luther, Zwingli, Calvin, and others to the extent that a prop like St. Peter's was more a statement of the church's dominance over errant forces than a sacred house of worship?

Late in the afternoon, the time change and hours of sightseeing in the congested city caught up with Justin. The guide returned him to his apartment where Justin anticipated an extended nap. Taped to his apartment door was an envelope with a telegram: "Meet me at Trattoria Roma, next to the Pantheon, at 9 p.m. tomorrow. A.G.

Calabrese." Below his name was his phone number and Vatican address.

Exhausted, Justin slept until dawn the next day.

∴

Tucked into a corner across the street from the Pantheon, the restaurant's dozen half-filled outdoor tables lined the sidewalk. The Pantheon, an architecturally perfect domed house of worship built by slaves around 25 A.D. to honor all Olympian gods, has sixteen stone pillars holding the triangular arch above the main entrance. It was transformed into a Christian church in 608 A.D., dedicated to Mary and all the martyrs. The wide cobblestone piazza that surrounded it spanned to several side streets, including the one where Justin spotted the Trattoria Roma. He tensed at the sight of Cardinal Calabrese and two other priests laughing and drinking red wine at a table nearly hidden by a full, potted fern. Illuminating the shadowy faces of the men circled in conversation, a single candle flickered in the center of the table covered by a white cloth.

Now stiffened with anxiety, Justin greeted the familiar cardinal and was introduced to the other priests, two American theologians whose names he recognized, Godfrey Diekmann and John McKenzie. Near Justin's age, they looked relaxed and welcoming, smiling with no guile. Despite their stellar reputations in church circles, in this setting, but for their black suits and Roman collars, they could have been mistaken for corporate executives enjoying a warm autumn Roman evening of al fresco dining. Once seated Justin remembered both Americans were scheduled to present at the Cincinnati conference over a year ago; Justin didn't last long enough at that meeting to hear them speak. Now he speculated whether they might recognize him as the priest who collapsed with the "seizure."

The coolness of the early autumn night seemed to want to bathe Justin, to calm him. At one point he stretched his neck to the few stars visible through the earthly lights of Rome. Then he refocused on the conversation at the table.

During the long meal, Justin let the cardinal order multiple courses for him, all the while wondering how much of the gourmet food he would be able to digest. He also let the three men lead the discussions about the council, the pope, and politics of the Vatican. In Hoosier parlance, Justin knew he was in high corn.

"What amazes everyone is he completely ignored the establishment. He called the council after consulting few outsiders. No one knows quite what to make of it," the Jesuit McKenzie said. His was an intense, kind face.

"It is either a stroke of genius or a fizzle of a demented old man," Father Godfrey, the Benedictine from Minnesota, observed. The noted scholar seemed serene, which Justin envied.

"He's not demented," the cardinal said. "He knows what he's doing. He's a very holy man with great wisdom. I sense the winds of change are the winds of the Holy Ghost." He spoke with a thick Italian accent and smelled of garlic.

At the end of the evening, as Justin walked alone to his apartment, he felt relief that the two scholars didn't seem to recognize him from Cincinnati. He also had a tingle of hope that perhaps the ancient, crusty old church could revive itself to be what it was called to be on the first Pentecost: holy people doing God's work in a broken world. Power, prestige, wealth, image . . . could they be replaced by simple service, humility, poverty, and authenticity? Justin doubted the church could change as much as he doubted he could change himself. But a struggling, small part of him was willing to put his best efforts into both endeavors.

CHAPTER 11

THE OFFICE WAS SPARSE. A simple, clutter-less desk with a small lamp, two upholstered dark green chairs that faced each other, a side table with a box of tissues, and a single tall window with a border of heavy satin burgundy drapes, trimmed in yellow, opened over a lush garden, park-like setting. Justin caught a whiff of lavender when he entered the office of Dr. Rudolph Goldberg. Lavender reminded Justin of the statue of Our Lady in his boyhood home on a doily covered side table in the kitchen. There his mother kept stems of the flowers in a vase as a simple shrine to the Virgin. And there she lit an azure glass votive candle nightly, and with her son, prayed the rosary. Praying the rote petitions next to his mother on his knees was the most peaceful time of each day.

"How may I be of help?" The bespectacled psychoanalyst spoke crisp English with a mixture of German and British accents, a reflection of his native country and his years in London where, as a Jewish war refugee, he studied his trade at Tavistock Clinic under Freud's disciples.

"I have physical problems." Justin looked at the tall window, opened enough to hear several birds chirping in the trees.

"Yes?"

Justin knew he was starting all over. It was like re-reading a familiar, unsettling book, spending hours and energy a second time, knowing the outcome.

"Not much can be done. I take the medicine prescribed. Let's just say I am not worse." Justin felt impelled to rush to solutions.

"Medicine for?"

"I have trouble with my digestive system, and I have headaches and I seldom sleep well."

"Can you tell me more?"

During this first meeting the psychotherapist took notes on a pad propped on his knee just as Miss Aaronheim had done in initial meetings. A short man in his sixties, his hair was thin and gray and his face narrow at the jaws. He possessed a brief smile that seemed genuine.

Still Justin felt uncomfortable. He had never fully trusted any man. With no father during most of his years in his childhood home and no church authority, whether the faculty in the seminary or fellow clergy in the archdiocese, worthy of trust, Justin was now in unfamiliar territory. At least with Miss Aaronheim some connection was possible early on; she had motherly qualities.

"Doctor, I am here because of my physical problems. My therapist from Cincinnati recommended you, as I think I mentioned when we set up this appointment. She thinks I need further therapy."

"For?"

A long pause ensued. Justin looked at his knees, uneasy. Comfort eluded him. He took a deep breath.

"I'm nervous a lot. She thinks if I receive more therapy my physical problems will maybe go away."

"That's what she thinks. What are your thoughts?"

The question was direct, but Justin couldn't distinguish whether it was a necessary inquiry or a move toward authoritarian control. How harsh would this man be?

"She may be right. I don't know." He shifted in his seat and crossed his arms over his chest. Through the opened window he heard a church bell toll; perhaps it was someone's funeral.

"Are you willing to try?" His voice was strongly masculine, yet bore a welcome tone.

He put down his pen and stared at Justin, who noticed his heavily starched French cuffs, with what looked to be ivory cufflinks, jutting from his gray coat sleeves.

"Yes. Yes, I'll try. This isn't easy."

Dr. Goldberg smiled with gentleness.

∵

That evening, as Justin tried to unwind with a stroll along the narrow streets around his apartment, he saw a young father, holding his son's hand, walk past him under a street light. The boy looked to be about three or four and both licked gelato on cones in between giggles. After they walked on, Justin stopped and turned to stare at their backs. A skip of joy marked the boy's steps. Seeing their figures diminish into darkness, Justin stood on the street and cried in silence.

∵

In the following weeks Justin began his classes at the Pontifical Immaculate Conception College, the internationally renowned training ground for theologians, future bishops, and cardinals from English speaking nations. Usually sitting in the back of the class room, he socialized little and kept quiet during lectures. Much of the material presented he'd studied privately over the last quarter century. What had been new theological thinking was now becoming mainstream, thinking that might coalesce at the council, two and a half years away.

Chapter 12

A T NIGHT HE RETREATED to his room to cook a lonely supper, read, pray, and sleep. If Mark thought Justin was in Rome on a reconnaissance mission, he'd be disappointed.

Twice a week, in the late afternoon, he scheduled therapy with Dr. Goldberg. After two months, Justin sensed a slow connection with him, but the name of Basil Epperman was yet to be uttered. The content of the sessions focused on adjusting to Rome and a review of his years at St. Peter's Hill and his brief period as vicar general.

In early December 1959, Justin walked in a chilling rain to his appointment with a headache worse than normal. The night before he'd gotten no more than two hours sleep and, despite medication, had spent most of the early morning hours with turbulent digestion.

Weak, underweight, and exhausted he sat across from Dr. Goldberg.

Neither said a word for several minutes; the therapist awaited Justin's lead.

Finally, filling his lungs with a mouth open to all available oxygen, Justin began. "I am miserable. I can't concentrate and my body is tied in knots. I don't know where to begin."

The low afternoon Roman sun streamed across the glass-covered bookcase behind the doctor. Bound answers to human pain, Justin thought about the books.

He looked at Dr. Goldberg and pleaded, "Help me."

"I want to. But I have a sense there's a burden you carry that either you aren't aware of or you are scared to tell me."

"Yes, yes." In a rush his innards stirred and he excused himself.

Upon his return he slumped back in the chair. "Something worse is happening to me. I don't understand. I can't control my body."

"Have you considered that perhaps what's happening is related to an issue we've not yet discussed?"

Justin recognized the diplomatic way the doctor steered the conversation. And Justin knew exactly what he had been withholding from the man in whom, after more than two dozen meetings, he felt the beginnings of confidence.

How much more suffering could he endure? When, he wondered, would the therapy on the real issue begin with Dr. Goldberg?

Turning, again, into himself, Justin bowed his head and slumped his narrow shoulders for several minutes.

In a sudden shift he sat up and blurted, "I was raped at thirteen by a priest in the seminary." With tearing eyes and a gaping mouth he couldn't believe the words had come out.

Dr. Goldberg said nothing for several minutes, waiting to see if Justin had more to add.

Nothing more came.

"When you are ready," the therapist said in a near whisper, "you can tell me more."

Justin moaned and wiped his eyes with his knuckles before grabbing a tissue from the box on the side table. Something had seized him; there was no forethought to what he had just said, and it frightened him. His style was always to be in control of his words and thoughts. The inner censor had failed him, leaving him vulnerable.

The session ended with no more words.

∴

The next few nights, curiously, Justin rested better, with four or five hours of sleep each night. The headaches persisted, but the gastric turmoil eased. His mind raced with disjointed thoughts, and he sat in classes in a daze.

∴

The night before his next therapy session Justin read his breviary under a dim overhead light in the chapel at the college, hoping to collect himself in anticipation of Dr. Goldberg's curiosity. Before a singular, scarlet glass-encased flame in the sanctuary, he opened the worn, leather bound book and prayed the psalms of lament. Pausing mid-sentence, he stared at the red, flickering sanctuary candle on its bejeweled, golden stand. Like a parting of Red Sea waters, his mind opened wide to a new vista. Relief filled him and he breathed deeply before closing his eyes. A presence . . . divine? . . . calmed and relaxed him.

∴

During the following months Justin revealed, little by little, hints of what took place in the secret meetings with Basil Epperman. The fullness of the trauma he withheld, however, suspicious that Dr. Goldberg would respond with rage and harsh judgment.

CHAPTER 13

B Y EARLY SUMMER 1960, Justin's hours in the classroom convinced
him he was learning nothing new; yet, to honor Mark's authority, he signed up for a new round of classes for the fall. At the last
session of the spring semester the guest lecturer was Father Yves
Moinet, the Dominican friar from France who many believed to be
one of the most influential advisors to the pope.

The high-pitched thick French accent did not diminish his insights and enthusiasm for the role of the church in the twentieth
century. He spoke of hope, engagement with the world, dialogue
with other religions, and a respect for the dignity and opinions
of those in the pews. Justin sat spellbound. The evolution of this
theologian's thinking, which paralleled Justin's own development
as a theologian, resulted in fresh concepts about key issues in the
church and God's ways of working in the world. The rote answers
to the ultimate questions, such as the existence of God, the meaning of life, death, the afterlife, the role of the church, were no longer good enough for Yves Moinet or Justin Zapp. To have Justin's
creative rethinking of these matters, acquired mostly from deep
research in the isolation of his ordered office at St. Peter's Hill,

confirmed by the words of this renowned master of the trade, energized Justin.

When he introduced himself at the small reception following the lecture, the older priest exploded with excitement.

"I know of your writings! I need you to help me!" He held a glass of local wine and was dressed in the black-and-white layered Dominican habit.

Justin stood stunned. He looked curiously at the bright-eyed Frenchman.

"You need me?" The social chatter of the other students all around them made Justin question his hearing of the priest's words.

"Yes! Yes! I have been asked by the Holy Father to prepare a paper for the Council on Jewish-Catholic dialogue. I had heard you were in Rome, but I did not know how to contact you. Can we meet to discuss this more?" He was bald with an oval face; deep-set, sincere eyes; and a toothy grin.

Justin agreed to meet the following week, unsure what was being asked of him and suspicious he might again be dealing with a self-absorbed cleric who wanted to use Justin to his own ends. The energy and excitement evaporated as quickly as they had erupted. He left the reception early; a fierce pain across his forehead would not stop. When he got to his apartment, he faced a sleepless night.

∴

At the next day's session with Dr. Goldberg, Justin immediately brought up the request of Father Moinet and his concern that it may be yet another up-the-ladder cleric using Justin.

"I am curious," Dr. Goldberg began. "Why would you be suspicious?"

"I'm suspicious of anyone who wants me to use my scholarship on their behalf." The tall window was fully open on this June day; a thick flock of blackbirds clattered in the trees across the street.

"Why?" The doctor's voice was absent any judgment.

A long pause followed before Justin began to tear up.

"You know how I've told you a little about being raped by Father Epperman? Well, I haven't been telling you all of it."

"How so?"

Justin had remained instinctively protective and cautious, still sensing Dr. Goldberg might rush to condemnation if Justin revealed the entire Basil Epperman story. The look on the therapist's face at this moment was anything but accusatory. Pure care is all Justin felt as he chose to reveal more, as if impelled by an inner power of unknown origin.

And so Justin told a second person the disgusting details of his rape at the hands of a sick priest. During the entire rendering the doctor never took his caring eyes off Justin and never said a word. Justin was collected and clear in his rendering of the brutal history.

At the end of the session the priest-patient sat in silence with a slow stream of tears on both cheeks, his head bowed.

∵

During the seventy-two hours between their sessions Justin spent long periods in solitude at his apartment window overlooking the manicured garden, pondering his life and the devils within that still refused to leave. His skin tightened with goose bumps at the thought of Basil Epperman, and his viscera roared in protest. He could smell the rubbing alcohol of the infirmary and feel the puffy hand of the drunken old man taking off Justin's clothes. The taste of the sweet-sour highball of whiskey and Coca-Cola was nauseous. He heard again the animal grunts that filled that darkened room thirty-seven years before.

Justin rushed to plug his ears, trying to block the sounds and the nightmare memories. He let out a howl and rushed to his bed to cover his head with a pillow, burying himself under the down comforter.

When he got up, hours later and well into the night, he was wet with sweat and depleted.

At prayer the next morning, with the sun breaking the eastern Italian sky with magenta and orange, there slowly emerged a shift in his understanding of Basil Epperman in his life.

At the next session, he launched headlong into the issue.

"He taught me, most of all, to be compliant," Justin said. "He was a mean, insane alcoholic who forced his body into mine and might as well have stuffed a sock in my mouth after it was over. God, I'm so ashamed. So ashamed." He elevated the volume to confirm his words.

"Ashamed?" Dr. Goldberg drew Justin out with skill and warmth.

"I took pleasure in it too, I remember. I didn't control my own sexual urges. Me, a seminarian preparing to be a holy priest!"

Justin remembered the smells of semen, booze, and cigarette smoke. He raised his voice in yet another self-indictment, but the therapist remained calm. "I'm a hypocrite. I let him do these things to me, I enjoyed it, and I didn't stop him."

The memory of a tingle at the sick priest's hands on Justin's body excited and disgusted him. He wanted desperately for the doctor to immediately confirm his distorted view of himself.

After a prolonged silence, Dr. Goldberg said, "I know this is hard for you to hear." Pause. "You were not at fault. You were a victim."

"You won't agree with me, will you? Miss Aaronheim told me I wasn't to blame either. But I know I am at fault too."

"No, that's a lie." The doctor had never before been so direct in his statements and eye contact.

The word pierced Justin like a lance. Lie. The one thing Justin fought all his life was the urge to lie. His conscience demanded truth. In an immediate, seismic shift he questioned whether he had gotten it wrong. All these years had he harbored the delusion that he caused Basil to rape him? He sinned by failing to refuse him and by not reporting him to someone who could have stopped the sick priest. Now Dr. Goldberg was telling him the opposite was true, as Miss Aaronheim did. But somehow his words sank in. Justin was not to blame. His whole identity rested on his guilt, his inadequacy, his shame, which Dr. Goldberg was denying. Unlike his therapy in Cincinnati, this time he felt the words, causing something to melt or wither inside him like the Wicked Witch of the West doused with water. And with that something's demise a feeling of open space—bright, wide, and limitless—rushed over him. Like that parting of the Red Sea experience in the college chapel.

He covered his face with his palms and wept. After a long silence he looked up, wiped his eyes, and said, in a near scholarly voice, "As I see it, when we are children, we're supposed to obey and not question our parents. I did that with my mother in my home and with my teachers. My mother, especially, was so good to me, despite her fears and insecurities."

"And as the child grows up?" the doctor said. Justin felt what must have been the remnants of a warm, father-son bond, even though Justin had so few clear memories of his own troubled father.

"As we grow we're supposed to think for ourselves. Outside of my scholarly work, I don't think for myself. I do what I'm told." Justin said. A delivery truck shifted gears and accelerated on the street below the window with a roar. Streams of diesel fume seeped into the room.

"So you're still a child in some ways?"

"Oh God, yes, I guess I am. I've never seen it like that."

"Are you ready to grow up?"

"I'm scared. But I'm not scared." The openness expanded more.

"How so?"

"Being a man means telling the truth, trusting my judgment, taking action!" There was now forceful energy in his words.

"Is that okay?"

"You're not a Catholic, so this may be difficult for you to

understand. But I fear what Basil Epperman did is not unique among priests. Maybe I need to do something about that."

"Educate this Jew." He smiled a small smile at Justin, putting him at ease.

"I suspect there are other priests who may be doing what Basil did. They may get reassigned mysteriously before their set terms at a parish are up. What am I to do? Do I betray my fellow priests?"

"Or save the lives of children?" The doctor stared at Justin. He had again laid truth in his patient's lap.

Another moment of silence before Justin said, "I know more than anyone what this sexual abuse does to a human being. I am a mess. It haunts me every day. He was a sick, sick man who should have never been allowed to be near children. I have no doubt he did to other boys what he did to me. Maybe worse. He should have been locked away until he dropped dead."

"And who would have taken on that responsibility?"

"I should have!" Justin shouted.

"But you couldn't." His voice was insistent.

In a near whisper Justin replied, "I know, Miss Aaronheim and now you have tried to convince me of that. I'm just beginning to feel it."

"Sit with the feelings."

CHAPTER 14

To escape the blistering month of August 1960, in Rome, Justin sought respite in the Umbrian town of Assisi. The train ride to the hilly region relaxed him; his inner wars had left him mentally and physically exhausted. In a tiny one room cottage, at the foot of the massive church built in honor of St. Francis, he slept twelve hours a night for three nights. At dawn, tranquil, he walked up the hill to say mass alone in the undercroft near the encased, tattered robe of the humble, thirteenth-century saint. He'd return to a simple breakfast prepared by Signora Clemente, the elderly widow who rented her single cottage to tourists. The solid little structure, built of native stone with a weathered orange tile roof, sat behind her fifteenth century villa, hidden from the street by several pale gray-green olive trees. The balance of the day he read, prayed, and napped. The prayers were for inner healing.

One cool night, strolling the cobblestone streets of the hilltop village, he spotted Tom Gentry, the young priest Justin had met at the Cincinnati event, sitting at an outdoor trattoria with a group of Franciscan friars in long black habits with cowls and white, three-knotted ropes about their waists. He wondered if it really was Tom, reluctant to accept the odds of running into the young priest thousands of miles from Indiana.

"Justin!" Tom yelled. Part of Justin had wished he'd not be recognized; it meant socializing with strangers and disrupting his time alone.

Exchanging introductions, Tom explained he was in Assisi after a summer Scripture course in Belgium.

"I'd heard the bishop wanted to send you for further studies. I didn't know it was this summer," Justin said. With reluctance he accepted Tom's invitation to join the group.

The young priest had maintained his athletic look. Justin was sure celibacy was difficult for this man with a chiseled face, a blonde flat top, and light blue eyes, who probably drew women like hummingbirds to nectar.

A half hour of casual conversation left Justin anxious and ready to return to his cottage.

Tom, full of supper and local wine, failed to notice his confrere's distress and said, "I'll be in Assisi three nights and would like to talk. Supper tomorrow night?"

Justin hesitantly agreed to meet Tom in the piazza the following night. Justin wondered if there were church developments in Indiana that Tom wanted to discuss.

∵

As vicar general Justin was familiar with one of the archdiocese's star young priests. Father Thomas Gentry entered the seminary when he was twenty-one. He'd been a small town basketball star in the 1950 boys state final, scoring a remarkable thirty-three points. Although his school was runner up in the tournament, he and his teammates were statewide heroes, returning to their hometown with a parade down Main Street and proclamations by the mayor and the governor. Despite his general apathy regarding sports, Justin, like most Hoosiers, followed the team's underdog spoiler role that year.

When he left Indiana University after two years for Presentation Seminary, Tom Gentry's fans were not surprised. News reports mentioned Tom never went with the drinking, partying crowd. He was recognized as a strong, honest young man who thought for himself and made his own way through hard work and persistence.

"Orvieto?" The waiter asked Justin.

"Minerale gasata." Justin spurned wine for local bubbly bottled water; he felt it helped digestion.

Tom had chosen an isolated café off the main piazza. Like the locals, he'd made reservations late on this warm summer night. The full moon was rising over the hills of Umbria, making long, soft shadows on the beige stone buildings of the small city. The smell of roasted garlic and burning hickory filled the air.

Justin's desire for a meal with casual talk was not to be fulfilled. Leaning over pasta, Tom launched into the topic that concerned him.

"Just before I left, a mother in the parish talked to me about Father Al Kremer's conduct with her ten-year-old son." Tom was still a new enough curate to address his pastor as "father."

Justin tightened as the words flowed from the young priest's mouth. He instinctively didn't want to hear what was being said but forced himself to put down his fork and look at Tom. The slow sounds of an accordion player across the wide piazza distracted him.

"It seems Father Kremer's taken the boy on overnight trips to his elderly parents' home several times."

"So? He's befriending the boy?" Justin sensed where this was heading but felt compelled to be the devil's advocate.

"More than befriending, I'm afraid." Tom took a sip of wine. "The boy has complained the priest has touched his private parts and has had the boy do the same to Father Kremer."

Justin's belly churned and his forehead tightened as the information flowed out. Justin knew Alfred Kremer, who frequented priests' meetings that Justin attended. He was one of the most respected priests in the archdiocese.

"Why are you telling me this?" Justin said with a bark that surprised both men. A violin had joined the accordion player in another slow tune to soften the evening.

"Because I don't know what to do. You know the archbishop. Do I tell him?" The young priest was calm and genuine.

Justin backed off. "Is the woman credible?" Justin secretly hoped she wasn't.

"Definitely. She is conscientious and well-respected."

"And she's told no one but you?"

"What difference does that make? I don't know who all she's told. I'm just concerned about the boy. He's ten years old, for God's sake. What kind of man plays in such a way with a child?"

"It happens, Tom. It happens." Justin looked down at his plate piled with stringy linguine and open beige clams. He wished with all his might that what happened to him was a one-time event and that no other child was ever abused by a clergyman.

"Yes, it happens. How's it stopped?"

Justin looked him in the eye and was direct. "The truth."

"What do you mean?"

"The truth. You tell the truth. That's how it's stopped." The words seemed foreign to Justin.

"Well, I'm now telling you the truth. You're still the vicar general, even though you are on leave for your studies right now. What do you do to stop it?"

"Look, this could be worse than we know. If it's true—and you'll have to make sure beyond all doubt—Kremer's a sick man. He'll have to be stopped."

Tom sat in a daze, his eyes like saucers, as he listened to Justin tell the positive side of Tom's pastor. Alfred Kremer was a kind, conscientious priest. He was comforting to the elderly, a great fundraiser for church buildings and projects and was known to deliver spellbinding sermons that drew in crowds on Sunday mornings.

Justin sat quietly to ponder ways to reconcile what seemed to be two entirely different Al Kremers.

Tom respected the silence until his impatience intervened. In a near demand, he asked, "Can we tell the archbishop now? Surely he'll want it stopped." His passion for righteousness, which Justin speculated Tom assumed every priest shared, was evident.

But Justin's conscience, long ago compromised by his own experiences of being violated, ruled for more caution than the innocent Tom wanted. This news was a bombshell. If either Tom or Justin reported it, events could spin out of control fast, leaving reputations and careers in the wake. As a priest of over twenty years, Justin knew the men of the cloth were not all saints. But to accuse one of the most esteemed of the clergy of molesting a boy would challenge the mores and status of the clerical culture he knew Mark O'Connell and bishops before him worked hard to maintain.

"Tom," Justin said, "I don't know what to do. Let me think about it and pray over it, and I will be in touch after I return to Rome." Justin hardly touched his meal.

Tom's face showed disappointment. "And in the meantime, what about the boy? What do I tell the mother?"

"Tell her the truth. Tell her you spoke with someone in the chancery. And tell her not to let her son ever be alone with Kremer. That much you can do now to protect him."

∴

Justin's body reacted with vengeance during the remaining days in Assisi. By the time he was settled in the Roman class room the next month, he'd lost weight and was exhausted.

Anxious to take Tom's challenge into therapy, Justin welcomed Dr. Goldberg's return from his summer vacation.

CHAPTER 15

"I T'S JUST SO COMPLICATED. Here I am thousands of miles away and I'm feeling guilty."

"Guilty?"

As if Justin was the most intriguing human on the planet during those fifty scheduled minutes, the psychotherapist focused on his every word. In Dr. Goldberg's presence, Justin knew no harshness of judgment. Nonetheless, as if by instinct, he remained guarded to ward off a possible castigation. A lingering part of him wondered if the doctor's single-word question prefaced a dressing down.

"Don't you understand? I could've stopped Basil and didn't. I can stop Kremer now and won't. What's wrong with me? I'm such a hypocrite. A fumbling hypocrite."

There. He'd judged himself before the doctor could do it.

The surprise response was as smooth as warm cream. "Perhaps we need to review both these issues, one at a time. Let's start with Father Basil. Your guilt?"

"Miss Aaronheim told me I was not at fault for what I did with him. You tell me the same thing. But I still feel overwhelming responsibility. Some nights I lay awake, tossing and turning and think of nothing but him . . . how he'd get me drunk and I'd know what was happening and I'd still keep drinking. He liked it when we drank together. He had a phonograph in his room and he'd play sweet melodies, romantic ones, over and over, and we'd have one drink after another. To this day I turn off the car radio when those 1920s songs come on. God, it was so sinful. How'd I do that?"

The clouds, growing darker, moved above the trees across the street. A September storm gathered.

Justin broke into tears. This talk of Basil was like stirring mud from the bottom of a farm pond that had long ago settled.

"And the drinking was only the beginning. Then the mortal sins began. He'd make me masturbate him, telling me I had to know how to do this to know what people would confess to me after I was ordained. I remember him telling me this was all part of my priestly formation. Oh, God, it was all so sick. And it was all my fault. . . . I let it go on and on."

"And who could you go to for protection from him?" Dr. Goldberg slid the question to Justin with such grace that Justin felt it merge with Justin's own thoughts.

"At the time I didn't think I could tell anyone." Thunder sounded from the outside the partially opened window.

"No one?" The doctor tipped his head slightly in an inquisitive look of care.

"Who? The rector? I'd gone over all of this with Miss Aaronheim, but it still isn't settled. That rector was going to listen to a freshman in the minor seminary? Basil threatened me. Don't you understand? If I told anyone, especially the rector, Basil'd deny it and have me expelled for lying. He'd paint me as a disturbed boy unfit to be a priest."

Justin stared into space and then added. "And here I am a disturbed, unfit priest. How ironic."

Lightning lit the sky. Rain pounded the glass of the tall window, which Dr. Goldberg stood to close.

The following weeks Justin attended the classes and spent most of his off hours alone in the library or in his room, reading and finishing a submission for *Theology Today*. The article was a summary of the ten major issues to be presented to the upcoming council, including Jewish-Catholic relations.

His nights were sleepless, the gastric turmoil continued unabated and the headaches, which became worse every morning, were as intense as ever.

Twice a week he caught the bus to go three miles to Dr. Goldberg's office, which was on the second floor of an office building several blocks from the Forum Square. When the crowded bus, smelling of dirty fumes, cigarette smoke, and sweaty bodies, neared his destination, Justin felt growing relief; his trust in the kind doctor had increased incrementally. The anticipated harsh judgments of the psychiatrist never appeared. He sensed the late middle-aged man may yet prove to be a competent guide in sorting the dark feelings and mangled past.

But despite several letters from Tom Gentry inquiring about action against Alfred Kremer, Justin procrastinated in dealing with that issue. In therapy, Justin avoided the subject as well. What he was really doing was wishing it would simply vanish like morning fog.

∴

In November, Senator John Kennedy was elected president, the first Roman Catholic ever elected to that high office, adding to the headiness of the imperial Roman Catholic Church. Convents, monasteries, and seminaries bulged with new members. The number of converts grew. The rotund, smiling pope won the hearts of everyone. And the Second Vatican Council was to convene in just twenty-three months, promising great things for the people of faith.

It was a high point for the universal church, the world's most respected moral authority.

∵

In mid-December he flew to Indiana for the Christmas break. It was to be a two-week vacation from what had remained boring studies. He had scheduled a spiritual retreat at the Lourdes Retreat House in an isolated region a hundred miles from the chancery. A requisite meeting with Mark was also scheduled.

On the flight across the Atlantic his thoughts turned to Tom Gentry and Al Kremer, for he knew Tom awaited a response. The issue had not receded. The thought emerged that Al's personnel file might offer clues to counter the mother's reports.

The first night back at the chancery, when Mark was at a dinner with major donors to the new college, Justin went to the administrative office on the first floor. It was dim from the weak hall light passing through the glass transom above the door. As he stepped in, the room held a dry, after-hours radiator-heat-stuffiness. He'd remembered from his pre-Rome orientation where the keys hung on the cabinet door behind the secretary's desk.

Feeling like a thief breaching private space, he turned on the overhead florescent lights and walked across the room to draw the metal Venetian blinds covering the window. The smell of lemon polish from the desks and wood panels assured him of the orderliness of the operations of the local church's seat of power.

With the turn of the key, the file room door opened to several rows of five-foot gray document cabinets. This was the living archive of the church in the sprawling archdiocese, including every priest, sister, religious brother, marriage, baptism, confirmation, Knights of Columbus charter, and parish history.

A black-lettered sign reading "Priests," stenciled across the top of one of the steel cabinets caught his eye straightaway. Under the Ks, he found a hefty folder with the name Reverend Alfred Joseph

Kremer on the tab.

Reading the contents Justin became nauseous. In it were dozens of letters, some handwritten, most professionally typed on letterhead, with complaints about Al Kremer's behavior with boys ranging from four years old to fifteen. Boy Scout leaders, school principals, lay teachers, nuns, coaches, parents, grandparents, and camp counselors. All with the same complaint against the esteemed priest: he sexually abused boys.

Justin dropped the file on the desk and rushed to the bathroom down the hall where he knelt before the commode and vomited his supper in heaves. Holding his throbbing head, he sat on the floor, his back against the wall, his mind whirling. He tried to take in the information he didn't want to believe.

Within minutes something gave him the strength to return to the room and resume his furtive task. The pattern quickly emerged: Al Kremer never completed the traditional six-year stint as pastor at any parish. After one, two, or three years he was reassigned, with a noted press release stating he was sent to a different parish to build a new school or new rectory or convent. No doubt the old archbishop recognized a skilled fundraiser in Al Kremer. There was no record of responses to any of the complaint letters. From the previous archbishop's point of view, evidently, there was no acknowledged abuse by Alfred Joseph Kremer, ordained Roman Catholic priest.

Justin's hand shook when he placed the overstuffed file back in its alphabetical slot in the drawer. He could take no more. He locked the chart room, opened the blinds, turned out the lights, and slogged up the carpeted stairs to his quarters, his head pounding and his belly churning.

Next to his window, he knelt and prayed. Sin seemed to pervade the official church's attitude toward Al Kremer. He prayed for mercy. But more importantly, he prayed for wisdom to know what to do in his own position of authority as vicar general of the archdiocese. His body trembling, he wept in confusion, disgust, and disillusionment.

The following morning, at breakfast with the bishop, Justin ate the creamy oatmeal and said little, despite his superior's jovial tone and inquiries about Rome and plans for the Council. Justin had no idea how to broach the subject of Al Kremer.

CHAPTER 16

O N A FRIGID, SNOWY January 20, 1961, Senator John Kennedy took the oath of office as president of the United States on the steps of the nation's capitol building, with Richard Cardinal Cushing, dressed in the biretta of the Princes of the Church, grinning behind him. The immigrant, poor Catholic Church, after decades of hatred and prejudice, had successfully climbed its way to the pinnacles of power in the wealthiest country on earth. Justin watched the news of the event on a small black-and-white television in the common room of the Immaculate Conception College with several other students.

∴

During the six months after Christmas 1960, Justin continued working with Dr. Goldberg. In a session the week before Mark was to arrive in Rome for his installation as archbishop on June 29, the feast of Saints Peter and Paul, Justin felt pressure building to the explosion point.

"I can't put it off any further. Tom will want to know what I've done about Kremer. He wants me to confront Mark and get Kremer pulled from all ministries where kids are present."

"And?" Dr. Goldberg asked. The early summer sky was deep blue, the window open to a cooling breeze.

"And what? Don't you understand what an atom bomb this is?"

"Explain." The doctor looked intently at Justin, eager to learn more about the ancient ways of Catholic bureaucracy and authority.

"Gentry tells Mark that he discussed this with me months ago. I've done nothing to stop it. Mark will tear into both of us for even bringing up the issue, knowing how he always wants to protect his priests. He might then punish us and spare Kremer. He and Kremer are tight because Al pulls in the money." Justin was making the links like the clerical culture was one big crossword puzzle.

"And the children?" Dr. Goldberg pierced through the ecclesial politics and placed the central issue directly in front of Justin.

Justin bowed his head with a long sigh. "God, you're right. The children. I'm such a disaster. I'm letting them go unprotected just like I was. I'm a hypocrite." A long pause. "A hypocrite worthy of hell."

He strained to look at the doctor, whose face spoke of sympathy.

"I'll talk with Mark myself. I'm still the vicar general, even if I'm on temporary leave. And I'll let Tom know what I am doing before he meets with Mark. Whatever happens after that, I can't control."

This new found determination seemed to emerge from nowhere.

That afternoon he walked to the Jesuit church near Dr. Goldberg's office. Since being in Rome he went to confession to an anonymous priest at the sixteenth century ornate sanctuary where the priest sat in the wooden box throughout the day, quietly awaiting sinners seeking peace.

"Bless me father, for I have sinned . . ." he began. With no forethought he rushed to confess his neglect in confronting his superior with the transgressions of a fellow priest.

"I have failed to be a responsible vicar general," he whispered to the man behind the screen. "There is a priest in my archdiocese that must be stopped from hurting children, and I have a duty to try to stop him. I've let this go on for months."

There was silence on the other side. Justin waited.

In a paced British monotone of an old man the words began.

"Father, you are correct. You must take action to stop the priest from hurting children. But do not be so harsh on yourself. To discern the right action takes time. You must ensure you do not rush to judgment and unknowingly hurt someone's reputation that may be innocent. Do you think you have ample evidence?"

"Yes, more than ample evidence. I have studied the personnel file and talked with a curate who knows of the abusing pastor."

"If you have evidence, then the matter must be brought before your superior."

"Yes. I have failed and am guilty of leaving the children unprotected."

The old Jesuit absolved him and told him to go in peace and sin no more.

∴

That night Justin stayed up late, praying over his decision. His headache was gone, and his abdomen was quiet. After an hour in silence with his God, a slow growing serenity settled over the weary priest. He got a good night's sleep.

CHAPTER 17

USTIN MET MARK IN a Vatican office a day after his superior arrived in the Eternal City for the pallium ceremony recognizing his elevation to the position of archbishop.

"Do you have an audience scheduled with the pope?" Justin made what he thought was small talk before bringing up the issue that most concerned him.

"Wednesday, the day after the ceremony, at ten in the morning. And you will be joining me."

Justin was stunned. Why would Mark want him in the room when he met the pontiff? As soon as he asked himself the question he self-scolded for his own naïveté. Of course the new archbishop would want his now internationally renowned scholar at his side when given an opportunity to impress the most powerful man in the church. How could Justin not have anticipated such an invitation?

"I'd be honored to be with you," were the only words Justin could find.

Fearing the Kremer issue would disrupt Mark's agenda, Justin rationalized saying nothing about protecting children.

∴

"I am a coward. I am an insensitive coward." Justin looked out the tall window of Dr. Goldberg's office at the deep green tree leaves stirring in the late June's muscled wind. The Roman sun seemed brighter than usual.

"More guilt?"

"Real guilt. I met with Mark, and he wants me to be with him at his audience with his Holiness tomorrow. I was too scared to mention Kremer."

"Scared?" The doctor's consistent mixture of empathy and nudging was again evident.

"Yeah, scared of what? I'm scared of my own shadow. I'm such a mess. I want to act, but I'm just such a passive jackass. God forgive me."

"Scared of what exactly?" Dr. Goldberg let the self-criticism pass and gently led his patient back to the core issue.

"Okay. I'm scared of myself, to tell you the truth. I think I'm frightened of the power I have and don't want to use. What can Mark do? Fire me? Demote me? Embarrass me? I guess he could do all those things. But you know what? I have some leverage too." Justin fell silent, as if to expose his secret weapon would risk its denotation.

"Leverage?" Goldberg pushed.

"Yes. I know he wants to get a red hat. If the decision makers in Rome know he's covering up the abuse of kids and it hits the newspapers, he'll be sidelined in a heartbeat." As soon as the words were spoken he turned scarlet.

"God, I can't believe I'd say such things. What's wrong with me?"

"Nothing." The doctor's word was solid.

"What?"

"I said 'nothing.' There is nothing wrong with you. What you are saying is you are an intelligent, caring man who will not permit the sexual abuse of children. To stop it you'll expose the archbishop if necessary. You have your values right. You were once one of those children, please remember, so you, more than anyone, know what action is necessary."

"It doesn't feel right. It feels soiled . . . to threaten an archbishop."

"Telling him the truth and expecting him to do the responsible thing is not threatening. It is what mature, mentally healthy people do. They protect children from sick sexual molesters."

Dr. Goldberg's words were sharp and crisp. Justin rushed to again judge himself, wondering why he failed to think with such clarity and then act with courage.

∵

Justin sat near the high altar in St. Peter's as the ancient rite, rich in baroque pomp and detail, unfolded. Pope John XXIII placed the pallium, a thick lamb's wool collar, over Mark's outer liturgical vestments, symbolizing his responsibility to be a caring shepherd. The new archbishop, now in full command of his flock, pledged in Latin to protect from injury the souls charged to him, each a vulnerable lamb. The annual event for new archbishops from around the globe reminded Justin of the courage needed to keep all from harm, especially the powerless children. Behind him a life-size tarnished statue of a seated St. Peter holding the keys of the kingdom seemed to be covering Justin's back.

The following morning at ten o'clock the pope's personal secretary escorted Archbishop O'Connell and Father Zapp into the papal study. The pope walked around his hand-carved wooden desk to greet them before everyone sat in a semicircle. Besides the two Hoosiers, the papal secretary and the pope were the translator, Cardinal Calabrese, and two of the pope's advisors.

After the archbishop delivered his report on the state of his

Indiana archdiocese, the pope turned to Justin to ask in Italian how his studies were progressing. Justin was enough of a natural linguist and had absorbed sufficient Italian since being in Rome to understand him.

Justin was surprised the aging pontiff knew anything about his being in Rome to prepare for the council.

"Your Holiness, the studies are progressing well." His Italian was choppy.

"I know Archbishop O'Connell has chosen you to be his peritus for the council, but I hope he will not be offended if I have you as one of my periti." The plump, round-faced pope offered a broad smile in the archbishop's direction.

The archbishop was wide-eyed with surprise. At that moment Justin realized Mark O'Connell may have felt his vicar general, who he had mistakenly believed he had shaped and guided to be an internationally appreciated theologian, had just leap-frogged him. What did this do to his superior's chances of one day being a cardinal, Justin immediately wondered. The pope's request confirmed Justin as a preeminent international scholar on Jewish-Catholic relations. He would help the pope set the agenda for the most important church gathering in a century and critique the working documents to be debated. The new archbishop surely knew this was a more prestigious and powerful position than being one of thousands of bishops in the crowd. The plotting Mark O'Connell's plan to use Justin to enhance his own advancement had just been derailed by the saintly pope.

"What an honor!" the archbishop said. But Justin speculated he was fuming and deflated on the inside.

If he had some leverage as vicar general to end the abuse before the meeting with the pope, he had even more now. Justin was now the pope's ally first, vicar general to Mark, second. The questions remained, though, whether he would use his new leverage and, if so, when?

CHAPTER 18

A T NINE THAT NIGHT Justin and Mark met at the Trattoria Reggio for a supper that had been scheduled weeks before by Mark's secretary. Something solid in Justin said this was the time to raise the Kremer issue with his superior.

He had prayed over it and tossed the questions back and forth in the therapy sessions. The obsessing was over. He now felt the Holy Ghost infusing him with fortitude and wisdom to speak the truth, more so now that his primary loyalty now rested with the pope.

"Cheers!" The archbishop raised a glass filled with Orvieto wine to Justin's clear water glass.

In an immediate shift of mood, Justin began. "I need to discuss something important." Justin leaned over the table with a straight, solemn face.

"Sounds serious."

A middle-aged waiter, in a black suit and crisp white shirt with a narrow ebony tie, slid menus in front of each priest, bowed, and returned to the kitchen.

"It is serious. It has to do with one of our priests."

"I'm all ears." He means to be charming, Justin thought, perhaps to minimize the gravity of the moment.

"A mother in Al Kremer's parish is reporting he has sexually molested her ten-year-old son. I am getting the story from another priest, who wants the abuse stopped."

Without pause the archbishop responded. "Hog wash! What's her grudge?" He arched back in an arrogant posture. A police car with a me-maw siren and flashing lights sped past. A steady stream of pedestrians strolled along the sidewalk between their table and the street.

"I don't know her . . . but the other priest says she's reliable."

"Says she's reliable! Why should anyone trust her?" His face and neck heated in deep pink. "Let me tell you something." He pushed his arms over the table, leaned into Justin's space as he glared at the younger priest with the weight of his office. "I've been a superior of priests as a dean for years and now I'm the archbishop. I've seen this kind. They've been offended by a priest in one way or another and seek revenge." His face was now scarlet in anger and his words curt. Shifting to a mocking high pitch he went on. "Their daughter didn't get the right day for her wedding in the church; they get enraged by a comment made when the pastor is having a bad day; the priest didn't make sure their son was altar boy for midnight mass. . . ." Sitting back and shifting to harshness, he added, "Whatever it is. Mostly silly stuff. What do they do? They can't get direct revenge because we hold all the cards, and so they turn to the oldest trick in the book: calumny." Now he stretched back in another haughty pose, deepening his voice. "Calumny, my friend. One of the great sins of the devil. They're out to destroy the reputation of the saintly priest. I've heard it all before. We get the complaints from crackpots wanting to extort money or settle a score or just be mean." He took a long drink of the pale yellow wine. In a paternalistic tone he added, "So, Justin, rest your troubled mind."

From his deepest self, Justin felt terrorized, like he was again in the presence of Basil Epperman in 1923. "While you are in Rome," Mark concluded, "all is well in Indiana. Al Kremer's reputation will not be soiled by some hysterical mother."

He held his empty glass in the air in triumph before pouring a refill. Placing his linen napkin over his mouth he belched into it, lowered the cloth, and smiled in deep satisfaction.

The similarities between Mark O'Connell and Basil Epperman had never shown before this moment. But here it was, in raw form. A mix of horror and outrage welled up in Justin as the archbishop's defensive monolog unfolded. The younger priest sat straight and looked his superior in the eye. When he finished, Justin took a deep breath, afraid to speak all he felt, but courageous to hold ground.

"I trust my source. This woman is not a vengeful crackpot. She is a loving mother whose son was molested by Al Kremer. I also reviewed Father Kremer's file the last time I was in Indiana. As you know, there have been other serious reports before you were appointed bishop."

"I'll not hear it, Justin. Get it out of your mind. I tell you, I've see this dozens of times. Lies, lies, lies, my friend. And those reports—yes, I know the charges. I can only assume my predecessor dismissed each of them. All lies, I'm sure."

"No, I don't believe they are all lies."

The waiter returned to take their orders and Mark discharged him with, "come back in a few minutes." He then continued, "Prove it. The easiest way for someone with no power to destroy someone with power is to spread scandal. Don't you understand that? We priests and bishops are men of power. We control parishes, schools, colleges, hospitals, and the souls of thousands. People in the pews know we have power and most are holy, gentle, and compliant. But every once in a while some nutcase comes along and wants to bring one of us down. Ignore it, my friend. Just ignore it."

This time he took a longer gulp of wine, lowered his glass and again grinned at Justin.

Justin knew where this was headed, worried the wine and Mark's entrenched attitude would make reasoning impossible. When the waiter returned again, he inhaled and sat back in his seat, gathering his composure while Mark ordered first.

With a rebuff of the topic of Al Kremer, Justin's superior moved to other topics: the laying of the cornerstone on the main classroom building of the new Catholic college, the plan to build a new shrine in honor of Saint John Vianney, the patron of priests, and the largest ordination class in the archdiocesan history from Presentation Seminary, thirty-six.

"God is good to us, Justin. We are building the reign of God in Indiana. We should be pleased with our efforts, as I am sure God is pleased with us."

During the extended soliloquy during the meal Justin held his tongue. When the Mark stopped, Justin softly stated, "I am always hesitant to claim I know the mind of God, your Excellency. All I know is, I want to be a good priest and be honest."

"Well, you're quite right. Yes, yes. And you are a good man. So don't let your mind be troubled with matters where you have no experience, okay?" His words now held a slight slur.

Justin said nothing. He felt these last comments culminated a litany of distorted twists of reality.

After cafe macchiato in the tiny espresso cups, the priests took separate cabs back to their separate quarters.

In his apartment, Justin hit the bathroom door with his rolled fist and gritted his teeth, sucking in air through his nostrils, a bull in a ring. "Why? Why? Why am I in such a sick life? He's power hungry! He's blind! I can't do this. . . ."

Angrily twisting his chair toward the window he collapsed and stared at the late June Roman sky, the crescent moon on the horizon above the trees in the park across the narrow street below. Gradually his breathing and heart calmed.

In a few minutes his skill at analysis took charge of his fury.

He was dealing with a resistant superior, unwilling to examine the claims against Al Kremer, leaving Justin to fortify his case with strong evidence. This task would take time and certainly be complicated by distance.

He prayed for more than an hour before the open window, seeking the gifts of the Holy Ghost, especially wisdom. His mission was set.

CHAPTER 19

"H IS POWER'S GONE TO his head." The assessment reflected Justin's emerging, yet fragile, confidence. "He might be right to say the church in his archdiocese is growing as the good Lord wants, but he won't listen to any criticism of Al Kremer."

Dr. Goldberg remained calm, giving space to this fresh side of his patient.

"The only way to deal with Kremer is to build the case against him with facts, which isn't easy when I'm so far away."

"Is it your responsibility to build the case by yourself?"

Sure it was, Justin thought. But he'd been in therapy with this skilled professional long enough to know his questions sometimes sparked alternatives. So Justin hesitated before he answered.

Why did he assume he alone was to build the case? Tom Gentry was living with the priest in question. Tom had the information from the concerned mother.

And what of the Catholics who had written the previous arch-bishop complaining of Al Kremer? Could they help? The weight of their testimonies alone should be more than sufficient to convince Mark to exile the abuser.

After a long pause Justin answered his therapist. "No. No, it's not my job to build the case by myself. I can work with others."

Fear and doubt, his perpetual enemies, did not paralyze Justin. But part of him knew diffidence still lived behind his strong words. Like a caged lion, it would do no harm unless Justin opened its pen and let its force dominate the jungle of his mind.

"Mark will minimize any facts we bring to him," Justin continued. "The goal is to overwhelm him with enough information that he can't deny it. Then he's forced to pull Kremer out of parish work. So, yes, it will take a team to do this."

"This is a different side of you, Father," the psychiatrist said. His bushy eyebrows arched with subtle delight.

"Yes. And I'm not sure I trust it."

"Perhaps it needs to be tested." Dr. Goldberg smiled and concluded, "Our time is up."

∵

At his apartment desk that evening, Justin typed a four-page letter to Tom Gentry explaining that the archbishop needed specific information on the case and requesting Tom to ask the complaining mother to meet at the chancery with Tom, Justin, and the archbishop. If she knew other parents or coaches, teachers, scout and 4-H leaders who could corroborate her allegations, he should enlist them as well. As sensitive as it might be, Justin also suggested children give testimony if Tom judged they could manage discussing their experiences without becoming emotionally distraught. More than anyone, Justin knew the victims may be the most hesitant to discuss their experiences.

The next morning, a Saturday, Justin walked to the post office several blocks from his apartment to mail the letter, its contents weightier than the postal scale reflected. As he turned from the counter he passed a Roman teenager who looked to be about thirteen or fourteen. A tsunami of memories washed over him.

"No good pastor can minister to his sheep without knowing the forgiveness of God for their own mortal sins." The booming voice of Basil rang in his hears. "So you must understand what you are doing is part of your training to be a good priest. Our strongest urge is concupiscence, young man! You must give in to it to know what your parishioners wrestle with every day." He rushed to a hidden bench under a shade tree and sat with his hands over his ears.

"No! No!" he shouted in whispers to himself. The blubbery jaws of the demonic priest flapped like Jell-O and his piercing eyes, with bristly gray brows, burnt through Justin.

"You don't become holy by prayer and fasting alone, my boy. Your soul must be shattered by sin so you know what real forgiveness is and be filled with grace. It is the necessary fault!" His perfect false-teeth grin reflected the single dim light in his room.

"God, no!" Justin shouted into the sky. Tears coursed his cheeks. He slumped and heaved pain for several minutes.

Once calmed he sat erect and looked through deep green shrubs to the see the young boy from the post office riding a bike along the street, nibbling a candy bar in one hand as he steered with the other. He looked carefree, happy.

Whipping his eyes with his handkerchief, Justin collected himself, got up, and walked to his quiet apartment to study papers in preparation for the Council.

Chapter 20

Y VES MOINET, THE DOMINICAN friar picked by the pope to lead the preparation of Council documents on the Catholic-Jewish question, had had a circuitous route to his position of influence.

"The Spirit has ways that baffle me." Moinet sat across from the American peritus in the House of Studies a few blocks from Justin's apartment. The centuries-old stone structure's thick walls helped cool the room from the July Roman heat.

"Just six years ago I was an outcast. The power brokers in the Vatican silenced me. Today the pope wants me to help alter history! Who would have guessed?" His thin white hair glowed in the window's filtered sunlight. His deep blue eyes spoke of serenity, honesty.

The parlor's auburn tile floor held a polished sheen. On the milky-colored plaster wall behind the theologian hung a five-foot-tall painting of St. Dominic, his order's thirteenth century founder. The saint's pose, with a contorted twist of his neck heavenward, spoke of a mysticism that was foreign to Justin in the mid-twentieth century. The painting's thick baroque frame, over a foot thick and gilded in gold, somehow defied the saint's teaching on the elevated virtue of poverty required of his friars.

"You're a prophetic voice. Prophets have histories of being rejected and misunderstood," Justin said. He was in awe of the man whose writings he had studied in detail for years. His research and now personal encounter gave promise that Moinet would not be another harsh man of authority exacting demands on a passive Justin. Justin sensed a truthful humility about the self-possessed scholar, fifteen years his senior. Perhaps this was no Basil Epperman or Mark O'Connell.

"Awe, but we are all called to be prophets, my American friend." Birds chirped a parallel conversation through the open window covered with a black grill of handcrafted ironwork. "And I need your own prophetic voice as we cobble together a more enlightened understanding of the Jewish people. This is an area of study where you know more than I. I want you to teach me, and I trust your voice on this matter more than my own."

It was difficult for Justin to imagine that he knew more about Catholic-Jewish relations than this internationally renowned theologian. Despite his years of scholarly research and publications on the subject, Justin couldn't imagine himself in the high echelons of ecclesial masters that included Moinet and the friar's patron, Cardinal Augustine Beal, rector of the Biblicum Institute in Rome.

Justin responded, "I'll help as you direct me." Sitting back in the leather upholstered parlor chair, Justin relaxed the more Moinet talked.

"I want you to be a peer with me. Together we must prepare a draft to submit to the cardinal and Pope that clearly outlines a shift in the church's position regarding the Jews. I need you to do the scholarly research to support an elimination of the idea the Jews are guilty of killing Jesus. And we need to frame an argument that they are the first Chosen People and are not required to be converted to Catholicism to be saved." He spoke with urgent compassion that Justin had not encountered anywhere. The doorbell rang and down the hall footsteps rushed to attend to it.

Justin focused again on the moment. "I may be able to help in both areas, Father." Justin knew he could put on paper tight, convincing arguments but still felt insecure sitting in front of Moinet.

"And let's do away with the 'father' titles, Justin. We are now colleagues and friends, are we not?"

"Yes, Yves."

∴

Indeed, Moinet was an expert in ecumenism, although not Christian-Jewish relations. Growing up in the French Ardennes, he told Justin he made friends with the children of his parents' Protestant and Jewish neighbors. Upon joining the Dominicans, he had studied in Belgium before moving back to France near the outbreak of World War II. During conflict he was a prisoner of war, having joined the French army reserve as a chaplain. In POW camps in Mainz, Colditz, and Lubeck he encountered Jews, many who would die in the Shoah.

"I saw things I never want to talk about. Such horrors," he told Justin.

His writings after the war, curiously, revealed little about the tragedy of the Jews in Nazi Germany. What they did reveal, however, were differences with the Vatican's theology police. He was silenced by Pope Pius XII in 1954.

When Pope John and Cardinal Beal called Moinet out of the theological exile, Justin didn't fully grasp that Moinet, although an esteemed academic, knew little about Christian-Jewish issues. Over the months they were to collaborate, Justin would be expected to draft a document that would win over conservatives wanting to retain the centuries old condemnation of Jews. This long-standing vilification had justified the persecution and discrimination of millions of the original Chosen People culminating in Hitler's slaughter. Justin and Moinet grasped that any reversal of the Catholic teaching on the Jews would be a cultural shift altering nearly two millennia of rationalized cruelty.

∴

Justin sequestered himself in the Immaculate Conception's impressive library the afternoon after the meeting with Moinet, determined to coalesce the necessary documentation to meet expectations. The main room, lined with stacks of thousands of books, smelled of binder's glue. The sun poured through the clear windows of the high-ceilinged chamber. Oak study tables and matching chairs, a mix of orange and brown hues, varnished and polished, lined the center, end to end. Two uniform black lamps with simple white shades were evenly spaced on each of the ten tables. Entering this room, Justin's adrenaline surged; a scholar in a library this vast was like a thoroughbred in an endless field of bluegrass. Justin's energy flowed without barriers. He was in his element, not just intellectually, but emotionally, gradually growing sure of his skills. No headaches or abdominal stirrings. Focused on the work at hand. Losing all sense of time.

"The library is closing."

Justin looked up from his books to see a tiny nun's soft face. Most of the lights of the cavernous room were out.

"Oh. I'm sorry."

"That's quite all right. The Holy Ghost must be busy in you."

"Yes. Yes, I am sure. I am sure." He rubbed his eyes with his palms then blinked several times.

The beads of her dangling rosary sang a soft clatter as she moved through the stacks.

CHAPTER 21

THAT NIGHT JUSTIN SLEPT a rare, deep sleep. The following morning, saying his private six o'clock mass at a crypt altar at the Immaculate Conception, he felt a rich connection to God. The musty undercroft, built of local stone decades ago, smelled of delicate incense mixed with subtle candle smoke. The dim space housed a dozen small altars in niches, stations of prayer for the priests of the college to offer their private daily Latin masses. Justin's masses here served to anchor his days in God, as on this day when he experienced a personal closeness and mutual care with the divine. It was a comforting thirty minutes.

Following his mass, he was eager for breakfast and a return to the library to pick up where he'd left off with the draft. As he placed the gilded green chasuble into the sacristy closet, an Italian custodian shouted, "Father, there has been an accident. A boy has been hit by a car."

"The oils?"

With a nod of understanding the custodian rushed to get a sick call kit containing the holy oils for the sacrament of Extreme Unction. Justin hurried up the stairs in his cassock to the tabernacle in the main chapel to retrieve a pyx containing the Holy Eucharist host.

The custodian, who spoke impeccable English in the Queen's accent, led Justin to the street in front of the school. Police surrounded the scene of a black Fiat sedan astride the sidewalk. Beneath the front bumper lay a twisted bicycle and a teenage boy.

"This way, Father," a police officer shouted in Italian.

Justin bent to the boy and felt his own blood drain from his face. Before him lay the same teenager he saw leaving the post office and later riding his bike with the candy bar on the previous Saturday when he sent the letter to Tom. What was happening? Justin thought. What was God doing?

As if by rote, he bent to anoint the shaking boy, still conscious, but with the gasping breaths of shock. Fresh deep red blood pooled around the teenager's full head of coal black curls.

"Can you take Communion?" Justin asked in broken Italian.

"Si, si." He opened his mouth to receive.

Justin carefully placed the wafer on his tongue and proceeded to anoint him.

Stunned, Justin sat on the ground and held his soft hand, praying for his recovery in audible whispers of English.

Abruptly the medical team arrived to examine the victim before placing him in the ambulance. Justin felt helpless.

∵

Later at the library his concentration never came, his mind filled with images of a boy one day carefree and today near death. His thin adolescent olive-skinned body. The deep brown eyes. The broad smile as he rode the bicycle munching candy. The brisk energy of leaving the post office. The boy-man blossoming before the world, innocent, curious, fun-loving, handsome, spontaneous. His represented the insouciant youth Justin never experienced.

Someone had stolen Justin's youth, leaving him constricted and anxious, ready to please and denying his own pleasures.

Anger rushed over him; it was delicately balanced by a determination to regain, bit by bit, what was lost. With Dr. Goldberg's help and by the grace of God, he would regain it. Justin closed his books and left the library, feeling tight all over. The headache returned and his stomach churned.

∴

Dark clouds surrounded the ancient city as Justin stepped from the bus in front of the doctor's office. The session began with the sounds of thunder cracking and bolts of lightning brightening the summer sky in an eerie display of God's force.

"I feel hopeless. After all this time in therapy, the feelings still hunt me like a bloodhound. They won't let loose. I started thinking of the ways Basil tried to justify what he did to me . . . what we did together. He said I had to know the mercy of God for my failure to contain my 'concupiscence.' That was the curious word he used, 'concupiscence'."

Dr. Goldberg stood to switch on a floor lamp behind Justin to brighten the room darkened by the storm. From his solid, upholstered chair he asked, "Tell me more."

The sound of his warm voice relaxed Justin. He sank deeper into his seat and took full breaths to quiet himself. With his eyes closed, he said, "I wish I could just run away from the world to a safe place like this and stay forever."

Dr. Goldberg waited. The rain beat against the tall window like fingernails on a wooden desk.

After several minutes Justin opened his eyes and told the therapist about the teenager involved in the auto accident. As he spoke, he cried.

"Something about that boy touched me in ways I don't understand. He seemed so carefree riding the bike and eating the candy. I've never had that kind of freedom and joy. I know nothing about him, but I just sensed his zest for life. His joy. Now it's all gone." He reached for the tissue box and yanked several.

"You're close to yourself at thirteen right now?"

"I'm about to turn fifty, did you forget?" There was an edge in his voice.

"I know your chronological age, but you mentioned earlier the thoughts of Basil trying to justify the acts he forced on you."

"Yes, yes. It makes me sick to remember. I don't think I understand you." He felt a sledgehammer hit his head at every mention of Basil's name.

"Can you see that the boy on the bike is a victim?"

"Why, yes. For all I know, the boy rode on the street in all innocence. The people at the accident told me the driver of the car was drunk." Rain now pounded against the window, and the trees across the street whipped in the wind.

"Sounds like the boy didn't will that the car hit him."

"No way is he guilty. Your point?"

"Do you see any parallels?"

He focused his eyes on Justin and awaited a response.

Silence.

"But I enjoyed it, don't you understand? I had plenty of reservations, but I gave in and let him do it to me. It makes me as guilty as he was."

The rain calmed to pecks at the window. The room brightened with a rush of sunlight.

Despite repeated sessions when Justin understood and accepted his innocence, the confounding feelings again refused to leave.

A long pause ensued with Dr. Goldberg looking at the priest with care. Justin looked up to see the soft eyes.

"Crazy, isn't it?" Dr. Goldberg said. They exchanged half smiles.

"I want to go to the hospital to check on the boy. I don't even know his name, but I'll find him. I pray he is healing."

"As you are," the doctor responded.

∵

After multiple explanations to hospital staff in his awkward Italian, Justin found Giuseppe Giovacchino in the intensive care unit at the hospital a few blocks from the Immaculate Conception. His parents sat at his bedside when Justin entered the area enclosed by bleached cotton curtains. A glass bottle of deep burgundy blood attached to a steel pole dripped new energy into the teenager. A gauze bandage encircled his crown and left cheek, swollen, bruised, red, and purple. The headband made the face like that of a failed, young prize fighter. Justin didn't know if the boy was asleep or unconscious, his breaths slow and even.

After introducing himself, Justin explained he was the priest who administered the sacraments to their son on the street. His mother, a slim, big busted woman in her thirties, bowed to Justin once she comprehended his broken Italian. Justin gestured for her to stop and reached to caress her hands, folded together as if in prayer.

"You saved my son's life!" Her voice was high and insistent.

"What?" Justin asked.

"Yes, you gave our boy Holy Communion and Extreme Unction and that healed him!" The father, a stout man in working clothes and a tired face, shook Justin's hand.

"No, no. I am not a physician. I am the priest. The doctors have helped with his body. My job was to help him with his spiritual needs."

"No, no, no!" The parents raised their voices in unison.

"Well, let's just say the hand of God is upon your son, working with the doctors and nurses and you and me." He looked at the patient as he asked, "How is he doing?"

"He is going to be better. He is sleeping now. You must come to our home for supper on Sunday, Father." The mother seemed pushy.

Justin stiffened at the command. He didn't want to get involved. He wanted to keep his distance.

"Let's just let Giuseppe heal. Then we can discuss other things."

With that he raised his right hand to bless the boy. The parents rushed to kneel at the bedside and make the sign of the cross on themselves. Giuseppe did not awaken.

Justin slipped from the room and found the hospital chapel near the front entrance. In the quiet space he sat for an hour in silence, reflecting on the session with Dr. Goldberg and the visit to Giuseppe.

Breathing evenly he felt his heart beats slow. He closed his eyes and felt calm. Yes, he knew he was not guilty. He wanted more than anything to know he too was a victim, a victim like the young Giuseppe was a victim.

Chapter 22

THE LETTER FROM TOM Gentry heartened Justin. Tom wrote of his eagerness to collect a group to meet with the archbishop about Al Kremer. He planned to prepare them to tell Justin their stories upon the vicar general's return to Indiana during the August 1961 school break.

During the remaining days in Rome, Justin's outpouring of work for Moinet remained steady. The energy flowed again, causing Justin to lose his sense of space and time while hunched over scholarly material in the library.

Arriving at the archdiocesan chancery in early August, Justin felt an immediate constriction when he put his suitcases on the oak foyer floor. The building's ornate furnishings and dark wall paper closed in on him. The freedom of being away from his superior failed to fully register until he stepped back into this bleak Edwardian limestone edifice.

On Justin's bedroom door the archbishop had taped a note: "At a meeting in Washington, D.C. until Saturday noon. Supper together Saturday evening? Mark."

Three days of no Mark O'Connell offered some consolation.

After settling into his room, he surprised himself by initiating a long distance phone call to Tom to arrange a strategy session. And he was eager to again review Kremer's personnel file to gather names of those who had written the previous archbishop with complaints about Kremer.

∴

"No takers." Tom Gentry looked tired. Now twenty-eight, he was supposed to be in the springtime of his priesthood.

"No one will meet me or the archbishop?" Justin sat across from his junior cleric at the conference table on the first floor of the chancery. The double doors of the large room were closed on Justin's second day back in Indiana. A small floor fan rotated back and forth at the other end of the room. On this sticky Indiana summer day, two tall windows opened to an alley below.

"Nope. I located four parents in the parish who admitted Kremer had abused their sons, but none wanted to help." Tom's face was deep pink from too much time in the sun, perhaps during picnics or softball games with the CYO of the parish.

"What's going on? Don't they want it to stop? Don't they care?" Justin's outrage swelled as he felt his head warm.

"I don't know. But our parish is tight, and living in a small town, everyone talks, mostly behind the scenes."

"What about the sheriff or the police? Have they gotten any reports?" Justin felt desperate as he leaned across the conference table.

"I checked. They know what's going on too. But they just smiled and winked when I brought up the issue. The chief told me there was no way he'd ever bring charges against Kremer because he loaned him money after he'd lost a paycheck gambling in Terre Haute last year. And the sheriff is up for re-election and doesn't want to stir up trouble. He can't win without the Catholic vote."

In his anger Justin considered alternate ways to confirm Kremer's sick actions.

"If I share the personnel information can you keep it confidential?" Justin leaned across the table at Tom, who wore a black suit and fresh starched Roman collar.

"Sure."

"As vicar general I reviewed Kremer's file and found letters asking the old archbishop to pull Al from his posts." The phone rang in the office down the hall and a muffled voice of the secretary answered.

"Give them to me and I'll track them down. If they're already on record they should be willing to help."

"But you've got to be discreet." A siren screamed from the open window then diminished.

"I understand. Trust me."

"Meanwhile . . ."

"Meanwhile I'll continue to caution any parent who gives me new reports."

"We won't give up. Kremer is sick and has no business being with kids." Justin spoke the words with a controlled disgust and rage that he'd never shown anyone.

Tom leaned back in the stiff meeting chair, soothing Justin's wrath with a wave of his right hand.

"No way will we back down," he said.

In a quick shift he added, "This probably isn't the best time to ask, but do you plan to attend Al's silver anniversary next weekend?"

Justin gave the young priest a cold stare. "You kidding? Great timing! Do I have to?"

"You know the way it works better than I do. People know you're in town and you're still the vicar general. The archbishop will say the mass."

"I'll be there." Justin capped his indignation.

∴

The twenty-fifth anniversary celebration was in Father Al Kremer's church, St. Marius, in the small city of Freiburg. Al gave the sermon to the Saturday morning standing room only crowd, thanking all who had supported him in his ministry since that day in September 1936 when the previous prelate ordained him "a priest of God forever," in Kremer's own words. The archbishop, flanked by a deacon and sub deacon, sat erect across the marbled sanctuary from the pulpit. He seemed to value every one of Kremer's words that enhanced the status of the priesthood to a mostly lay audience.

Justin and dozens of his fellow clergy sat in the front pews. Incense curled through the large Romanesque house of worship built 90 years before by German immigrants. The limestone had been quarried near Bedford and hauled by mule drawn wagons the seventy-five miles to Freiburg. Through the years coal soot had diminished the exterior's off-white sheen to a dirty gray.

Lined up like penguins in the loft, a boys' choir, wearing black cassocks and white surplices, sang impeccable Gregorian Latin chants in harmony accompanied by heavy organ music. Justin kept his head down as Kremer deflected his self-adulation by acknowledging the hundreds of lay people who "helped me raise over $5 million to build new churches and schools at . . ." The location list seemed interminable to Justin.

His imagination carried him to each of Al's assignments, wondering whether boys had been assaulted, one by one, clandestinely, at each parish. How many boys, or perhaps now young men, wrestled with the demons Justin still wrestled, unable to feel serenity and joy? Looking at Al Kremer in the ornate pulpit, preaching to hundreds of devotees, Justin felt disgust.

At the Elevation of the Host, following the consecration, the altar servers rang two sets of high-pitched hand chimes and the massive bells in the steeple clanged loud enough for the farmers to hear in fields a mile away. The deacon stepped toward the altar, with its white linen cloth embroidered with purple grapes and brown shocks of wheat, to tilt the thurible back and forth, emitting clouds of sweet incense, symbolizing the prayers rising to the Divine.

At the lunch banquet in the basement of the church after the two-hour Latin mass, Justin sat with Tom Gentry and four other priests. The large room, filled with smells of cigarette smoke, roast beef, and women's sweet perfumes, was decorated in carefully twisted silver and white crepe paper with silver paper accordion bells dangling from the light fixtures. A twelve-piece orchestra played below the stage where the guest of honor sat with his parents and other family members to his left. The archbishop sat to Kremer's right, his gold cuff links and pectoral cross reflecting the spot lights shining on the head table.

As the meal began, Justin's stomach roared. He excused himself, exiting to the men's room. While washing his hands before returning to his table, four boys, probably classmates, about twelve or thirteen years old, stormed through the door. Before they saw the priest at the sink a stocky one said, "Come on, Patrick, tell us what the Queer Kremer did to you?" The words were prepubescent alto.

As soon as they caught sight of Justin in his black suit and collar the talking ceased. Justin flipped the water from his hands above the sink and dried them with a paper towel, not acknowledging them. The boys were eerily silent at the urinals as he pulled open the door to leave.

Back at his seat, Justin caught sight of them on their way to a table at the other end of the crowded dining area near the stage. They sat with three other boys. The sign planted inside the floral centerpiece in their midst spelled out in big letters, "Four-H." From his position next to Tom Gentry, Justin watched them laugh and heard verbal jousts the way all adolescent boys do. The one he recognized as the possible victim, based on the men's room comment, remained expressionless.

After the lengthy toasts and laudatory speeches, which irritated Justin as indulgent puff, the event closed with everyone standing to sing "Holy God We Praise Thy Name," accompanied by the mini orchestra. The guest of honor stood with the others at the head table, now cluttered with dirty plates, dessert bowls, half-filled coffee cups, and water glasses. Mark O'Connell and Al Kremer, both wide open-mouthed singing the words of the triumphant hymn, beamed.

Before the last verse Justin pulled Tom aside and pointed to the stone-faced boy at the Four-H table.

"What's his name? The one who is not singing and has his head bowed." Justin leaned into Tom and spoke into his ear above the music and singing.

Without stretching, Tom, a head taller than most, scanned the boys.

Bending down to Justin he said, "Patrick Gardner. Nice kid. Quiet. Why?"

The last lines of the hymn rang out and the crowd applauded.

"I need to ask him some questions. I think Al may have another victim."

Justin made his way to the Four-H table. In an out-of-character outgoing gesture, he approached Patrick. The youth had thick, rigidly combed and oiled orange hair and a face splashed with freckles. His boy-body appeared stretched in a way that early adolescence demands: lanky arms, narrow shoulders, pencil legs, and high waistline. His thin face appeared neutral, neither joyous nor morose, and his thin lips kept his teeth hidden.

"Young man, I am Father Zapp. Could I speak with you for a moment?"

The boy seemed stunned, and the others at the table remained silent in curiosity.

"Yes, Father."

He stood as Justin shook his limp hand. The boy looked away.

The other boys remained silent with staring, curious eyes on Justin.

"Can we step outside the dining room?" Justin pointed toward a side door. Patrick's eyes showed confusion, his forehead wrinkled, and his eyebrows lowered in a stare at the floor. Every move the priest and their classmate made grabbed the curiosity of the other boys.

The two walked to a lit hallway leading to several rooms used for overflow grade school classes. Justin led him into one of them and closed the door. Stepping to the teacher's desk, he gestured for the boy to take a seat at a student desk. Patrick sat with his head lowered, as if ready to be dressed down.

"Please don't be alarmed," Justin said. He wanted his words and smile to calm the youth. "You are Patrick, right?"

"Patrick Gardner. Yes. I didn't do anything wrong, did I, Father?" He reminded Justin of a wounded puppy.

The rumble of the departing crowd came through the closed door.

"No, no, son. I'm not here to scold you. I want to ask a favor that could help a lot of other boys."

"What, Father?" The boy grew rigid, sat up, and seemed suspect, tilting his boy-face to one side.

"Well, I want you to be honest with me."

"About what? I didn't do anything." Now a shallow tone of defiance.

"No, I'm not accusing you of anything, Patrick. Please calm down and listen. I want you to know nothing we say to each other will be repeated unless you give me permission, okay?"

"What is it?" He shifted to a slouch and kept looking away.

"I work with the archbishop at the cathedral. I am worried about your pastor, Father Kremer. I think he may need some help with a problem."

"I don't know what you're talking about, Father."

"Please, Patrick. I want to be honest with you as you are with me. Earlier this evening I overheard you with some other boys in the lavatory."

"We were just joking. It was nothing. I think I have to go. My ride's waiting." He wrestled himself from the too small desk seat and got up to leave.

"Please, Patrick."

The boy rushed into the hall and disappeared.

Tom Gentry continued to socialize as Justin returned to the table. The crowd had thinned. Justin waited until Tom walked to the exit. Outside he tugged his elbow and drew him aside.

"Tell me more about Patrick."

"What makes you think Al's gotten to him too?"

Justin relayed the incidents in the men's room and the classroom.

"God! He's a nervous type. Shy at times. Home life is rough. His mother drinks and the dad works two jobs."

"Can you get to him?"

"I'll try. He seems reluctant to get close to me compared to the other boys in Four-H. Maybe for good reason."

"Maybe. I'd like to know what these boys know. If he'll agree to be interviewed, it'll help a lot."

Tom said he'd meet with Patrick and get back to Justin before Justin returned to Rome.

∵

That night at supper back at the chancery with the archbishop, Justin couldn't eat. His head throbbed at the temples, and his stomach renewed its turmoil.

"Too much partying at Kremer's shin-dig?" The archbishop chuckled as he forked a piece of fried pork chop into his mouth. The room air conditioner blew cold air across Justin's neck.

"I think you know how I feel about Kremer."

"Let it go, my friend. You have no evidence, and you'd have to question the motives of anyone who accuses him."

"I'm concerned about the boys. The boys are the damaged goods in this situation."

Where were these words coming from? Justin felt like another person, more noble and candid, had invaded his body and spoken.

"You're fretting about boys who are being manipulated by conniving, vengeful parents. I've learned to trust none of them. I ignore them because they are a pack of liars."

"How can you say that when you've never even met them?"

"Pastoral experience, that's how." He put his fork down and brushed his mouth with his napkin. "You've spent your priesthood with your head buried in books. You don't know what real pastoral work is. I do. So trust me and forget about Kremer."

"I'm not hungry." Justin pushed his plate to the center of the table, stood erect, and walked from the room.

CHAPTER 23

Justin stared into space. The room was dim in the late after-noon. Traffic sounds muffled through the window, opened slightly to a modest breeze.

Dr. Goldberg remained silent, his gentle eyes set on Justin.

After several minutes Justin said, "I'll bring down O'Connell if I have to. Kremer has to go. I'll do whatever it takes." His voice carried weight.

"And what will it take?" Dr. Goldberg showed no excitement. He sat back in his cushioned chair, his elbows resting on its arms.

In an immediate shift he whispered, "A lot more courage than I feel today."

Dr. Goldberg waited.

"Epperman haunts me. He's like a ghost that never leaves."

"And the ghost won't let you be courageous?"

"I don't know. It's some vague threat, I guess, if I try to be brave."

"Anything similar to the nights in the seminary?" He, too, was now almost whispering.

"Yes. Yes, he really didn't have to threaten me then. I was so intimidated by him—his bigness, his deep voice, his position as spiritual director. God, he was crazy."

A steam shovel on the street roared, and Dr Goldberg got up and closed the window.

Upon his return he continued, "You were a boy. Now you are a man. Basil Epperman is dead." He said "dead" in a way that felt terminal.

"Yes, yes. He's buried and gone to face his creator. I don't have to feel like he's scoring everything I do."

Dr. Goldberg kept quiet. The steam shovel's continuous roar was now mute.

The strong voice returned. "War's raging. I have got to get rid of Kremer, and I will. I can't let Basil fight me while I'm pushing Mark." Pause. "Ah!" Justin pressed his temples with his palms.

"The same headache?"

"Yes." He squinted and bent over in the chair with his knees pressed together. After a pause he sat erect with his eyes closed and his hands in his lap.

"Can you remember the first time you experienced these headaches?"

"Yes. Yes. It's the same pain I felt each morning when I awoke in the infirmary after a night of Basil. I don't want to talk about that now."

"A hangover?"

"Probably. I don't want to discuss it."

"The pain after nights of abuse?"

"Stop! Nights of sin!"

"Of dominance and abuse."

A long pause. A siren blared from the street and then faded.

"But I took pleasure in it!"

"You were an adolescent boy, easily aroused. And you were used and abused by a sick man."

"Stop. I know that."

"Yes, you know it, but you've sealed the rage. The rage wants out."

Another long pause.

"It'll come out when I get angry at Mark. It will. That scares me, really scares me."

"Get angry at him. Anger can be healthy. Responding to an oppressive, cruel act with rage can lead to a healthier relationship. Mark is no different than Basil, unless you respond differently than you responded to Basil. As a boy you didn't have the tools to stop the cruel priest. As a man you can stop your superior, if you choose. The headaches and, I dare say, the gastric difficulties and insomnia are your body's way of telling you that you should remain a young boy, be passive, and let self-centered, cruel men have their way. These physical symptoms erupt when you are on the verge of acting responsibly against oppressive superiors, when the mature side of you wants to expand."

Justin felt himself slip into a daze as he tried to absorb the analysis.

"Maybe you are correct. Maybe. I'll think about it."

"Maybe this is correct? You'll think about it?" Dr. Goldberg leaned forward in his seat in a confrontational posture Justin had never seen. "Look, we're past this. You've already thought about it . . . too much! You know the truth. The time for action is now."

∵

That night Justin tossed for several hours before getting out of bed to pray the office. His window opened to the street below, he heard revelers singing songs in Italian with a slur of words he could not decipher.

He closed his breviary and stared at the moon sliver over the park across the street. He once again prayed for guidance, but there was a stronger prayer for fortitude. The battle over Kremer's removal would require time and effort, but mostly fortitude to stand against Mark O'Connell. He'd never engaged in such a deliberate attempt to stop evil.

Knowing he'd failed to act against Basil had defined him. He felt he wasn't up to the task. It should be left to the strong and saintly, not to him, a socially backward egghead scholar. He didn't possess the energy nor the knowledge to maneuver his way through this ecclesiastical mine field. He rushed to the toilet but didn't arrive in time, soiling his pajamas, the seat, and the floor.

"Why, God? Why!" He cried cleaning the dark, wet mess.

After a shower and fresh pajamas he fell asleep in his chair, holding his breviary.

∵

The following week he began his last class at the Immaculate Conception. Each weekday morning he was in the classroom and three afternoons a week in the library preparing the drafts for Moinet.

Once into the rhythm of school and research, his preoccupation with Al Kremer diminished, as did insomnia, headaches, and digestive upset.

Back in Indiana Tom had agreed to contact each person who had complained about Kremer to the previous archbishop. It was a period of quiet investigation to build the case for Mark against the abusing priest. By Christmas break Justin knew he and Tom would be working together to present their case to their prelate in a high stakes confrontation.

Until then, Justin relished the time in the library with his books.

∵

But with a letter from Tom Gentry in early December, the Kremer storm clouds gathered quicker than Justin had anticipated. Tom reported he'd spent days locating those who had written the previous archbishop with complaints. Patrick Gardner withdrew from Four-H and refused to talk with Tom. Rumors of Kremer's misconduct continued, but when Tom sought out the parents of children thought to be abused, none would talk.

More surprising, of the teachers, a principal, scout leader, and a coach who had put in writing their requests to O'Connell's predecessor for Kremer to be reassigned, each had been pulled from their posts within days of the postmark of their letters by orders of the previous archbishop. The three teachers and principal, all nuns, were immediately reassigned to distant dioceses, two in rural New Mexico and two in isolated parts of Colorado. The scout leader was quickly fired and subsequently left the parish. The coach resigned under pressure and Kremer publically defamed him, despite his winning basketball record. None agreed to meet with the new archbishop to discuss Kremer.

The pattern was clear. "As for reporting, the archbishop would find it troubling to remove a highly esteemed clergyman based on the word of a child, so we may have to pressure the previous accusers to give us what we need," Tom wrote in the conclusion to his the letter.

∴

Justin returned again to Indiana for the Christmas vacation. Instead of staying at the chancery, he asked to stay with Tom in the rectory he shared with Kremer in Freiburg. Justin felt he was going into the belly of the beast.

Freiburg, Indiana, at the end of 1961, was a thriving small city of 7,000 souls. The early German settlers had built their large church, fit to be a cathedral with its vaulted roof and high steeple as witness to the enduring faith of the conservative Catholics in the isolated town set amid forests, rolling corn, and soybean fields. The children of the immigrants had ensured their temporal financial security with wood manufacturing plants that employed hundreds in nonunion piece work that numbed the mind and deadened the soul. Cabinets, office and home furniture, television, hi-fi, and radio consoles flowed onto railcars and tractor trailers across town, supplying America the wood products it demanded.

The business owners, doctors, lawyers, and bankers isolated themselves from the poverty-paid workers in a gated community with a private country club at the edge of town. People understood the town's caste system to be impenetrable.

The exception was the parish priests. They accessed the private parties of the wealthy and the hidden shacks of the poor, if they cared to.

∵

Tom Gentry picked Justin up from the airport two days before Christmas. On the two hour drive to Freiburg, with a gentle snowfall covering the harvested fields, Justin rushed to get more details about Tom's investigation.

"Can I meet with any of the ones you've identified?"

"You can try. But I think we're facing a stone wall. Either people see this as a private matter they'll deal with on their own, or they've been ostracized by Kremer or the chancery's discredited them. And in the case of the law enforcement people, they just don't want to get involved."

The closer to the town, the more intense the headaches.

"Can you pull in the next service station?"

As soon as the car stopped, he rushed to the men's room on the side of the cinder block Gulf station. The door was locked and he tried the women's, which was open.

"Nice move," Tom said when Justin was back in the car.

"You do what you gotta do." They both smiled.

CHAPTER 24

B Y THE TIME THEY reached the palatial rectory, several inches of wet snow covered the Hoosier countryside and roads. It quieted the town like a quilt quiets a restless baby.

Justin knew there was a small window of time to enlist someone to talk with the archbishop, which was his sole purpose in spending the holidays in his homeland. If he'd stayed in Rome, Christmas would be tranquil in his apartment, which suited him well. His conscience alone forced him to be in Freiburg with Tom.

"Great to have you with us, vicar general!" Al Kremer had an engaging smile and demeanor. Standing nearly six feet tall, he possessed a bronze face, as if he lived in the Caribbean instead of gray Indiana in December, and had a tall, thin, yet muscular frame. He welcomed Justin in the large foyer set off with white crown molding and detailed floral wallpaper of green, yellow, and pale blue. The immediate subtle smells of pine and burning oak seasoned the setting.

Justin's stomach soured as he shook the pastor's small, limp hand.

The rectory was furnished in a style equivalent to a Park Avenue suite. Indirect lighting; sunken chairs; and a couch in oranges, greens, and cranberry graced the parlor. Modern original paintings on the walls interspersed with contemporary renderings of the Virgin and the Holy Family. A fire cracked in the sleek, yellow brick fireplace while Andy Williams's Christmas album played on the corner Hi-Fi. The colored lights on a perfectly coned Christmas tree completed the holiday scene. Justin figured Kremer either had his own interior decorator or possessed style himself.

"Highball?" Kremer was graceful in everything he did and said. Calm, collected. Each gesture and move choreographed.

"No, just ice water."

Kremer raised his eyebrows as if slighted and turned to Tom to make the same offer, which he accepted in the form of 7 and 7.

A thin, forty-something woman, dressed in white with a brief, frilled apron, came through a swinging door with a tray of Christmas delicacies, including Trappist cheeses, fruitcake, and water crackers.

Justin wasn't hungry. He wanted to get the welcoming formalities over and go to his room to sleep after the long flights.

∵

The next morning, after each priest said his individual Christmas Eve masses in the large church, Tom used the pretext of showing Justin the town to discuss in private their common mission.

The streets had been cleared of the melting snow and the late morning sun's reflection off the remaining white cover blinded Justin. Tom pulled an extra pair of sunglasses from the glove compartment and handed them to his colleague.

"I couldn't tell you at the rectory but we buried Patrick Gardner last week."

Justin, sitting in the passenger seat, felt stunned. "What happened?"

"He hung himself in his basement."

"Oh, my God. No."

Tom drove toward the gate of the national forest outside of town. The road was slush and the car tires watered the shoulders with an icy spray. He stopped in an empty picnic ground with the engine idling. In the sun, a half dozen wooden tables leaned sideways against each other like performing circus elephants, stored for winter. The melting snow left them dark gray with water stains.

"Did he leave a note?" Justin leaned toward the dashboard, looking at the black, naked trees, the snow dropping in clumps from limbs.

"Yeah, his parents let me read it. In essence it said he had committed a sin with Father Kremer that was too awful to live with. Since he was going to hell anyway for the sin, it wouldn't make any difference if he committed another mortal sin with his suicide."

"No mention of what the first 'sin' was?"

"Unfortunately, no."

"Does Kremer know about the note?"

"No. No one does except the parents and me. They called me when they found him because of my work with the kids in Four-H. They're devastated."

Justin put his hands over his eyes and shook his head. "What now?"

"I have some ideas, but I wanted to run them by you first. You're the vicar general."

"Yes, the man with all the power." He kept his eyes covered and spoke to the floorboard.

"I'm not sure anyone has the power to get rid of Kremer."

He looked up at Tom. "Mark does. Yes, he does."

"Yes, and you and I know we're the only ones who can stand between Kremer and more Patricks. Here's what I've come up with. The parents of the boys abused who've come to me might talk if I call them individually and tell them Kremer was implicated in Patrick's suicide. I'll just ask them directly how many more suicides they want."

"But you've already said they won't talk."

"Let me try this. If several agree to help, we'll meet the archbishop in a group. If they're all in the same room and the archbishop sees how many are affected, it could take on a different meaning. And they might feel stronger as members of a group."

"I don't want to discourage you, but we both grew up in small towns. You can't accuse the esteemed pastor of a town's parish of molesting kids and not think all hell won't break loose. You'll open up something that will affect these people the rest of their lives. This whole place will be changed forever."

"But you're the one who suggested we have the parents meet with the archbishop to report what Kremer is doing."

"That's different. They can do that individually behind closed doors. No one needs to know except the man who has to make the decision about Kremer, Mark O'Connell. It's kept under wraps. Gathering a bunch of parents in a room won't be confidential. The whole town will know the second they leave the room."

Tom looked into the wet, bare woods, deep in thought.

"Tom, let's pray over it the next few days. I don't know what to do. Let it settle and we'll discuss it after Christmas."

"I just feel so sorry for Patrick's family. God, it's so bad."

"You have no idea the hell Patrick was in before he died. Our God is merciful. I have no doubt he's with God right now, perhaps praying for us to make sure we do the right thing to stop Kremer."

The priests returned to the rectory in time for the noon meal. That night Al Kremer led the parish in prayer at Midnight Mass. The celebration, Justin reflected, of God entering our messy world as one of us.

CHAPTER 25

T HE MORNING AFTER CHRISTMAS, Kremer left town to be with his sister in Chicago. A stocky teenager with light complexion and cheeks filled with pimples rang the rectory's front doorbell and asked to see Father Gentry.

After an hour-long meeting in the front parlor, the boy left and Tom went to Justin's room.

"Can we talk? Downstairs in my office?"

Gray covered Freiburg. The snow had melted and a moist sunless chill settled over Southern Indiana on this, the feast of the church's first martyr, Stephen. Tom and Justin sat across from one another in the cluttered office. Framed *Life* magazine cover pictures of John Kennedy and John XXIII hung next to each other above Tom's desk.

"I think we have some help," Tom said.

"Help?" Justin leaned to listen.

"Richie Schultz, a friend of Patrick's, stopped to see me just now to go to confession. After he confessed, he asked if he could talk privately. He's still in shock at Patrick's death, but he's also feeling responsible."

"For?"

"Patrick told Richie the details of being raped by Kremer."

"So it's true."

"Seems Al took Patrick to St. Louis for a baseball game the week before the twenty-fifth celebration. He got him drunk in the motel room and raped him. Patrick remembered enough of what happened to tell Richie in confidence. Said he felt he led Al on and it was part his fault because he enjoyed it."

"God, my worst fear." Justin shook his head in silence.

"I asked him why Patrick didn't say something to a grown-up, and Richie said Patrick didn't think anybody would believe him. And as I think about it, I noticed Patrick changed last fall. He used to be easy-going and you could joke with him, even though he was quiet. Then, a few weeks after the school year started, he'd shut me out."

"Will Richie help?"

"Yes. He's feeling so much guilt for not doing something to save Patrick that he said he's willing to talk with you and whoever we suggest. He thinks Kremer is still pursuing boys, but he doubts he can get anybody else to squeal."

"I'm here till Saturday. Can we rush this?"

"What do you want to do next?"

"I'd like to meet Richie now."

Tom picked up the phone and connected with Richie at his home. The boy agreed to return to the rectory, which was six blocks away.

∵

Richie Schultz was a football prospect. He had short Marine-cut brown hair, a round face with a button nose covered with light freckles in between all the pimples. His crooked front teeth filled his face when he smiled.

After introductions, Richie sat with Tom and Justin in a closed office used for marriage preparations. Tom began by telling the boy that Justin was the vicar general, the number two man in the archdiocese and that everything they discussed would be private unless Richie said it was okay to repeat what was said.

"I know Father Tom told me I'm not responsible for Patrick's suicide, but I should've done something about Father Kremer after Patrick told me what happened in St. Louis. Maybe that would've saved him." The smells of frying hamburgers seeped into the room from the kitchen where the housekeeper had started lunch preparations.

"I don't think you could have saved Patrick. Patrick must've had a lot of worries and problems to do what he did." For a young priest, Tom held a capacity for empathy that impressed Justin, who let him lead the discussion.

"But he changed after St. Louis. I saw it." Richie's voice cracked with insistence. "He wasn't fun anymore and didn't want to do anything with his friends. He didn't go to the football games or bowling or just hang out with us. All he wanted was to stay home and read or watch TV or listen to his transistor."

A door slammed across the hall, making Richie jump.

"I couldn't get him out of it. Maybe I could have done more. Maybe, if all his worry came from the St. Louis stuff, I could have done something and he'd still be here."

"I got a feeling there was nothing anyone could do. But we may be able to prevent future St. Louis situations if you tell Father Zapp what you know happened."

Richie squirmed in the chair and looked over at Justin, who was sitting in his black suit and collar, patient for the information to flow. The room's light green carpet, heavy drapes, and overstuffed upholstered furniture seemed to lend to the secrecy of the meeting, as if guaranteeing the absorption of any echoes.

"Here is what I know. The day after Patrick got back from St. Louis, he called me to say Father Kremer treated him like a buddy.

He took him out to eat at a fancy place downtown before the ball game on Saturday afternoon. Then they went back to the motel and that's when Father Kremer made drinks for Patrick and told him it was okay to drink together because they were not in public and he was a priest who would supervise him. When Patrick had two drinks Father Kremer started touching him. The next thing he knew, Patrick woke up in the morning with no clothes on, and Father Kremer was asleep in the other bed."

Justin asked, "Did Patrick tell you that Father Kremer touched him in private areas?"

Richie blushed and lowered his head, "Yes."

"Can you be more specific?" Tom whispered.

With his head nearly between his legs, Richie said, "He said Father Kremer put his penis into his bottom."

"Thank you. It is important that Father Zapp hear this from you."

Richie was ghostly and stared at the pale green wall.

"Richie, I'd like you to share what you've told Father Tom and me with the archbishop."

"I won't get in trouble, will I? Will Father Kremer pull me off the football team?"

"No, Richie, no. No one will harm you. All that you have said is confidential," Justin said. "We think it's important the archbishop hear your story, though. If we arrange a meeting with him, would you tell him what you've told us?"

"Will my parents know?"

"It may be helpful to let them know. I'm sure they love you and don't want something like this to upset you." Again, Tom's gentle style was perfect.

"If you let us talk with them, we'll make sure they know you're helping us so other boys won't end up like Patrick," Justin said.

"No, no. They'll be mad, I know it. They love Father Kremer," Richie answered.

"Father Kremer is loved by many people," Tom said. "But he has a big problem, son. Unless we get Patrick's story to the archbishop, we can't stop Father Kremer from hurting others, you understand?"

"Yes, but I'm scared. I don't want to get kicked off the team."

"Trust me." Tom leaned toward the boy. "As long as I am assistant pastor and chaplain of that team, and as long as you play well, you'll be on the team next fall."

Richie smiled a weak smile with his big crooked teeth and nodded his head.

Before leaving the rectory Tom let the housekeeper know to keep the lunch warm in the oven for the two priests.

CHAPTER 26

Pıus and Mary Frances Schultz lived on a side street in the seedy end of Freiburg. Their cement block, two bedroom house sported moldy white paint and casement French windows. Deep muddy tire tracks scarred their front yard.

The two priests and Richie arrived unannounced near noon.

"You in trouble?" Mary Frances asked her son. The priests, both in Roman collars and black suits and dress coats, flanked the boy at the front door.

"No, Mrs. Schultz, Richie is not in trouble," Tom said.

She wore a frayed housecoat and her hair, brown with streaks of gray, hung to her shoulders in tangles. Just over five feet tall, she looked old enough to be Richie's grandmother with a weathered face and deep sunken cheeks. Her eyes were dark craters and a cigarette perched between two fingers at the end of her pale, thin arm lined with raised veins that looked like a parade of night crawlers.

"I apologize. This place is a mess what with Christmas and all." Justin smelled alcohol mixed with cigarette smoke. She moved dirty dishes and newspapers from the dining table to make room for the priests.

"What'd Richie do now?" she asked in a low, tobacco charred voice.

"He did something right, that's what he did, Mrs. Schultz." Tom looked around. "Is Mr. Schultz here?"

"He'll be back anytime. He's getting off early at the factory because it's Christmas week."

The backdoor opened and Pius Schultz walked in with a cigarette in one hand and car keys in the other.

"Somebody die?" he said. His was a sober face with a beige coating from the sawdust at the factory. He was stocky and had the same Marine buzz haircut and soft blue eyes as Richie; he looked uneasy.

"I don't know. They ain't said yet. Sit down and listen." Her beer breath made Justin queasy.

"Mr. and Mrs. Schultz, you have a great son. He's honest and hardworking and a great athlete . . . ," Tom began.

"Get to the point, Father. What's he done now?" The mother's words slurred.

Richie stood near the front door with his arms crossed and head bent, studying his frayed Converse All Star shoes.

"As you know, Richie was a good friend of Patrick Gardner. . . ."

"Yeah, that was a shame. What makes a person do that, Father . . . ?" Justin noticed her speech fading.

"No one can ever be sure," Tom said.

"Mary Frances, be quiet and let the man tell us what Richie did wrong," Pius said.

"Your son did nothing wrong. But we're learning from him that Patrick may have been so upset with what was done to him that he took his own life," Tom said.

"How do you know this, son?" Pius glared at his son.

"Let me explain. Please." Tom was making sure the meeting stayed focused. "Patrick and Richie were close friends, as you know. When Patrick returned from a trip with Father Kremer to see a ball game late last summer, he told Richie that he was hurt by Father Kremer."

"I kept it a secret because Patrick asked me to. I should have told somebody because Patrick was never the same after he got back from that trip," Richie said. His voice was nervous.

"What'd Father Kremer do, beat Patrick? Maybe he got out of hand or something and needed to keep him in line. Nothing wrong with a good whipping." Mary Frances's head bobbed back and forth like wheat tops in a gentle wind.

"Patrick was not out of line, Mrs. Schultz. Father Kremer may have been though. Richie, can you tell your parents what Patrick told you about the trip?"

Richie proceeded to relate to his parents what he'd told the priests the hour before.

"I don't know if you need to tell anyone about this, son," Pius responded. "I think we just forget about it. The boy is dead and we'll never know the truth and anything you say is just hearsay."

Mary Frances's head stilled on the top of the dining table, cushioned by her forearm. She began to snore.

"But we believe, if the story is true, that Father Kremer has a serious problem and could hurt other boys," Tom said.

Pius looked at Tom with a doubtful eye.

"It's important the archbishop hear from your son directly. That's why I'm here." Justin was serene. "I work with the archbishop and we're concerned about all our priests, but we are most concerned about the boys, to make sure that nobody harms them, including Father Kremer."

"Look, Father, I'm a friend of Father Kremer. He's helped me in ways no one will ever know. I don't want his reputation in this town to get damaged."

Tom jumped in. "No one will know your son met with the archbishop. Father Zapp and I intend to make sure everything is confidential. Please. Please, let us take Richie to the chancery to meet

the archbishop. We'd like you to go with us and sit in the meeting."
Tom glanced at Mary Frances as if to acknowledge her incapacity to
meet with anyone.

A long silence ensued. Tom's eyes looked to Richie, then his
mother and settled on Pius, who looked out the window.

"Fine. You can have your meeting and I want to be there." Pius
shifted his stare to his son as if to say he'd gotten both of them in
a fix.

"Can we all arrange to go tomorrow?" Justin said.

Pius looked surprised.

"The quicker we deal with it, the better," Tom said. "If necessary, I'll call your foreman."

Tom and Justin were a team.

∵

The archbishop's secretary set the meeting for the next afternoon at
one at the chancery. This gave Justin and Tom that evening to prepare; Justin wanted nothing to go awry. Together the priests briefed
Pius and Richie on how to address the archbishop and practiced
with them what they were to say, making Richie's story succinct.

Justin wanted them to wear dark suits and ties, which neither
owned.

"They'll be there this afternoon for the fittings," Justin said over
the phone to Hank Bowe, who owned the only men's clothing store
in Freiburg.

"I'm not sure I can get the alterations completed in time, Father," he said.

"I realize this is the week after Christmas and your seamstress
may be taking a few days off, but please tell her I will pay her double
if she gets the job done on time."

The next morning the suits were delivered to the Schultz home
before the two and a half hour drive to the chancery. Justin footed
the bill, including a bonus for the seamstress.

..

"There is a bit of a change in plans," Pius said. He leaned down to address Tom through the open car window. He wore the new suit, but his narrow navy tie was askew around his thick neck.

"You're still going?" Tom asked. Justin felt himself tighten.

"Yes, Richie and I are going, but Mary Frances insists on going too."

Tom looked over at Justin with concern.

"It's a long trip, Mr. Schultz," Justin said. He stretched his neck to look through the driver's side window from his shotgun seat. "We'll be in the car about five hours, maybe longer if we run into bad weather."

"She says she's going. I don't think you can change her mind," Pius said. He placed his hands on the car door below the window and shrugged in compliance.

During the long drive to the chancery the two priests, Pius, and Richie were silent most of the way. Mary Frances slept.

Stopping for lunch at the Tee Pee Diner south of downtown, Justin felt unsure of the outcome of the meeting with his superior. If there was a way to assure Mary Frances would be as disciplined in the meeting as Pius and Richie, there was a chance the archbishop would be open-minded about the facts. If Mrs. Schultz slipped herself a drink or two, everything would be in jeopardy.

At the diner she stayed in the bathroom for over fifteen minutes while the men ordered from the menu.

"I'll let her order for herself," Pius told the waitress.

The large diner sported American Indian décor, with colorful feathered headdresses, tomahawks, bows and arrows, and a large buffalo head mounted on the walls. Smells of fresh coffee, grilled onions, and fried hamburger and bacon mixed with cigarette and cigar smoke.

Mary Frances returned to the table with fresh lipstick, pink cheeks, and a toothy grin. She wore a faded blue pill box hat wrapped in brief netting over her brushed, oily hair. With her floral purple and pink dress and white cloth belt, Justin felt she looked presentable for the archbishop.

Little was said during the short lunch. Justin picked up the check and gave the waitress a nice tip. Leaving, he stopped at the door behind the others, closed his eyes, and said a brief prayer for the success of the meeting. He felt his head begin its familiar pounding. By the time he was in the car his stomach emitted a sharp pain as it processed lunch.

CHAPTER 27

T HE FIVE WAITED IN the same chancery conference room where Justin had met Tom to plan their common mission. Justin noticed the Schultz family members staring at the ornate room with its dark portraits of dead bishops on the polished wood panels as if it was a museum. The air held a brief scent of lemon furniture polish mixed with mildew and stale tobacco smoke. The radiator clanged a few times to push warmth into the chilly room. The subtle overhead light of the single crystal chandelier gave orange tinges to the room.

"Good afternoon and blessed Christmas season to each of you!" The archbishop entered the room wearing a black cassock with violet piping and waistband, his gold neck chain with a dangling pectoral cross penned at the third button. His gait held a slight spring, his combed oiled silver hair obsessively perfect. He extended himself to each person, shook hands, personally welcoming them with kind words and a broad smile. He possessed a warm poise that Justin admired.

Seated at the head of the long table, he began, "And what brings all of you here today?"

"Your Excellency," Justin began, "Father Gentry and I wanted you to meet with Richie and his parents to discuss a serious incident that happened to Richie's friend, Patrick Gardner."

The archbishop turned to Richie to listen.

"Your excellency," the boy began, reflecting the proper way of addressing the prelate which Justin taught him the day before, "My friend Patrick committed suicide the week before Christmas. He hung himself in the basement of his home."

The archbishop was expressionless while continuing to listen.

"When school started last fall Patrick told me . . ." Richie stumbled. The words refused to come out. "He told me . . ."

"Patrick told Richie Father Kremer got him drunk and raped him in the behind, Mr. Bishop." Mary Frances fired the slurred words across the table like a series of tactical missiles.

Justin realized the credibility of the accusations immediately crumbled.

The archbishop glared at Justin. "Perhaps Father Zapp and I can meet in my office for a moment. If you will excuse us?" He stood without looking at anyone and walked from the room. Justin followed.

Standing face-to-face in Mark's closed, private office the shouting began, "What in God's name are you trying to do? Make a fool of me and the Church?" His scarlet face and wide eyes Justin recognized. Had not Basil Epperman the identical look when he flared at Justin over thirty years earlier?

Justin froze in the presence of heavy rage and power.

"Answer me!"

"I . . . I . . . I" Now his words failed him.

"Sit down!"

Justin sat across from the massive desk facing his superior.

"You're playing with high stakes. You are trying to ruin the career of one of our most valued priests. You're trying to tarnish the sanctity of the holy priesthood itself. You want to scandalize the people in the pews?" As the litany continued his voice rose. "You are trying to put me in a corner to force me to harm Father Kremer! And you are about to get yourself pulled out of Rome and exiled back in some remote cornfield! Is this what you want? You want all this destruction to rain down on all of us?" He swiveled his chair around and looked out the window.

An extended silence ended when Justin, from an unknown place deep within, said, "There are children being hurt. I care about these boys, your Excellency." He spoke with calmness, took a deep breath, and realized his forehead and entrails had calmed.

In a slow gesture, Mark turned his chair to face Justin. "I want you and Tom to take that drunken woman and the other two back to Freiburg. Then I order you to never mention Al Kremer and boys in the same sentence ever again. And I want you on the next plane to Rome. As far as I'm concerned this issue is over. You can stay with your egghead scholars in Rome for the rest of your life for all I'm care. Just leave."

"No. No. With due respect . . ."

"Yes! Justin. Due respect requires you do exactly as I order. Now leave."

"I will leave. But this issue will end when Al Kremer is put in a place where he can never again harm boys." Justin didn't know where the words came from.

"Enough! Leave!" He stood and pointed to the door.

CHAPTER 28

O N A COOL JANUARY day in 1962, Justin gathered his mail from the locked box in the foyer of his Roman apartment building. A letter from the chancery in Indiana stood out. Below the archbishop's letterhead the official announcement declared:

> Effective immediately: Reverend Alfred Kremer is
> assigned pastor of St. Thomas More Parish. Reverend
> John Kreiger is assigned pastor of St. Marius Parish,
> Freiburg. Reverend Thomas Gentry is assigned assistant
> pastor of St. Peter's Hill Parish, St. Peter's Hill. A new
> assistant pastor at St. Marius Parish, Freiburg, will be
> assigned in June, 1962.

The notice had the signature and seal of the archbishop.

Justin reacted with disgust. Mark's way of dealing with Kremer's sickness was to move him to the wealthiest, largest parish in the archdiocese. To arrest the swelling threat in Freiburg he moved

Tom to the remote St. Peter's Hill as an unneeded assistant. It was ministerial isolation for the energetic young priest; a demotion of the most grievous nature in the springtime of his priesthood.

That night sleep refused Justin. The radiator, which was on just a few hours each evening, cracked and banged, got too hot, and then cooled. So, it seemed, did Justin's mind. By four-thirty, wrapped in a dull green wool blanket, he was finally asleep in his lounge chair.

∴

"I did what I could. But it backfired." Justin explained the chain of events to Dr. Goldberg in a calmness that was out of character. He wore a gray sweater over his black shirt with Roman collar.

"What did it feel like to say no to the archbishop?"

"At first I was scared as the strong words came from nowhere. Later, I realized what he was trying to do to me was exactly what Basil did. At thirteen I let Basil do it. But now . . . I don't know. It's different."

"Different?"

"He's my superior. I pledged obedience to him the day I was ordained a priest. But am I to obey an order that is morally wrong? From the time of Augustine to Aquinas until today Catholics have a long tradition of respect for the individual conscience. Assuming the conscience is well formed, the individual, and the individual alone, is accountable to God to make sure the conscience is followed."

"And?" With his hint of a smile Justin wondered if Dr. Goldberg savored the intellectual explanations of his patient.

"Well, I know the archbishop is morally wrong. I've done what I can do to tell him."

"So, your reaction?"

"I feel guilty for snapping at him. He's been good to me, in some ways like a father I never had. But he has some of Basil in him too. He can be domineering, arrogant. He's also a climber in the church, which makes me leery. . . . Maybe I could have been more diplomatic." Justin stared out the window, deep in thought. It was a dreary, winter Roman day, sunless and chilly.

"Your insomnia?" Dr. Goldberg asked. Justin wondered what connection his therapist wanted him to make with this change-of-topic question.

"Yes, I couldn't sleep last night. Restless. That's not unusual, as you know. Kept thinking about O'Connell and Kremer. What next? How to deal with my angry boss? Tom Gentry? One thought bumping up against another until my muddled mind just wore down and I went off to sleep."

"What about all those bumping thoughts?"

"That's where I'm stuck. I do feel that by doing what Tom and I did with the Schultz family and by saying what I said to Mark, I'm getting better. I'd have never thought of doing such things before therapy."

"But now?"

"Well, now I have all these things stirred up because of therapy and don't know what to do with them."

"Can you sort them out one at a time?"

Justin noticed Dr. Goldberg ignored Justin's misgivings about their work together. His was a gentle, inviting voice steering Justin back to the issues at hand.

"Where to start?" Justin let himself be steered.

"What's most pressing?"

"Al Kremer. He'll do the same thing at the new parish. Guaranteed. I'm sure Basil went from one assignment to the next finding victim after victim. I know it. A man doesn't change just because his environment changes. Kremer's sick and I don't know what the cure is, but I know a new, bigger, more prestigious parish isn't the answer."

"So you start with Al Kremer?"

"Yes, but where to start? I'm still thousands of miles away and have my work cut out for me with Father Moinet and the pope."

"No other allies in Indiana?"

"No. With Tom in exile, I have no contacts in Freiburg or in Kremer's new parish. Besides, I really want the whole thing to just go away. I'd like to crawl under a bed and stay hidden until the storm passes. This isn't what I wanted to do as a priest—to act like J. Edgar Hoover and build evidence against another priest. I think Mark has set up a situation where Kremer can't be touched. I'm sure no one in Freiburg will help, especially after what happened with the Schultz family. None of those who protested to the old archbishop can help—they've all been exiled too. I think I'm powerless, which really doesn't bother me."

"Are you sure you're powerless?"

"Yes. And I really don't want to discuss it anymore."

"You may want to think about what power you still have."

"Why are you forcing the issue?"

"Because you have a history of avoiding people who dominate you. You find your way into comfortable work, safe spaces, as a means to avoid dealing with anyone who wants to control you."

"What's wrong with that? Who wants to pick a fight all the time?"

"I'm not talking about picking a fight. I'm talking about engaging life as you live it. Running away from conflict isn't healthy. You did it with Basil, before you had the ability to confront him. But you've never changed. Now every time you meet a domineering person, you want to react the same way you did with Basil, even though you are a grown man now and have the ability to deal with conflict."

"But I did confront the archbishop."

"Yes. You did it very well, to your credit."

"So what's your point?"

"My point is Father Kremer will keep abusing boys."

"And what more can I do to stop him?"

"That is the question that must be answered. You are still the vicar general." Dr. Goldberg spoke the final words of the session without expression.

CHAPTER 29

EXCELLENT WORK!" IVES MOINET beamed as he reviewed the draft schemata. "You've grasped the essence of the argument and substantiated it with solid research. I couldn't ask for more."

"I'm pleased you like it." Justin continued to feel inferior to Moinet, despite the Dominican friar's warmth and compliments.

"I think we are ready to meet with Cardinal Beal and the pope."

"What? Shouldn't we get some other experts to read it?"

"Why? Don't you understand? You are the expert. You know more about this issue than anyone. Why do you think His Holiness selected you for this job?"

Justin's narrow categories about life shook again. Working with Father Moinet challenged how Justin viewed himself. Perhaps Justin was more competent than he was ever willing to admit.

∵

During the following weeks, the sessions with Dr. Goldberg seem to drag, directionless, sterile.

"Why do I keep coming to see you? We're getting nowhere."

"Where do you want to go?"

"I think I'm finished with therapy."

"You can end our work at any time."

"What do you think I should do? Do you think I'm well?"

"You have improved in many ways, yes. But you and I know the overarching issue you must address is not being discussed. You are avoiding it again."

"And I've told you, I don't know what to do about it. It's dead for now. If I get word that Kremer is raping more boys, I'll deal with it then."

Dr. Goldberg pressed no further.

∴

Maria Giovacchino arranged for Justin to have supper with her husband and their three children the evening after Justin met with Moinet. It was an event Justin dreaded, but he felt a priestly obligation to go as a gesture of appreciation on the family's part.

"Father, you are so thin! We will fatten you tonight!" Her authentic enthusiasm startled Justin.

Aromas of simmering tomato sauce, rich with olive oil, basil, garlic, and oregano, wafted in the foyer of the three story apartment building, a ten minute walk from Justin's own Roman residence. The priest braced himself for what he anticipated an awkward evening at best. Their tiny home, with rooms smaller than Justin's, had been rearranged to accommodate him for a multicourse meal prepared by Maria. In the center of the living room a folding table was set with a pale blue cloth, patched and mended in several places. A fresh bouquet of red, yellow, and orange garden flowers in the middle of the table spoke of the care Giuseppe's mother had invested in the occasion. The place settings, orderly arranged, consisted of mismatched plates, drinking glasses, and silverware, with frayed cotton napkins pressed and folded.

"Won't you sit down? And would you like a glass of red wine?" Paolo Giovacchino asked the double questions with a gesture for the guest to take his place at the head of the table.

"Just water, thank you." Justin took the seat as directed. His head began to pound.

"No wine?" His host looked wounded.

"No, thank you. I must avoid alcohol." The explanation seemed to satisfy.

Within minutes the children filed into the tight room to greet Justin. Giuseppe, his ten-year-old brother and seven-year-old sister each wore clean, starched, and ironed clothes and broad grins. Their deep black heads of hair, smooth, fair skin, and chestnut eyes spoke of a special beauty that was rare among the descendants of Northern European immigrants back in southern Indiana.

As the meal progressed, comfort settled over the room, a comfort Justin felt and acknowledged within himself. The pasta, a handmade fettuccine that Giuseppe explained his mother kneaded and sliced, was smothered in the deep red tomato sauce and link sausages, and capped by fresh Parma and ground pepper. During his time in Italy, Justin had not tasted a dish to compare with this one. More important to him, however, was the serene milieu in which the six of them ate. The family conversed with one another in a civil tone. They politely asked a score of questions of the priest: What do you study? What is Indiana like? What is this Council thing that is about to happen? Do you like Rome? Do you have a family? On and on. Based on the anxious moments at the hospital when he first met the parents, Justin anticipated a rowdy clan that would overwhelm him with inappropriate attention and demands. Instead, this family was composed and attentive. He felt their genuine interest in him.

When he prepared to leave, Paolo showed him to the door. "We would like you to consider us your family in Rome. We're not important people, who you may be accustomed to, but we enjoy your company and are so grateful for what you did for Giuseppe."

∵

As he settled into his apartment that night, he knew he'd been mistaken about the evening. He wondered if he could learn to appreciate the Giovacchinos' interest and develop a connection with them in this lonely city. It made him only a little anxious to think about the prospects.

When he finished compline, he stilled himself in prayer. Deep within, the sharp edge of loneliness grew. Reflecting on the gentle, veritable Giovacchinos, he recognized the beauty of family love. Growing up an only child in a home with three older women, he had not experienced the respect and care a mother and father can have for one another, a respect and care lived, as if by osmosis, by the children. He knew there was no loneliness in the Giovacchino family; the word was probably foreign to them.

Just being there for a few hours awakened in him a surprising desire for connection, for breaking down the thick walls that protected him from everyone. Despite the undefined risks, he knew he needed love. At his core, however, he questioned whether he'd ever be loved by anyone.

∵

The meeting with the pope was set for the feast of the Conversion of St Paul, January 25, 1962, in the lofty Vatican office with burgundy damask wallpaper, polished marble floors and rococo furnishings. The centuries-old chamber smelled of burnt beeswax candles from an adjoining chapel and smoked meats from the palace kitchen.

On this chilly overcast winter day, the windows, with their heavy ornate gold trimmed drapes, remained closed.

The pope looked tired compared with the first time Justin met him. And his heavy face sagged more, as if his life was slowly receding. Justin wondered about the state of the seventy-nine-year-old man's health. Would he live to open the council? To close it? He wore a white cassock that covered all but the tips of his shoes, his wide girth wrapped in a simple broad cincture. A pectoral cross hung from his neck and rested over his belly when he sat, and a tiny white zucchetto covered the top of his round head.

After formal greetings at the large table in the center of the room, the pope began, "I am to understand that the first schemata meets everyone's approval?"

Father Moinet and Justin nodded. Cardinal Beal interjected, "Your holiness, the document is everything I could hope for. But you know it will not be received well in some quarters." He narrowed his eyes at the pope.

"I understand your concern, your Eminence. There are some in the Curia who will find this unacceptable. But we must remember we follow the movements of the Holy Ghost as best we can discern them. If there are those who will stand in our way, we must listen to them with respect, pray over the matter, and then act. If it is the work of God, it will happen. We are but instruments for God to work in the world as God sees fit. I refuse to be curious or anxious about the shape of things to come."

Justin felt his eyes go moist as the pope spoke. In these words Justin recognized a man steeped in a rich faith he'd not found in clerical circles, nor in himself. He spoke with absolute trust, resulting in a freedom from worry and anxiety. This is what Justin longed for, to be free of all distress and to fall into the arms of God, liberated from his own individual plans and schemes that he used to confirm his value, his legacy. The man seated at the head of the table appeared to be much more than the leader of the largest organization in the world. Justin felt at that moment he sat in the presence of a living saint.

∵

Augustine Beal was six months older than the pope. A Jesuit who once refused Pius XII's offer of the red hat of a cardinal, he was forced by John to take it in January 1960, three months into John's pontificate. Justin imagined that any revolutionary changes that might come from the council would no doubt need the mind and influence of this fragile octogenarian. He was bent with osteoporosis and his turtle-like face was rutted with the lines of a doddering man. Justin had heard that he, having lived in Rome since 1924, knew the inner politics of the church, yet had kept some distance from power struggles by being the confessor of Pius XII. Justin thought John had wisely appointed him head of the Preparatory Commission for the purpose of steering the pre-council work in a direction to amaze not just the Curia, the inner Vatican power elite, but also the pope himself. In this position Justin surmised Beal might be able to bridge the Pius XII loyalists and the John XXIII reformers.

Sitting in the room with the pope, Beal, and the previously exiled theologian Moinet, Justin knew he was witnessing the power of the Holy Ghost breathing health and freshness into a wounded, stale church. And Justin was part of it, far from the tragic circumstances he left in Indiana.

And that was fine with him.

CHAPTER 30

B Y EARLY APRIL 1962, Justin escaped Rome for a much needed retreat. He chose a Jesuit center in a remote village of Lust-muhle in eastern Switzerland, a day's train ride away. The center held a good reputation among English speaking clergy in Europe, but most notably in Rome. As he left his apartment building for the train station, the postman, head bowed in concentration on a fist full of mail, bumped Justin.

"Pardon, padre, pardon!" he said in a rush. He shoved several letters toward Justin and moved on.

In the cab Justin sorted the correspondence. An American aero-gram of flimsy pale blue paper trimmed with dark blue and red had St. Peter's Hill return address on it.

> *St. Peter's Hill, Indiana*
> *March 30, 1962*
> *Feast of St. Henry*

Dear Justin,
  More trouble. The assistant at Tom More, Fred Klein, who is my classmate, tells me Kremer's at it again. Three parents have come to Fred with specific accusations

concerning their sons in the grade school during this summer. Your advice?

In Christ, your brother,
Tom

Justin proceeded to the station anguished by the news. During the ride to Zurich, rain pounded the roof and windows of the train. Justin had hoped to view the early spring Italian vineyards and rural villas, the tranquil northern lakes and wide vistas of the Alps to help him transition from bustling urban life to his anticipated serene destination. Instead he was left to ponder the brief, explosive comments of Tom's letter with heavy showers and fog masking the landscape. During most of the past few months he could distract himself to avoid his obligations as vicar general to deal with Al Kremer. Fred Klein's reports to Tom affirmed Justin's worst fears about Kremer: geographic cure was impossible. Kremer had evidently picked up right where he'd left off.

With this letter, the issue Dr. Goldberg had been forcing Justin to deal with since the first of the year again exploded in front of him. His forehead and digestive system didn't react well. He turned inward, tied in knots.

Was he to try again to get parents to make demands on the archbishop? Was it Justin's job to return to Indiana to coordinate the confrontation? Who was Fred Klein and could he be trusted? Would it do any good to remind Mark again of the files accumulated on Kremer under the previous archbishop?

In the simple retreat house outside the village, tucked among low mountain pastures, Justin anticipated he would find an isolated area of beauty and tranquility to pray, relax, and restore his soul. Not that the work in preparation for the council was exceedingly taxing, but he did need time to reset himself before God. The letter from Tom immediately threw him off plan, took him where he'd refused to go in therapy.

Sitting on the fourth-story balcony of Gonzaga Center, over-looking the spring green, rolling fields of the farms surrounding the village, Justin tried to gather himself. The bells of the dairy cows gave gentle clangs with each aimless step of the grazing herds. Soft clouds spiced the clear blue sky as the afternoon sun started its chore of casting long shadows. Couldn't life be this serene always? He wanted more than anything to deny the existence of Tom's news.

Following breakfast the next day, Justin met with reluctance his assigned spiritual director for the eight-day retreat, Father Hugo Peters. A short Englishman with a thick, bushy white beard, Justin knew of his solid reputation in Roman circles for working with priests in discerning the movements of the Holy Ghost in each individual.

Justin had not had a spiritual director since his ordination, and he didn't want one. In the seminary, students were assigned faculty members as spiritual directors, which is how Justin ended up with Basil Epperman. But Justin had never permitted any director there to know his inner self. He had successfully stayed superficial, reveal-ing just enough to capture their approvals to progress to ordina-tion. With training finished, he secretly pledged to himself never to engage in formal spiritual guidance again. He planned to let Father Peters know during the first meeting that he'd like to make the retreat without his services.

The screenless window was open to the cool country air as Justin entered. The slight scents of the season's first-cut grass and fresh manure filled the room. The old man sat in a deep-cushioned, worn leather chair next to a table cluttered with stacks of dog-eared books. He removed his reading glasses and looked up at Justin with a serene smile.

After exchanging introductions, Justin began, "I appreciate your offer to guide me during this retreat, but I prefer to just spend time here on my own."

"Sounds unusual. I respect your wish. But if you don't mind, can I ask, what are your hopes for this retreat?"

"I just need time away from my work in Rome. This is a beautiful setting and I think I can rest my mind here."

"You may well need to decompress a couple of days. But the purpose of a good retreat is to give yourself space to listen to the Holy Ghost within you by being away from all of the everyday distractions. My job as director is to be your companion during this time, to give you a second set of eyes and ears, so to speak, to understand how God is working in you."

"That's fine. And, again, I appreciate the offer. I'll let you know if I need you."

∴

That night was again sleepless. Thoughts of Tom's letter and Dr. Goldberg's admonitions filled his wobbly mind. He got up and went to the chapel to pray. The sanctuary lamp, a candle encased in a blood-red glass with a baroque gold base, flickered next to the altar. It was the only light in the simple chapel, but the flame gave enough brightness to cast dark shadows on the life-size, wood-carved crucifix over the tabernacle and altar. He sat in silence, awaiting direction, any direction, from God. He felt spikes across his forehead. His entrails made noises with pointed pain. Images of Basil, Mark, Tom, Richie, Patrick, and Mrs. Shultz in an alcohol stupor, the pope, Moinet, and Justin's anxious mother floated about in his mind then contracted into a violent whirlwind. Around and around and around. He shook with fear and then covered his eyes and cried.

Exhausted, he returned to his bed and slept until ten the next morning, awakening with a curiosity about the prospects of meeting with Father Peters a second time.

CHAPTER 31

THE AGED, SANTA CLAUS-BEARDED Jesuit stood hunched before the window, his back to the room as Justin walked in. Justin knew his footsteps announced his presence. The spiritual director turned around.

"You're back?"

"Reluctantly, yes."

Justin again sat across from the old priest, whose breathing seemed hesitant.

"I don't know where God is leading me. Perhaps you can offer guidance."

"Perhaps. Any hints from God?" There was an elf-like quality to his expression-filled face.

"No."

With that Justin began a summary of the situation in Indiana and the opinions of Dr. Goldberg. He said nothing about his experiences with Basil. Father Peters expressed interest in his every word but gave no hint of an opinion on the unfolding story.

"So, I don't know where to turn for guidance to stop Father Kremer. What does God want? Why won't he tell me?"

Father Peters took a deep, raspy breath. "We know God uses circumstances and people to communicate to us." Justin tried to focus on every word. "God led you to your position of authority in your archdiocese, and he led you to Dr. Goldberg. Perhaps you can pray over the Father Kremer situation, and we can meet again tomorrow to see how the Holy Ghost is working. Sit in silence and pay attention to the stirrings within you, trusting that God put them there, and what God puts in us is there to produce fruit. We may not know what kind of fruit, but we must trust God to accomplish it. As you pray, keep in mind the importance of the safety of the children involved. That, Father, must be primary."

None of the words penetrated. Justin left feeling like the guide had offered bromides, nothing more.

∵

Nevertheless, during the next twenty-four hours Justin took time to pay attention as the priest instructed. During a long walk in the afternoon, along the centuries-old paths through the pastures and woods surrounding the Jesuit house, he paid attention to the sky and birds. He noticed the bees scurrying from blossom to blossom. A rabbit crossed a lush meadow, in no hurry, but casting a curious eye toward Justin as he softly ambled by.

At the top of a hill Justin looked over the village, clustered in the valley. A bicyclist rode along the black ribbon-like highway, bordered by low stone fences. The clock tower struck three. Shouting and laughing, a handful of children played soccer in a field next to the tiny school. From a second-story window a young mother called for her child to come home. Between the clang of their neck bells, cows mooed. A distant rooster reminded him of the peaceful days at St. Peter's Hill and nosey Mrs. Mayer, who now, Justin imagined, was preparing meals for Tom Gentry. What Justin wanted—that quiet, near monastic life of scholarship he savored at St. Peter's Hill—he couldn't retrieve. Life had gotten chaotic since those days, and Dr. Goldberg's efforts to push Justin into the very arena of messy church power and its sinfulness weighed heavy.

∵

"I don't know what God wants now. I'm confused. My thoughts are cloudy. The answers aren't coming. I just want to go back to Rome and finish my work for Father Moinet." Justin felt weary from hours of trying to clear his mind of obsessive thoughts about Al Kremer.

"It's all right to be confused. God doesn't work on our schedule. Patience is important." The frail Jesuit spoke in soft, deliberate words.

"I'm impatient. I'll be returning to Rome with that letter in my hand. More boys are being abused." Justin felt a crescent of tears fill his eyes.

"God may be letting you know you are not the one to fix this tragedy."

"What do you mean? I've assumed all along it is my job to fix it because I'm the vicar general and the archbishop won't touch it." Justin pulled his handkerchief from his back pocket to dab his eyes.

"Yes, God may want to use you to resolve part of the issue, but it is God doing the work. You are merely God's instrument. You are not God."

"I don't trust that. I need to know how to fix it myself."

"That may be the exact place where God wants you to change." He smiled a loving smile.

∵

The week after he returned to Rome, news of the death of Cardinal Domenico Trifiletti stunned Justin and the entire inner circle of the Vatican. Trifiletti had been the pope's superior when then Bishop Angelo Roncalli, now John XXIII, served in the Vatican diplomatic corps. As pope, John elevated him to cardinal and, to win the graces of the Curia, made him secretary of state. But since the announcement in January 1959 of the opening of the council, Trifiletti had used his skills as a diplomat to sideline the progressive council agenda the pope envisioned. Justin was particularly concerned that his months of preparatory work for Father Moinet would be cast aside by Trifiletti, who wanted to maintain the status quo. So with his death, Justin secretly felt relief. Trifiletti's passing almost seemed a *deus ex machina* moment in church history. But it also set in motion events that would directly impact boys in Indiana.

CHAPTER 32

S PRING'S MILD TEMPERATURES AND clear skies welcomed pilgrims from around the world to the Eternal City. Justin dove back into the preparations for Father Moinet, not out of urgency for the scholarship; already, the volume of work he'd produced had exceeded Moinet's and Cardinal Beal's expectations. He was well aware the work helped him avoid thinking about Al Kremer.

In his response to Tom's aerogram, Justin simply wrote that he would pray over the issue and give a full answer soon. Justin had no idea what to do, and his faith in the guidance of the Holy Ghost, as suggested by Father Peters, had not grown.

·.·

A bold afternoon sun filled Dr. Goldberg's office. The windows open, the sounds of the street enlivened the room. Chatting pedestrians, motor scooter buzzes, car horns, and singing birds created low-level background noise for Justin's first therapy session since his retreat. A slight scent of diesel exhaust came through the window as well.

After describing the contents of Tom's aerogram, Justin said,

"This is what I feared would happen and I really don't want to deal with it."

"No, you don't. Does that surprise you?"

Refocusing on the moment, Justin said, "I guess deep down I knew this had to come back. So, no, I'm not surprised. Just . . . just angry."

"How so?"

A police car with a blaring siren passed along the street.

"I just want it to go away. I'm not going to go looking for evidence to force the issue with Mark."

"So, what happens to Father Kremer?"

"Let Fred deal with it. He's a big boy."

"Alone?"

"Alone what?"

"You want the young curate to report to the archbishop the raping of boys in the parish by his immediate superior?"

"I wish you wouldn't say it like that."

"Is there a polite way to say rape?"

"You know what I mean. Anyway, Fred will have to deal with it. I can't let myself get caught up in it."

"If I understand, you are the number two man in the archdiocese, and you could not convince Mark to take action against Father Kremer. What makes you think a freshly ordained associate pastor can convince the archbishop?"

"He'll have to find help elsewhere."

"There is nowhere else. And this in no longer a matter of praying for guidance. You know what you have to do, and you are on the edge of letting yourself down."

Justin's head pounded as he left the doctor's office. He rushed to the men's room in the hallway of the office building.

∴

When he returned to his apartment a telegram posted on his door informed him that Cardinal Amleto Calabrese scheduled a meeting with him the next day at the Vatican.

Justin recalled the moment he met the kind prelate on Justin's first Pan Am flight to Rome, his care in orienting Justin to the Vatican and the supper near the Pantheon with the renowned theologians Godfrey Diekmann and John MacKenzie. Now Calabrese was the new secretary of state, replacing the rigid-thinking Cardinal Trifiletti. What interest would the powerful diplomat have in meeting the country priest from Indiana? Justin wondered.

Distressed by the session with Goldberg and anxious to know the reason for the meeting with Calabrese, Justin took a long walk through the noisy streets to the park near the Immaculate Conception. Small groupings of college-age Romans sat on the emerald grass, eating fruits and Italian pastries, drinking Coca-Cola from small glass bottles. They giggled and chatted, oblivious to the mothers pushing strollers, old men and women walking alone with their memories, and teenagers, carrying their books, returning home from school.

Justin sat on a bench near a fountain to collect his thoughts in peace. He looked up at the cloudless September sky. Swallows swooped and dove in their eating rituals, snaring unaware insects. The fountain's gurgle, steady and soft, should have soothed him. He knew in his mind he needn't re-analyze the origin of the demons he feared fighting. Miss Aaronheim and Dr. Goldberg had plowed that ground more than enough. Now he must get on with the battle and take action again. Be bold and fearless. But his bowels had other plans. Within minutes he was in the men's room inside the Immaculate Conception classroom building.

He returned to the empty apartment, showered, and walked in the cool, late afternoon to a church around the corner. There were several beggars asleep in its shadowed entrance. He entered and walked to a seat in an alcove behind a supporting pillar, blackened, like the rest of the interior, by centuries of candle smoke.

The ancient wooden seats creaked on their own as if to alert sleepy petitioners. The stoic statues on the main and side altars, beautiful to behold, refused to speak. The galleries of lit candles before them held vigil in the absence of the faithful ones who kindled their flames and left. From his seat Justin could see the tabernacle on the altar, but he figured few of the dozen or so others scattered in the dim church, mostly people closer to death than to birth, could not see him.

He closed his eyes and rested his busy mind. His breathing slowed. Little by little, like an open meadow with the increasing light of dawn, his thoughts grew clearer. His struggle to deal with Al Kremer was about much more than Al Kremer. He knew it was about his responsibility as a man before God. He was no longer a passive teenager forced to surrender to a drunken, sick old priest. In therapy he'd learned he had to directly confront Mark in an attempt to resolve the Kremer problem once and for all, or bury the issue at his own peril. This was not just a spiritual concern, as Father Peters guided him to understand. This was, one in the same, a mental and physical health issue as well. When all his emotional clutter cleared, the essential question before him was to act or die. His own abuse led him into a pattern of passivity before immoral authority. It had never worked, causing his physical distress and a stunted mental and spiritual life. Act or die. This was the essence of all his years of psychotherapy. The choice was his. Both prospects terrified him. But his faith dictated he act with courage and trust God would supply what he needed. Good Pope John, Justin knew, lived his entire life based on this trust. He would step up and imitate the living saint.

As he left through the church door, one of the beggars had awakened, holding a small metal cup up toward Justin. He reached in his pocket and dropped in several coins. In Italian Justin asked the man to pray for him. The smelly man in rags nodded and said, "God will protect you, Father."

∵

Reminiscent of his scheduled meetings with the pope, Justin passed through several layers of Swiss Guards, bureaucratic check points to the loggia of the Papal Palace with Raphael's frescoes on the ceiling, before entering a salon office of the secretary of state. The elderly cardinal, just two years younger than the pope, greeted Justin with familiar warmth. They met without the cardinal's staff. Having spent an unprecedented twenty-five years as apostolic delegate in Washington, he had grown up in rural northern Italy and spoke impeccable English. He also had friends in high places besides the pope, for his was a personal acquaintance with the new First Family of America.

"I need your assistance." He was graceful in speech.

"I will help if I can, your Eminence," Justin said. Despite the man's warmth, Justin felt anxious in the presence of this influential cardinal dressed in red, sitting behind an ornate, massive desk.

"Since moving into this position I realize I would like to build my own group of advisors. I need knowledgeable, cooperative men to fill the void left by Cardinal Trifiletti."

Justin's imagination kick-started as he listened. Was Calabrese going to ask Justin to work for him? Would this lead to Justin being ordained a bishop? Was his life to be a Vatican bureaucrat? His mind jumbled with speculations. His distress mounted.

"So," the cardinal continued, "I need you to draft a confidential profile of your superior, Archbishop O'Connell. He is one of a dozen candidates I am considering bringing to Rome on a permanent basis to be assistant secretary of state."

Justin was speechless, both relieved and troubled. He immediately understood he, personally, was not part of a personnel reshuffle. But what the cardinal had in mind was a major promotion for his archbishop. Also, if Mark did even an adequate job in the Vatican, he would be in line for the red hat within a few short years.

The secretary of state proceeded to outline what he wanted in the profile and the deadline for the report: July 1, 1962.

Justin agreed to cooperate.

CHAPTER 33

THE NEXT AFTERNOON IN therapy, Justin felt himself in yet another complex predicament. As much as he wanted to retreat into tranquil contemplation, he realized, by prayer and conviction, he had to act.

"What next? Lie about Mark? Calabrese must consider him a stellar candidate or his name would not be mentioned. Mark's an ambitious man; I've known that for years. This is his dream job—work in one of the most powerful Vatican offices for a few years, mentored by an influential cardinal, then, poof! He gets a red hat with his own post in Rome or his pick of major American cities." Justin shook his head and stared out the open window at the cumulus clouds moving with the strong wind across the sky's ceiling.

"What's your decision?" Justin felt Dr. Goldberg didn't have to confront him about his fear of taking action against Kremer. The real-life circumstances were doing the confronting.

"This is a nightmare. My conscience, my physical and mental states all tell me to face up to it . . . to go back to Indiana and meet with the parents who have complained to Fred and get on with it."

"So, what's your decision?" Dr. Goldberg repeated.

Justin felt tight all over. He wanted to escape. Go hike the hills of Switzerland again, anything for relief.

After an extended pause, he responded, "I can't make the report on the cardinal until I've given Mark another chance. I've got to go home and face it. But God!"

He put his hands over his face and shook his head.

The night before his flight to the States, the Giovacchinos invited him to supper. Since the first meal with them in the summer, Justin had stopped in several times for brief visits. Each visit confirmed his impression that they were congenial, authentic. The noise and energy of the children and the warmth of the family's hospitality drew him closer, as if their home was a safe, temporary cocoon from the whirlwind surrounding him everywhere else. And it all contrasted with his life of books and clerics in ways that lifted his spirits.

Sitting with Justin on small metal stools on the balcony of their apartment, Paolo asked, "Why the trip to America tomorrow, Father?" He sipped grappa and puffed a small cigar.

"It is church business, Paolo. It is my duty."

"You always seem so busy with church business. Curious, I don't think the Lord was so busy this way. Seems like his business was mostly teaching and mingling with the people he met. Being kind and healing people who hurt. . . ." Then, in a lower voice he added, "But, then, you know more about that than I do."

Justin was struck by the simplicity of this working man's observations. "I think you're right. I don't know if Jesus would recognize the big church machine his followers created in his name during the last two thousand years and all the busy churchmen rushing around to keep it all going."

In a few minutes Maria joined them on the small balustrade with three bowls of chocolate gelato on a wooden tray. The balcony extended out from the apartment building about six feet, and Maria had secured pots of red begonias around its sandstone rail.

Three stories below, children played soccer on the side street, yelling in high pitches. Smells from other apartments, above and beneath them, revealed menus of garlic, grilled beef, sage sausage, fried onions, simmering tomatoes, green peppers, and fresh baked bread.

"A little treat for our American priest so you won't forget us on your trip." Maria grinned as she extended the tray to the men.

"You spoil me," Justin said. "And I like it."

In silence they all relished the dessert.

∵

On the flight across the Atlantic, Justin prayed his breviary and read several journal articles on theology. The middle-aged woman next to him seemed absorbed in a novel. During the first few hours of the trip, he made several trips to the lavatory. After the stewardesses served supper, the lights of the coach cabin went off and Justin reclined his seat, hoping his head and bowels would ease and sleep would come. Instead, his mind raced with thoughts of meeting Fred Klein and plotting ways to convince Mark.

Justin had written Tom in advance announcing his trip home and asking that he, Tom, and Fred meet away from the chancery to discuss strategy. Justin had never met Fred so Tom was acting more as a liaison than a participant in this latest mission.

∵

Father Fred Klein's face was baby soft with pink cheeks and few whiskers. His seminary days at Presentation started like Justin's, as a freshman in high school. His professors there suggested and the old archbishop agreed that he be sent for advanced studies after ordination in 1959 so he could teach at the new archdiocesan college. He had been assigned to live in the rectory at St. Thomas More and say weekend masses in the wealthy, large suburban parish.

Weekdays he worked on his doctorate in physics at the state

university. Some priests, Tom told Justin, suggested Fred would be a better Jesuit than diocesan priest, given his high intelligence and interest in science.

Tom Gentry agreed to meet Justin and Fred in a private room of the country club a mile from St. Thomas More rectory, deep in a sprawling subdivision filled with big Cape Cod and low-level ranch homes surrounded by manicured lawns.

"Nice," Tom observed as he stared at the English country manor décor of the large club house.

"Yeah," Fred said. "The priests of the parish received free membership and food allowance, compliments of a Sam Radenour, the parishioner who owns Radenour Ford dealership," Fred said.

Justin listened as the two classmates caught up on mutual friends, then Tom shifted to the subject of the hour.

"We're all concerned about Al. You know his history at Freiburg and other places?" The waiter brought Fred and Tom glasses of beer. Justin had iced tea.

"I only know he's a superstar fundraiser, has built dozens of buildings across the archdiocese, and is as charismatic as Kennedy. He's now raising pledges for the new college and an addition on Tom More's school. I like the guy." Fred loosened and removed his Roman collar.

"We all like him. But there's a history with him," Tom explained. Turning to Justin he asked, "Can you catch Fred up on what you know about the years before Freiburg."

Justin cleared his throat, not sure how much to reveal to a near stranger. After pausing a few seconds, he said, "Let's back up. The three of us must keep a lid on everything we say here."

The two priests shook their heads in agreement. Justin kept quiet until the waiter left the small dining room with its wide picture window opened to the golf course outside. The maple and sassafras trees shaded the terrace with a heavy green lushness.

"Yes, there's a history, but when Tom researched the people who reported Al's abusing boys before Freiburg, every one of them was exiled or defamed by the old archbishop. When Tom and I dealt with the kid's suicide in Freiburg, we got nowhere with the current archbishop. Perhaps Tom has filled you in on that fiasco?" Justin looked at Tom.

"Yeah, we discussed it."

"So where does this leave us?" Fred asked.

"You tell us," Justin said.

"Look, guys," Fred began. "Sounds like nobody's able to break him. I've gotten three reports over the last few weeks, and yesterday I got another one. This time it's a twelve-year-old altar server who Kremer took on an overnight trip to Al's parents' house. The kid's mother says he came into the boy's room at night and fondled him. Scared the kid to death. Tried to bribe him to keep quiet, but the kid had sense enough to tell his parents."

"Will any of the parents meet with the archbishop?" Justin asked.

"Don't know. I can ask." Fred didn't appear flapped by the request.

"I think I need to stay out of this," Tom said.

"You're probably right," Justin said. "No need in you getting your hide blistered again. These kids are not in your parish."

"What about you?" Fred asked Justin.

"You need me?" He hoped Fred would say no.

"It will definitely add weight to the case." Justin heard this as a direct request.

"Well, know this," Justin said. "I've approached him twice about the issue and gotten rebuffed both times. But you'll need horsepower, which you don't have going in alone with the parents. Admit it, as a baby priest, you'll have no influence with this archbishop."

Justin remained circumspect about the Vatican appointment being considered for Mark by the secretary of state in Rome; a potential elevated status was at risk because of the issue at hand.

As soon as he had explained the limits of Fred's influence, Justin knew he'd put himself into the arena. If he joined in the meeting of Fred and the parents with Mark, he felt there was a slim chance they would succeed in stopping Kremer. More likely, he thought, it would result in hurting Fred and Justin in ways similar to what Tom experienced. Fred may not have yet fully understood it, but Justin and Tom knew Mark was not afraid to use his immense power to keep the worsening scandal from erupting.

∴

Fred acted quickly to gain the trust of the four sets of parents. Unlike Freiburg, small-town concerns about reputation and recrimination didn't seem to be factors in these suburban parents' willingness to act on their children's behalf.

Justin learned from Fred the parents were wealthy, educated, and had professions: one a physician, one an accountant, two nurses, one an insurance agent. Fred assured him the parents were articulate and anxious to stop Al Kremer.

CHAPTER 34

JUSTIN KNEW CLERICAL GOSSIP spread faster than beauty-parlor, small-town gossip. Although he had sent Mark a telegram saying he'd be in the archdiocese, ". . . to attend to ecclesiastical and personal business . . ." he suspected Mark knew his mission was to collect some sort of information for Calabrese on Mark's appointment to Rome. In making such appointments, Justin, and surely Mark O'Connell, understood the normal protocol included testimony from local clergy familiar with the candidate's character. Despite a thick veil of secrecy around all episcopal and other hierarchical appointments, rumors spread. Mark, Justin assumed, was aware the new secretary of state, the man who hand-picked Mark to be bishop and archbishop, saw qualities in him that could be useful in the Vatican.

But Justin treated his reason for returning to Indiana like the seal of confession. If Mark got rid of Kremer, Justin could give a favorable recommendation to Cardinal Calabrese. If not, Justin wasn't sure what he would say about his superior. To ensure the secrecy of his mission beforehand, Justin planned for Fred to initiate the meeting with Mark without letting on Justin would also be present.

The archbishop, dressed in a hand-tailored black suit with a gold neck chain, its pectoral cross tucked into his chest pocket, entered the same conference room where Tom, Justin, and the Schultz family met him the previous year. Justin felt tense, his head and innards rebelling at the circumstances. Part of him wanted it all to disappear. Stronger parts said stay and see this through. These stronger urges he identified as the workings of the Holy Ghost, as Father Peters might have observed.

Before Mark masterfully worked his way around the conference table greeting each guest, he caught sight of Justin in the corner. Immediately Justin sensed his superior may have felt trapped. The prelate's eyes widened and then refocused on each person in front of him. When he reached Justin, he smiled a wry smile, shook his hand, and said, simply, "Reverend Vicar General."

With his usual poise and grace, he sat at the head of the conference table and began, "How may I help you fine folks of St. Thomas More today?"

Fred, intelligent, inexperienced, and genuine, began. "Your Excellency, these parents of our grade-school students have some serious concerns to raise with you about our pastor."

The archbishop sat attentive. Justin saw him glance up at him, and Justin wondered what was going through his mind.

Each parent described their son's experiences. The stories varied little except for the location and extent of the sexual interactions. One mother, Fran Watkins, a nurse, wept trying to describe what her seventh grader reported to her. Unable to complete her story, her husband, Dr. Randy Watkins, the physician in the group, held her hand and finished.

"Once Father Kremer was alone with Michael in the sacristy after mass, he said he wanted to give him special instructions on how to serve at benediction. Michael told him he'd served benediction many times and needed to get home because he and his friends were going to the country club to swim. Father Kremer stalled him until the church was empty. Then he forced himself on Michael and later told him if he reported it he'd make sure he'd get pulled from the tennis tournament. Thank God, Michael had sense enough to tell us and ignore the threat."

At the end Father Klein stated the wish of the parents, which they had all previously agreed to, that the pastor be removed. "It is too dangerous for our children to be near him, Your Excellency. He is a sick man and needs professional help."

"I've discussed this with several of my psychiatrist friends. All agree the man is disturbed and needs time away to get help," Dr. Watkins said, confirming what Fred had said.

Justin kept silent. Fred and the parents handled themselves and didn't need a word from him.

Everyone awaited Mark's response. He sat with his head bowed, as if in deep prayer.

After a long wait he spoke. "First, let me thank you for meeting with me today. You are busy people, and I understand your sons feel they have been hurt by their holy pastor." He seemed calm, as if the information had failed to fluster him. He went on, "I want to investigate the matter. Your accusations are serious and involve a man ordained by Holy Mother Church to be a mediator between God and man. His hands have been anointed to change ordinary bread and wine into the Body and Blood of Jesus Christ. To report that the Devil himself has used these same hands to scare or hurt your sons is a grave charge." As he said the last sentence, he looked squarely at Justin. A chill ran through Justin.

"So, you will remove Father Kremer or not?" This was the insurance agent, Sam Macey.

"I don't know, sir. This is serious. I must study it."

"Our children are at risk, your Excellency," Dr. Watkins stated.

"I will study the matter, doctor." The archbishop's words were now cold. "If you will excuse me, I have important matters to attend to. Thank you for coming. Father Zapp, would you please show your guests to the door?"

Justin startled himself by overriding Mark's quick closure to the meeting. He stood erect, at the end of the long conference table, parents to his right and left, and the archbishop at the head position. "Your Excellency, with all due respect, there is nothing more to study. You and I know the testimonies you are hearing now are not new or surprising. You must remove Father Kremer immediately to protect these parents' children and perhaps dozens of other children yet to suffer abuse at this man's hands. The parents, Father Klein, and I all need your assurance you will act today on our behalf and on behalf of the children."

As soon as Justin finished, the archbishop, silent, stern, and red-faced, stood and left, looking at no one.

The two priests and the parents talked on the sidewalk in front of the chancery after the meeting. Cars, buses, and delivery trucks roared passed, a few feet from them. A spring thunderstorm threatened from the west with distant rumblings.

Fran Watkins dried her eyes with her crochet-bordered, pink hanky as Dr. Watkins put his arm about his wife's waist.

"I think we set a deadline for his removal," Sam Macey said. Justin thought Sam was the strongest of the bunch. His voice was defiant.

"Give him a week and see what he does. No point in putting deadlines on him," said Dr. Watkins.

"No, no," Fran interrupted. "These are our children. These are not some pet dogs or cats we're talking about. Sam is right. We demand his removal by a certain date or we go to the police."

Dr. Watkins dropped his arm from her waist and took a step back to listen to her as she spoke.

Fred offered a middle ground. "Why not set a deadline, but wait a week to see if he acts without an ultimatum from us. If he does not decide in a week to remove him, we tell him our deadline." The wind stirred the trees in front of the chancery, and the birds chatted a pre-storm telling of the pending rain.

They accepted the target date fourteen days out. If the archbishop did not take action in one week, they would inform him in writing of the deadline the following week.

Justin was silent until after they made the agreement. "I have but one question." His voice from the edge of the sidewalk huddle seemed to surprise the parents and Fred. "If the archbishop fails to remove Father Kremer on his own and if you set the deadline and the archbishop ignores you, you all agree to go to the legal authorities?"

They looked at one another as if confounded, perhaps realizing the public crisis this would create.

Finally, Father Klein said, "We'll let the Holy Ghost guide us."

"The Holy Ghost," Justin told them, "wants us to use every weapon in our arsenal to stop the molestation of our kids. This is a legal matter as well as a church matter."

They nodded their heads. But Justin wasn't sure they fully comprehended how obstinate Mark was. The parents all thanked Justin for arranging the meeting and for speaking so forthrightly to the archbishop before dispersing in expensive cars: a Cadillac, Chrysler Imperial, and Lincoln Continental. Father Klein went home in a ten-year-old Studebaker, and Justin walked into the chancery where the archbishop eventually awaited him.

Chapter 35

THAT EVENING, AS THE archbishop and his vicar general dined alone in the elaborate chancery dining room, neither man mentioned the event that marked the day. The table conversation consisted of updates on the new college; the expected number of ordinandi in the spring, thirty-seven; and the purchase of a new, life-size statue of Our Lady of Fatima for the archdiocesan retreat house chapel. Over dessert and coffee the archbishop mentioned coming to Rome for the meeting of Catholic Relief Services board, for which he served as chairman.

Justin joined in the table conversation as if the mid-day meeting never occurred, but throughout the meal he pondered the various options available. He wondered if his superior felt Justin had shoved him into a trap with only one exit. If Mark suspected Justin was one of several to report to Calabrese on his worthiness to be assistant secretary of state, Mark would surely hesitate to be captious toward Justin for speaking so defiantly at the gathering of parents and Father Klein. Any criticism by Mark could be taken as scolding Justin for trying to protect children, Justin surmised, a charge for which Justin already had plenty of evidence. After the confrontation following the Shultz family meeting, the archbishop might suspect Justin would be bold enough to include that kind of information in any profile sent to the Vatican. If Mark removed Kremer immediately from St. Thomas More, however, he may think this could redeem him in Justin's eyes, leading to a positive report to Calabrese.

The housekeeper swung open the kitchen door and poured each man a final cup of coffee then retreated without a word. The archbishop reached to pour cream into the steaming black liquid.

Justin's supper-long ruminations pushed him to speak the truth. "Perhaps you should take action worthy of higher office in the church." Mark looked stunned. "I'd hate to paint you as a prelate who's covering up a priest with a serious problem. I doubt that would play well in the Secretary of State's office."

Mark's face reddened. He sipped the coffee and looked directly at his vicar general. After he lowered his cup, he paused and said, "Perhaps we can get together for supper in one of your favorite cafés when I'm in Rome in a few weeks."

"Perhaps we can, your Excellency. Let me know the evenings you will be available."

"Yes, yes, we'll plan it."

∵

The following Monday, four days after the parent meeting and two days after Justin returned to Rome, the archbishop sent notice to Fred Klein that he was being reassigned as assistant chaplain to the cloistered Carmelite Convent on the south side of the city. He was to continue his studies at the university. Justin learned this news in an official chancery announcement and more troubling news in a letter from Fred.

May 1, 1962
Feast of St. Joseph the Worker

Dear Justin,

This is to let you know that I have heard from my sources that following my immediate reassignment as assistant chaplain to the Carmelite Sisters, the archbishop arranged individual meetings with each set of parents who attended our chancery meeting several weeks ago. When I followed up yesterday with each parent to find out how they wanted to respond to the archbishop's failure to meet the deadline we all agreed to, each seemed to be reading a prepared script over the phone. They said as far as they were concerned the issue was closed, and they would have nothing more to say on the matter.

To say the least, this is upsetting. Kremer is still the pastor. It is difficult to determine, but I suspect the archbishop worked his charm on the parents, told them he had a heart-to-heart talk with Al and that Al pledged to improve his behavior around boys.

Seems there is little you or I can do from our current posts. If the parents have in fact worked a deal with the archbishop, perhaps the best we can do is to wait and see whether the whole thing erupts again.

Between you and me, I find the situation disgusting. I am devoting my life to the church. I am sacrificing a successful career in the world and giving up marriage and children. But the church isn't what I was taught it was. My former pastor is repeatedly sexually molesting vulnerable boys. My archbishop works his magic to keep the abuser as pastor in the highest status parish in the archdiocese so he can raise millions for the archbishop's pet projects, and I get punished for trying to do the right thing. Is this an organization I want to give my life to? I'm not sure this is God's church. I wonder if the

Devil has already taken possession of it. If so, I won't be around long.

Pray for me. I trust you.

Sincerely in Christ,
Fred

p.s. Thanks again for being so courageous with the archbishop at our meeting.

Justin threw the letter on his desk. He felt like a failure. Not only had he set the stage for Tom Gentry to get demoted, he now was a major participant in the punishment of Fred Klein and perhaps his abandonment of his vocation altogether.

His breathing quickened as he slammed the desk with the base of his fist. Who was he and what was doing, he wondered. And how had this whole troubling issue of Al Kremer whirled out of control?

CHAPTER 36

WALKING TO THE LIBRARY at Immaculate Conception in the coolness of the early May morning, Justin's thoughts weighed heavy. The reading of Fred Klein's letter the day before demanded he reassess everything. By the time Justin arrived in the main room of the well-lit library, with its inviting row upon row of books and journals on scholarly biblical, ecclesiological, and theological matters, Justin, in a complete reversal, decided to ignore the critical issues in Indiana and focus exclusively on preparations for the council.

Without intense prayer or consultation with Dr. Goldberg, he determined the months of emotional toil and clerical diplomacy to stop the abusing Al Kremer had utterly failed. Instead, his irresponsible actions had resulted in the disruption of the lives of two priests who'd been demoted, one who felt tempted to abandon his priestly vocation. And the widening rift between Mark and himself promised long-term problems for Justin when he eventually returned to the archdiocese. Who knew what revenge his superior would exact once Justin was out of the protective shadow of Pope John? Most tragic of all, he knew better than anyone, was the ongoing threat to boys. The archbishop, as far as Justin knew, had placed no limits on Al Kremer's behavior, save perhaps a mild scolding as implied by Fred Klein's letter.

His planning, prayer, therapy, and confrontations had only resulted in more complex problems erupting. The most prudent course, he concluded, was to drop the entire matter. The boys would remain at risk, but Justin decided in that moment of profound insight on his way to the library, he'd exhausted his abilities to protect them.

He opened his briefcase on the polished oak table, took out his pen, notebook, and two theological journals and got to work. The quiet little nun, who tidied the periodicals and replaced returned books to their catalogued posts on the shelves, walked in front of him and smiled a hello. Her dangling rosary sang a low rattle with her passing. She smelled clean.

∵

"There is nothing more I can or will do. It's over." Justin's voice carried a hint of defiance. The window of Dr. Goldberg's office was cracked, letting in a trace of cool, moist May air.

Dr. Goldberg sat like a statue, still and cold, Justin thought.

"What's your reaction?"

"Why do you care about my reaction?" The psychiatrist's words were flat.

"You don't approve, do you?" A bird's soft trill from a tree across the narrow street seeped through the window.

"I didn't say that." His eyes stayed with his client, showing no judgment.

"Well, you're right. Your reaction doesn't make any difference. I know this is the best choice. It'll only make matters worse to try to force the archbishop to remove Kremer, which he's shown he won't do. So, I'll just do what I can do, prepare for the council, finish my work, and eventually go back to a quiet parish in Indiana." Justin was determined to believe his own words.

Dr. Goldberg listened and closed with a single observation. "I think you must do what you think is best. If it is a bad decision, your body and mind will let you know."

Justin left feeling his therapist did not approve.

∴

The following weekend Justin invited the entire Giovacchino family to dine with him at a trattoria near the Roman Forum.

"It's my way of thanking you for all the delicious meals you've given me," Justin had explained to Maria.

Justin, sitting in the front seat, instructed the cab driver to pick up the family at eight o'clock at their apartment building. Sighting Justin in the taxi from their doorway, the two younger children ran to the curb to greet him. Their beaming faces gave Justin a tingle of joy.

Piling into the small blue Fiat, with the two younger children sitting on their parents' laps in the back seat with Giuseppe, Justin gave the driver the name and address of the restaurant.

"I've never been in a cab before," said the youngest, Filomena. At six every new experience still excited her, making her dark eyes widen and her dimpled smile grow, showing the two gaps where baby teeth once found a home.

The car's open windows let in the constant fumes from diesel engines and periodic whiffs of variations of urban life: stale urine, cooked garlic, burning oak, and sour milk, perhaps left in gutters for stray cats, which number in the tens of thousands in Rome. The street lights gave a golden hue to the ancient stone buildings hugging the streets. Justin stretched upward to see lines filled with drying clothes, like a web of flags flapping in the breeze from the distant Mediterranean, three and four stories above the moving cab.

The taxi driver, with a cigarette dangling from his lips, swerved in and out of intersections, dodging cars, buses, and delivery vans, speeding through narrow, one-lane ancient streets and around sharp curves, arriving at the simple outdoor eatery with a sudden stop. Potted palms in barrel-size stone containers bordered the front entrance and hid the cozy patio lined with dozens of tables, sporting votive candles, small bouquets of yellow roses, and red tablecloths. The string of translucent light bulbs on black wires woven above Justin and the family added to the festive decor. About half of the dining area was filled with young parents attempting conversations above their children's chatter and giggles. A mauve-gray haze of cigarette smoke was building around some groupings, and the scents of the burning tobacco mixed with fresh baked bread tickled Justin's nostrils.

Lost in the excitement of seeing the Giovacchino children anticipate filling their stomachs and their curious stares at the variety of people and their movements, Justin let the tensions of the session with Dr. Goldberg slip from his mind.

An accordion player and violinist moved from inside the restaurant to the piazza with a slow shuffle, playing a sanguine tune. Each of the Giovacchinos looked from their plates to listen to the soft melodies of Puccini. Justin sat back and watched the five smiling faces of his Roman family, all content with the simplicity of the moment: good food, good music, cool evening, wrapped in love. A rush of jealousy passed over him. He wondered if Paolo and Maria had made the better choice. Hardworking parents raising three exceptional children, creating a family of simple faith and authentic affection. He wasn't so naïve to think their lives were without sorrows, but the burdens he'd been carrying all his life seemed inequitable compared to what this young couple had.

In an instant he shook resentment from his mind.

∴

That night, after praying compline, he called on that same self-discipline to closet his Epperman scars and the crusade against

Al Kremer and all it represented. He would pray his way out of the problems. Sitting in quiet, his mind filled with criticism of Dr. Goldberg for leading him so long down a fruitless path to force his superior to remove Kremer. Had he never continued therapy after being hospitalized, nothing would have been any different than it was at that very moment on this day in the spring of 1962 . . . except that Tom Gentry, Fred Klein, and Al Kremer would all still be in their old assignments. Mark remained in charge, Al Kremer, although in a different venue, still had access to victims, and Justin was still sequestered in Rome, doing his scholarly work.

Before crawling into bed, Justin prayed for the Holy Ghost to guide him. As he prayed it came to him to end therapy, write a complimentary profile of his archbishop for Cardinal Calabrese, forget about Al Kremer's behavior, and continue his work for the pope and Father Moinet until the council began in October, just five months away. After that he'd return to a quiet life in Indiana for the remainder of his days, writing and attending to the pastoral needs of any small congregation to which his archbishop assigned him. He made an act of contrition and tried to sleep.

CHAPTER 37

THE NEXT MORNING, AFTER his private mass in the dimly lit crypt under the chapel of the Immaculate Conception, Justin sat upstairs in the main sanctuary for over an hour in front of the tabernacle in the quiet space of prayer. This prayer was for God to lead him to inner peace. As he prayed, he reflected again that the whole idea of therapy had probably been a mistake. As a priest of God his source of guidance and strength should have been God alone, not a psychology developed by an Austrian Jewish atheist, Sigmund Freud, whose disciple was Dr. Goldberg.

Justin figured his abuse by Basil Epperman was his sorrowful path to God, his Way of the Cross, and he should accept it as such. He wanted to wash away thoughts that he was passive in the face of authority. In fact, maybe being passive was what God wanted of him. After all, was not the Lord himself passive before Pilate and the Jewish authorities prior to his murder on Calvary?

And who was he, a lowly diocesan priest, to question whether his archbishop was worthy of moving up in the hierarchy at the urgings of Cardinal Calabrese? He'd write a courteous profile of his archbishop and be done with it. If the cardinal wanted further information, he'd have to gather it himself. If Mark eventually got a red hat, that was God's doing, not Justin's.

Justin felt peace; the burden of acting like God to fix and direct events and lives lifted.

∴

"It is your choice." Dr. Goldberg gave no hint of disapproval of Justin's announcement to end his treatment.

"But after all these years, don't you care? Just a couple of weeks ago you were still telling me to do something about the archbishop." Part of Justin felt disappointed, wanting his therapist to push him to stay to show his attachment to Justin, if nothing else.

"My reaction is that you must follow what you think is best for you," he said. It was raining outside. The window was shut, but the drapes open, revealing the busy drops hitting the glass and sliding to the sill.

"No predictions of gloom and doom?" Justin wanted him to fight back.

"Father Zapp," addressing him formally, a rarity, "you are quite aware of the reality of your struggles, their origins, and their symptoms. You know what you must do to heal. You can make a decision for yourself."

Justin couldn't tell if this was a counterpunch or a statement of the confidence he had in Justin's abilities. And what did it matter anyway?

"I've made the decision. Thank you for trying to help me."

As he descended the stairs from the familiar office, Justin realized this ended an important chapter in his life. He left with resolve to follow a spiritual path to healing, having concluded the secular psychotherapy method led to nothing more than unnecessary disruptions and pain. Sitting on the bus to his apartment, he closed his eyes and envisioned Dr. Goldberg's strong Germanic face, serene, warm, and accepting even while confronting him in ways that

Justin now rejected. Justin realized he'd probably never see him again.

·.·

That evening before he ate his silent meal in the isolation of his apartment, Justin typed the profile of Mark O'Connell according to the guidelines Cardinal Calabrese had given him. He proofread it with no doubt about this action or its consequences. With deliberateness he sealed and stamped the envelope and dropped it in a sidewalk postal box on an after-supper stroll in his neighborhood. The earlier rain left Rome with a chilly May evening, a gentle time of year in Central Italy when the clear Mediterranean sunlight is strong enough to warm the days for wearing short sleeves, but the nights can be made for sweaters. As he passed cafés and shops, in the Italian tradition of evening meanderings, hundreds walked off their meals with him. He had learned to blend into this culture in ways that comforted him, making him curious how well he would readjust to life in rural Indiana once his work ended in the Eternal City.

Before going to his apartment he stopped in the church where he'd met the beggar a few weeks before. He sat in the same seat before the tabernacle. The sacred space was silent except for the occasional sneeze and cough of a praying soul in the nave behind him and the creaks of the wooden seats. A fragrance of sweet incense lingered from benediction held the hour before.

He felt a peace enfold him. He knew the day's events had redirected his life. His bowels and head were calm. He asked God to keep them that way and to not lead him into the temptation of trying to fix things that were out of his control.

As he left the church, the same beggar held up his tin cup, asking for alms without saying a word. Justin smiled, asked for a prayer, and dropped in two coins.

"I've been praying for you, Father," the old man said without smiling. "You will be given a trial soon and will need my prayer."

"I have trials every day, my friend. I need your prayers every day." The quick notion of a prophesy passed over Justin.

The man shifted the stub of what remained of his left leg and nodded his assurance.

Justin slept well that night, a rare good night's sleep. He proceeded through the next day, addressing his assigned work for Father Moinet with ease. His sense of inner consolation reassured him that all the emotional eruptions and attempts to influence his archbishop had in fact been useless diversions, spending his precious emotional energies in unproductive endeavors. He was determined to pray more to ensure his work for the church stay focused. This, and this alone, he knew was God's will for him.

CHAPTER 38

A RCHBISHOP MARK O'CONNELL AND Justin met for dinner at a small cafe a block from Vatican Square, within a hundred yards of St. Peter's Square.

"The international relief efforts in the Congo are the biggest concern right now," Mark told Justin. He was on his second glass of Orvieto wine. "Not enough money. The civil war there is devastating."

He dabbed a piece of bread into olive oil and took a large bite. The tiny space of the cafe felt cool to Justin, a welcomed shelter from heat of the day. The waiter asked the prelate if he'd like a second bottle of wine. Mark nodded his head.

Since the last confrontation in the chancery, Justin had dreaded this meeting. He intended to avoid any mention of Kremer and hoped Mark would too. By his silence on the issue perhaps the archbishop would surmise Justin's war over Al Kremer had ended.

"We can't get the good wines in Indiana. I wish I could store it somehow in my body and carry it across the pond." He burped and covered his mouth with his linen napkin.

Justin listened with as much interest as he could muster. But his thoughts floated from the Giovacchinos to Father Moinet to the curiosities of Vatican power struggles with just months before the council began. Spiced among these thoughts Al Kremer came and went in his mind. "Custody of the thoughts, custody of the thoughts," he kept telling himself, using a focusing technique he learned for praying while in the seminary.

"I'm glad you enjoy it," Justin said, trying to stay with the conversation.

Unless rumor gave him the news, Justin thought Mark had no way of knowing Justin had submitted the profile to the secretary of state weeks before. Mark avoided any mention of Kremer, which pleased Justin.

After the meal the archbishop lingered with a jewel-colored liqueur. Justin drank ginger tea.

"Does the pope still want you to stay for the council?" Mark asked.

"If the pope needs me and it is all right with you, I will stay. But I expect I'll be back at work at the chancery in December, after the first session."

"You want to return as vicar?" The question caught Justin off guard.

"Do I have a choice?" Justin welcomed the prospects of returning to a setting like St. Peter's Hill and planned to wait for the appropriate moment to convey that to Mark.

"No, not really. But out of curiosity, do you want to?" An elderly woman with a basket of long stemmed roses skipped their table. Her customers were men dining with their lovers.

"I'd have to think it over, but the thought of going back to St. Peter's Hill is appealing." Justin now oozed with diplomacy.

"That's interesting. I would have guessed that you would have caught 'Tiber fever' by now and want to stay around all this power in Rome."

"No," Justin bit his lower lip and looked into his tea cup, wanting the subject to change.

"We'll have plenty of time to talk later. Who knows where either of us will be after the first of the year?"

The meal concluded without Al Kremer's name being mentioned, much to Justin's relief.

∴

On Friday, July 6, 1962, the Vatican office of secretary of state announced the appointment of an obscure bishop from Denmark as the assistant secretary of state. Reading the story about the new addition to the Vatican diplomatic corps in l'Osservatore Romano, the official daily newspaper of the city-state, Justin felt relief. Despite his praise of Mark in his profile to Cardinal Calabrese, a different prelate was selected to be groomed to move up the church's bureaucracy. Had Mark been chosen, Justin knew he personally would have borne some responsibility, not because of any praise he offered about his superior, but because he had avoided the mention of the mishandled case of Al Kremer. The Danish appointment confirmed Justin's belief that by not trying to stop Mark's advancement, God had intervened and taken charge in some curious providential way.

Reflecting on the events of recent months, especially this July 6 decision by Calabrese, Justin felt somewhat vindicated about his decisions to quit therapy and stay out of the Al Kremer controversy. His body seemed agreeable as well, his headaches and bowels at relative peace. Nights were restful. He was even gaining a few pounds.

∴

The regular internal newsletter from the Indiana chancery to all the clergy in mid-July included the simple announcement of Fred Klein's indefinite leave of absence from the priesthood. Justin assured himself the young cleric's departure probably had multiple causes and was beyond Justin's capacity to reverse. The following morning Justin offered a mass for Fred in the crypt of the Immaculate Conception, praying God would guide him back to his vocation.

∴

The following week, Tom Gentry arrived in Rome with a group of pilgrims from the archdiocese. As with many priests, Tom took advantage of free travel by gathering a group of tourists, mostly the elderly with too much retirement money, for guided visits to Rome, Assisi, and Siena. Some pilgrimages included the Marian shrines at Fatima and Lourdes as well.

The young priest broke away from the tour group one evening to visit Justin in his apartment. Justin worried Tom would rekindle the Kremer controversy, and he determined to rush to deflect the issue if Tom brought it up. To help lend a fresh direction to their meeting, Justin tried for the first time preparing a meal with a local recipe Maria had given him; she had assured him he shared her talent for creating good food when he helped her in her tiny kitchen.

Justin's small apartment's dining table was large enough for Tom and Justin, or so Justin assumed. But when Justin met Tom at the door, Tom's appearance stunned him. In the months since Tom, Fred, and Justin planned the meeting with the archbishop about the abuse at Kremer's new parish, Tom had put on considerable weight, sporting a puffy face with bright pink cheeks and a pillow-like neck that overflowed his Roman collar.

During supper Tom, who struggled to sit at the small table, commented that Justin's lasagna was different than any in Indiana, with fresh tomato sauce made with Northern African tomatoes and local cheeses, herbs, and sausages. After Justin's appropriate portion, Tom cleaned the deep dish of the remaining helpings.

Justin had bought a bottle of high quality local red wine for the occasion, which Tom alone consumed before his second serving of lasagna.

"Excellent choice, Father Zapp!" Tom said with a raised empty glass. "Do you happen to have another bottle?"

Justin suspected trouble. He went to the cabinet to retrieve a second bottle, which he'd bought for the Giovacchinos. Tom finished his meal with most of the next bottle.

By the time Tom finished three cannelloni and lit a cigarette, Justin confirmed his hunch of something terribly wrong. The vibrant, optimistic, athletic young priest he'd known since before his ordination in 1959 had changed into someone of sloppy self-neglect.

Justin also realized, thankfully, Tom had not uttered Al Kremer's name all evening. And in Tom's alcohol-saturated state of mind, Justin hoped he would not broach the subject Justin most wanted to avoid.

But in a surprise shift Tom said, "Justin, I don't know if you are ready for this." His voice slowed and held a slight slur. God, this is exactly what Justin feared. "Richie Schultz wrote me." Justin's heart rate sped up. "One of his class mates in Freiburg is getting with Al Kremer once a week."

Justin didn't want it to be so. "Stop, Tom. Do you really want to tell me this?"

Tom's eyes widened at Justin's abrupt question. "I thought as vicar general . . ."

"Yes, technically I am the vicar." As he began, Justin wondered if any logic could penetrate Tom's alcohol haze, but he continued anyway. "But let's face it; I'm vicar in name only. You and I know our archbishop does everything himself. I'm in Rome, remember at the request of the pope, not Mark. After what I did with and Fred, Mark would have me out at St. Peter's Hill with you had his way. Once the pope is finished with me here or he be back home again in Indiana faster than A.J. Foyt doing Indy."

Tom laughed too loudly and sucked another drag from el. He exhaled a thin line of smoke toward the pale

Reaching for the bottle, he refilled his glass and took several gulps. "Well, just for the record, of which there is none, Kremer has a new boy lover back in Freiburg, far from the big city parish. The boys at the school know it, but nobody's talking to any grown-up. Richie knows all about it. And now I've done my duty and told you."

"Stop. Please." Justin spoke with firmness.

Tom held up his hands above his head in a sign of surrender.

"I'll call a cab," Justin said.

∴

After Tom left the apartment, Justin's head pounded for the first time in months. The lasagna churned in his stomach.

He fell asleep sometime after three in the morning. He dreamt of Richie Schultz and Al Kremer kissing and awoke in a sweat.

CHAPTER 39

T
HE NEXT MORNING JUSTIN phoned the Intercontinental Hotel
near the Spanish Steps, where Tom and his pilgrims were staying, only to be told the group left at day break for Siena.

Frantic to find him to learn more details about Kremer's latest
mischief, he called every hotel in Siena until he located the one the
group had booked.

"No one has checked in by that name, sir," the clerk said over
the phone.

"Has the tour director checked in? Can you connect me with
him?"

The director answered the phone and explained that Tom
wasn't feeling well and they had left him in Rome.

When Tom failed to answer his phone at the Intercontinental,
Justin took a cab there.

∵

"Answer, Tom! It's Justin!" His repeated shouting and pounding at
the door got no response. Justin worried for Tom's safety.

At the front desk, in his black suit and Roman collar, he asked the hotel security to open Tom's door.

Inside Justin found Tom asleep in his street clothes and shoes, curled in bed. On his night table was an empty fifth of Seagram's 7, an ice bucket half filled with water, and an empty Coke bottle.

Justin had an urge to vomit. Must he now bear the responsibility of yet another priest falling from the path of his vocation?

He whispered a prayer and pulled himself together. Instead of awakening his fellow priest from his stupor, Justin sat at the room's desk and jotted a note on the hotel stationary asking that Tom call him as soon as possible. He sealed the envelope, marked Tom's name on it and shoved it under the door as he left.

At dusk Tom stood at Justin's apartment, well groomed, wearing a pressed black suit several sizes too small and his too tight Roman collar. He smelled like a cocktail of Aqua Velva and Vitalis with a hint of whiskey and cigarette smoke.

"Sorry, Justin. I've been fighting a cold. You know, jet lag and bad Roman germs. Tough combination." He spoke with a confident humor that Justin questioned. It was obvious Tom wanted alcohol off topic.

"Come in and have a seat. Cup of coffee?"

"Sure."

"Rough night?"

"Yeah. Feeling better today, though."

Justin wanted to use what may have been limited minutes of sobriety. "Tell me more about the boy in Freiburg."

"He's a friend of Richie Schultz. Name's Larry Hall. Lives alone with his divorced mother in a trailer at the end of a dead end road outside of town. I know the kid and mom from the grade school. Poor, frightened little woman who cleans houses for the doctors over on Pill Hill. Larry's probably in the eighth grade, I'd guess, and evidently Al connected with him and his mother shortly before Al went to Tom More."

"Is Kremer involved with the mother too?"

"Naw. You kidding? It'd be a lot better if he was. Just the kid. Richie says he bribes Larry, takes him on overnight trips and afternoons in the national forest."

"How's Richie know so much?"

"Richie's on to Kremer. You know that. For God's sake, his best friend hung himself because of Kremer. Richie'd kill Kremer if he wouldn't go to hell for it."

Justin's head pounded and iron fingers seemed to twist his bowels.

Tom continued, "What can be done? The archbishop won't listen to any of us." He sat wide on the couch, his legs spread apart and his hands dangling over his crotch. He reminded Justin of an overgrown walrus.

"I don't know for sure. But I do know any evidence you get from Larry Hall could help," Justin said.

"That'll be tough. I live an hour and a half away."

"And I live thousands of miles away!" Justin raised his voice as he felt spikes driven into his forehead. He stared at Tom.

Tom stood up. He was a head taller and twice the weight of Justin. "Look, have you forgotten you are the vicar general of our great archdiocese and you can't get Kremer corralled? And now you want me, a lowly curate in the boonies to fix this for you? For Christ's sake, Justin, wake up. Do your job. Stop hiding out in some library, man." Tom was red with rage.

"I'm not asking you to fix it," Justin calmed his voice. "I'm merely asking you to get more information from Richie. Is that too much to ask?" Justin tensed all over.

"No. No, I guess not. When I have an airtight case, I'll let you know, Reverend Vicar General." He walked toward the door. "I have to meet the tour group."

"Wait. We need to talk this though."

Tom slammed the door.

∴

The Tuesday after Tom's visit, Justin met with Cardinal Beal, Father Moinet, and the pope for another review of the document draft.

"Are you sick, Father Zapp?" Father Moinet seemed alarmed at Justin's appearance.

"I'm fine. Just an upset stomach," Justin lied.

That morning while shaving Justin noticed the deep circles under his eyes from the re-erupting of his inner war. From his bathroom scale he knew he was down nearly twenty-five pounds. He felt nearly as many years older too.

As the meeting broke up, Pope John gestured for Justin to come near. The nonverbal motion surprised Justin. He approached the head of the ornate table where the pope sat alone.

He signaled for him to sit closer. Justin placed his chair at the pope's arm and put his hands on the table top, folded over one another.

"My son, you do not look well," he said, as he leaned into Justin as if he was hearing a confession. His Italian words were soothing. "Is there something about your health that the Holy Father needs to know?" His eyes spoke gentleness and compassion, set deep into his round face.

"I am fine, your Holiness." Justin was embarrassed by the pope's question and felt his face grow hot.

"If you are working too hard, my son, please rest. If it is something else that troubles you, I would like to know." He put his hand on top of Justin's in a light squeeze.

"Holy Father, you have the whole world to concern you," Justin said in his still faltering Italian.

"But I am concerned about one person at a time, my son." His mouth broke into a broad smile.

"Please pray for me, Holy Father. I may need your help at some point."

"Come to me as if coming to a caring parent." His smile lifted slightly his soft double chins.

"I will. Thank you." Justin got up and moved the chair back to its original position, genuflected, and kissed the pope's ring and left.

∵

On the way back to his apartment Justin stopped to pray in the same church where he'd seen the beggar. But the beggar wasn't at his post near the front door.

Sitting again in the spot where he could least be seen, Justin in fact wished to be invisible, to be out of his body and pure spirit in the face of God. He longed to dispel again the sins of Al Kremer and be at peace. For weeks he had felt a sense of consolation by ignoring the sick priest's behaviors. Surely this peace is what God would want for him. Now the whole issue had been dropped on him again with the update from drunken Tom Gentry. Couldn't he just ignore it again? Let someone else deal with it? And what of the consequences of any action he would take now? More good priests like Tom turning to booze and gluttony to stave off depression and loneliness? Another vocation like Fred's threatened?

He rested for nearly an hour before the voiceless tabernacle, awaiting any word on what he should do. No voice spoke.

As he left, the familiar beggar held up his empty cup. Justin gave him several coins.

"Thank you, Father. What is your name?"

Justin's surprise must have been evident to the old man.

"I won't hurt you. What is your name?"

Justin told him and asked him the same.

"Giovanni Salvano. I will keep praying for you. You look ill, Father. God will protect you."

CHAPTER 40

"Maria, I am not well tonight," he said over the phone from his chair overlooking the Roman streetscape.

Justin was scheduled for supper with the Giovacchinos and had promised to take the family for dessert at a pastry shop near their apartment.

"Do you need anything? I'll bring your meal over to you. I have it prepared. No trouble."

"Not tonight, please. Also, apologize to the children. We will plan it for another night."

∴

He tried to read and pray in his room. His thoughts and feelings swirled in his throbbing head. He mistrusted all the self-knowledge he thought he'd mastered in therapy. It led to no good. For all the effort spent, Al Kremer continued his ways and, nearly as tragic, Tom had been sent into a dark, alcohol-saturated place. Fred was exiled and questioning his faith and vocation, choosing the rare act of a leave of absence. And all the while Mark O'Connell used his skills as a diplomatic church bureaucrat to maintain the status quo for Kremer and save the Roman Catholic Church in Indiana from public scandal.

Another confrontation with his prelate was more than the good Lord required of him, right? In recent weeks had he not felt the Holy Ghost's consolation, as Father Peters described it, when he was out of therapy and focused entirely on the council work instead of the issues in Indiana? Surely the physical and spiritual peace he'd experienced were signs of God's approval. Surely.

∴

The following morning the bulletin board at Immaculate Conception posted a flyer with the unique portrait of a familiar bushy bearded Jesuit. That night Father Hugo Peters was to lecture at the theological school on "The Discernment of Spirits." Justin questioned why he had failed to notice the flyer before. Providential?

He took a seat in the back row in the air-conditioned theater where distinguished theologians and church leaders had lectured for the last quarter century. The students, faculty, clergy, religious men and women in a variety of habits and robes chatted, mingling like a flock of chickens waiting to be fed. He recognized many but wanted to not be recognized. He possessed neither the interest nor energy to meet anyone. Slouching in his seat and with a fist over his mouth, he waited until the lights dimmed and the spotlight shown on the podium before he sat up. Monsignor Martin O'Daniel, the rector, stood to introduce the small, old Jesuit.

As Father Peters began to speak, Justin leaned forward and prepared to take notes.

"The Spiritual Exercises of St. Ignatius Loyola have guided thousands in growing close to God since 1576. If one is guided correctly to follow the exercises, they can be a source of wisdom and consolation."

Justin hoped to learn something, anything, to reinforce his deep desire to stay out of the controversies in Indiana. He didn't need all the preliminaries on St. Ignatius or a primer on the Exercises. Give me the words of reassurance so I can forego any responsibility for the children back in Indiana, please, that's all I want, he thought. He slouched back into his seat as the sage continued in a monotone.

After about fifteen minutes the Jesuit's voice shifted. "Now I want to turn to a little known or discussed part of the Exercises concerning what I term 'Spurious Consolation.'"

Justin perked up.

"In my work as a spiritual director I notice some souls think they are doing God's will if they feel a sense of peace, or consolation, after making an important decision. This may well be true, but untested. Without knowing, these souls could be caught up in the pride of their own thoughts and the self-centeredness of their own desires."

He went on, "So we must test the serenity we feel after an important decision. Evil may result from the decision which was made primarily to avoid pain, confusion, and chaos. The person may really be afraid to make the decision the Holy Ghost wants. God provides what we need to face the suffering necessary to achieve the larger good God wants. When the evil spirit attempts to interrupt our carrying out God's will, we experience inner and sometimes outer confusion and emotional upset."

Justin was with him, alert.

Father Peters continued, "The consolation one experiences in doing God's will can sometimes only come after great struggle and pain. This is what we must seek to understand and act on with all our being."

Justin sat speechless. It was as if the old man was speaking directly to Justin's heart. Fear overtook him, and he left the auditorium in a rush.

CHAPTER 41

"YOU NEED THIS, FATHER." Paolo Giovacchino sat next to Justin on the patio overlooking the Mediterranean just south of Cinque Terra. The family had included Justin on their early August holiday to the resort. These coastal villages filled during late summer with European tourists eager to escape their daily labors and routines.

"You think I haven't noticed you've lost weight?" Maria asked with a motherly smile. "I'll prepare a special recipe tonight to put on some kilos."

The three children were splashing in the cove below the patio with several other children. Their giggles and screams told of their joy at getting out of the hot, dirty city.

Justin relaxed with the family for two weeks, sleeping until seven each morning and hiking the nearby rocky cliffs with Paolo and Giuseppe. During the afternoon siesta time he read and prayed, in a retreat state of mind.

One evening, when Giuseppe walked his siblings to town for gelato, Maria, Paolo, and Justin sat in silence watching the star filled night.

After a long pause, Maria asked, "Paolo and I can tell you have been carrying a heavy burden the past few months. We are happy to see you relax."

"I am at peace when I am with all of you. The world of a priest in Rome is so closed. If I let myself, I'd be consumed by church business and fail to appreciate so much of the beauty of the rest of life. Just look up there. A few months ago John Glenn circled the globe three times in a little metal capsule. And beyond this tiny earth there are probably billions of stars shining just for our pleasure."

"I don't have to look up there," Paolo added. "I can look in the eyes of people I love and find the greatest pleasures of life." He smiled at Maria, a seductive smile, and then winked at Justin.

"You shouldn't flirt in front of a priest," Maria said with a soft giggle.

"It's all right. God smiles when you two flirt!" Justin said.

They all laughed.

∵

Justin returned to Rome for a final six weeks of preparations for the opening of the Second Vatican Council on October 11, 1962. The event had been anticipated with a mixture of excitement and trepidation, depending on whether one longed to awaken the sleeping church or keep it in its slumber.

He determined to stay focused on his job for the pope while his internal combat over his superior and Al Kremer raged on. His body quickly weakened under the strain. A week later, he was admitted to Salvator Mundi Hospital for rest and attention to his diarrhea. He received fluids as he did when hospitalized for the similar dehydration in Indiana several years before. After four days under the care of the Salvatorian Sisters, he rested in his apartment where Maria brought him simple meals appropriate to his system: homemade apple sauce and cottage cheese, farina, water crackers, Jell-O, and ginger ale.

As he grew strong enough to return to work, he considered

scheduling another meeting with Dr. Goldberg but decided against it. He knew what he needed to do after praying over Father Peters's comments.

Indeed, Justin found his solace to stay resolute while in quiet prayer. In his now familiar spot in the ancient church, he sat for several hours. The words from Father Peters about 'spurious consolation' pierced him. In the stillness of the sanctuary he let himself surrender to something more important than himself. It was as if a space within him opened to a clearing. He entered it and ran free, unencumbered by the power and threats of Mark O'Connell or anyone else. With his eyes closed, he envisioned the old pope walking into the open space with him, to let him know he was not alone in facing the difficult mission.

When Justin left the ancient church in the late September twilight, he saw the old beggar smile. Justin pulled several bills from his wallet and stuffed them into the beggar's empty cup.

"You are at peace, aren't you, Father?"

"Yes. Yes, I am."

"My prayers are working." His broad smile had several missing teeth.

"Yes. Yes, they are. Thank you, Giovanni."

CHAPTER 42

J USTIN ARRIVED AT ST. Peter's Hill on the weekend before the annual turkey shoot, a fundraising carnival highlighted by competitive shotgun target shootings. Fresh dressed turkeys were the winners' prizes.

The parking lot surrounding the old church, school, and rectory displayed a children's Ferris wheel, carousel, a roped path for pony rides, as well as booths with numbered spinning wheels for winning homemade cakes, candy, and quilts. Bingo tables in the basement of the school awaited several hundred small-time gamblers. In the far grassy corner of the parish campus, the eight-by-eight-inch square white paper targets, stapled one each on separate wooden posts, stood like British soldiers in a row, awaiting battle.

Justin spotted Tom under a tarpaulin-shaded area where hundreds of chickens would be fried the next day. Surrounded by several muscular men with swollen bellies in sweaty white tee shirts, Tom fisted a beer bottle with one hand and pinched a cigarette in the other.

The men remembered Justin and offered him a beer from the red, metal Coca-Cola cooler topped with crushed ice.

"Thanks, guys, but not today," Justin said with a hesitant smile. He was on a mission.

"Oh-oh, guys, Father Zapp looks serious," Tom said with a beer giggle. He followed with a deep draw from his cigarette.

"You'd better go talk priest stuff with him, Father Tom," one of the younger men said.

Tom led Justin to the rectory where they sat in wicker cushioned chairs on the screened front porch. On the shaded porch, with the scent of smoldering leaves in the valley and hum of a farmer's corn-picker in a nearby field, Justin was flooded with tender memories from the less conflicted days of four-and-a-half years before.

Mrs. Mayer greeted him with a genuine hug and brought the priests iced tea. After setting the drinks on the end tables, she left and shut the tall wooden front door separating the house from the porch.

"I thought you were needed in Rome. Isn't the council about to start?" Tom's red eyes spoke of several beers' influence.

"I am needed there. But Kremer is more important. I want you to help me contact the Hall boy and his mother."

"No problem, big guy." Tom's informal address, Justin knew, was the result of the alcohol lubricant.

"Can we go tomorrow morning?" Justin recognized Tom to be in no state to talk weighty matters with Larry Hall or Larry's mother on this Friday.

"The turkey shoot's tomorrow!"

Justin gave him a serious stare.

"Okay. Yeah, you stay here tonight and we'll leave after breakfast," Tom said with a heavier slur.

"I'll be in town at the motel, but I'll pick you up at nine sharp. You call the mother to make sure they'll be home."

"Damn! I'm gonna miss the turkey shoot. . . ."

"And I might just miss the Second Vatican Council! So what? What's most important?" Justin's energy surged, but he wondered if Tom would remember any of the conversation at nine the next day.

∴

Mrs. Mayer met Justin at the St. Peter's Hill rectory door a little before nine.

"Father Gentry just finished breakfast and asked me to tell you he'll be down in a minute," the matronly housekeeper said. She'd put on a few more pounds in intervening years but maintained her warmth and efficiency.

"We're good. Called the mom last night and she said to call her when we get close to town," Tom said as he walked with Justin down the rectory steps.

Justin drove Tom in the rented car to Freiburg, a seventy-five-mile trip from St. Peter's Hill, giving the two men time to discuss what they were undertaking. Tom seemed tired and distracted.

It was a cool, crisp last Saturday in September. The trees' colors through the Hoosier National Forest seemed to shift into vivid scarlet, burnt oranges, and bright yellows and purples before their eyes. The dry autumn air, smelling of burning wood and leaves, blew in the priests' faces from the window vents.

"Katie Hall is about thirty," Tom began. He lit a cigarette and inhaled. "She was a teenage mom and has raised Larry by herself in the little trailer. Larry's been at the parish school since first grade."

"What's Kremer's hold on them?" Justin asked.

"Seems he's helping her with her bills, buying Larry's clothes. I don't know what she does with the money." Tom seemed coherent and focused now.

"How long's it been going on?"

"Richie said it started before Patrick's death. Al may have had several boys he was seeing at the same time."

"Richie still reliable?"

"Straight as an arrow last I knew. I don't see him much and teenagers change fast, you know."

"Tom," Justin said, "I've let you down. I should have stayed with this Kremer mess all along. I'm not balking this time. I need facts on Larry, and we need to have his mom and, if necessary, Larry, go with us to the archbishop. You ready for more punishment from the chancery?"

"Look, I'm at the bottom. What more can the guy do to me?" He pulled the ash tray from the console and tapped the end of his cigarette into it. "This crap disgusts me. We don't need Kremer in our brotherhood of priests. This is not the church I want to be part of. We're better than this, you know. He's destroying these kids."

"I understand that more than most." Justin looked squarely at the road.

After several minutes of silence, Tom took a final drag and crushed the cigarette into the ash tray before exhaling gray smoke toward the window.

∵

When they pulled into town, Justin stopped at a Texaco station for gas as Tom went to a pay phone to call Larry's mother. As the attendant washed the windshield and checked the car's oil and tires, Tom reported Larry and his mom were home and would welcome them.

The priests drove five miles along the highway going west. Justin turned onto an unpaved county road, a road easily missed because of the overgrowth of trees and brush surrounding its entrance. The thin layer of gray crushed limestone sprayed a dust cloud behind the car as Justin drove a mile further to the trailer. A canopy of maples, oaks, walnuts, and sassafras sheltered them along the way. A raccoon crossed the gravel road, causing Justin to brake in surprise. Tom slid forward and caught himself before his forehead bumped the windshield.

"St. Mary, save us, Justin! We're not in that much of a hurry."
Justin ignored him and kept driving.

Where the road ended, a narrow brown creek rock drive descended several feet to the pale blue, rusty trailer sitting on orderly stacks of concrete blocks. A bent hackberry tree, half its leaves already shed, shaded the home of Larry and his mother. Three lines of laundry hung in back of a wooden shed several feet behind the trailer; shirts, blue jeans, underwear, and socks flapped in the dry fall breeze. A black, rusty 1948 Dodge sat on the brown lawn near the trailer's main door.

When the priests got out of the car, a small dog, white and black with a tail full of burrs curled over its back, barked.

"Don't mind her, Father. She don't bite," Katie Hall said. "Here, Daisy! Here! Shush!" she said as she clapped her hands. "I'm sorry. She's just scared." She reached down and held the mixed breed by her collar to keep her from jumping on the two men. "You go on in and make yourselves at home." The dog calmed. Once the priests were inside, Katie let the dog free and followed them in.

Young Larry stood as the men, dressed in their black suits and collars, entered the tiny space. After Tom introduced the mother and son to Justin, everyone sat around the small, cluttered dining table.

"Larry, I hope you trust me. I need your help." Tom's approach was similar to how he handled Richie Schultz nearly two years before, gentle and genuine.

Larry, a pubescent boy of thirteen, was lanky with thick, chocolate hair cut close to his ears. He wore a plaid, pressed long-sleeved shirt with a small hand-sewn patch on the right sleeve. His hairless ivory face was narrow; he had dark blue eyes and thick black eyebrows. Several of his front top teeth had a yellow hue and bent one over another.

"Yes. I trust you. I've known you most of my life." He spoke with the high pitch of a choirboy.

Justin let Tom lead. Katie sat in a kitchen chair next to her son. She was thin with a high beehive hair style that added seven inches to her height; she wore a cotton floral patterned dress that had lost its once bright colors from too many washings.

"Yes, we trust you," she said.

"Well, Father Zapp and I need your help in making sure your friend Father Kremer gets help for a problem he has," Tom said. At the mention of Al's name the mother and son turned rigid.

"We don't know nothing about Father Kremer's problem." Katie was missing an incisor tooth and her pasty complexion told Justin she wasn't well.

Justin watched Tom to see how he was going to steer around Katie's obvious fears.

The engaging young priest did not disappoint. "It is healthy for grown men to be attracted to grown women, wouldn't you agree?"

"Yes, I guess so. But you priests aren't supposed to be attracted to women."

"Well, we're human too. We can be attracted to women, but we have chosen to be celibate, which you know means we can't date or marry."

"I can tell you that ain't always true." She seemed bold in contradicting Tom.

"You're right. We aren't perfect. But Father Zapp and I have serious concerns about Father Kremer not keeping his promise to be celibate."

Justin noticed Larry's face turning red. He fidgeted and rubbed his hands together with his head bent.

"We are wondering if you and Larry could help Father Kremer by meeting with the archbishop to let him know that Father Kremer is having trouble being a good priest." Tom seemed to be pushing enough to make his point without throwing the boy and his mother into a tailspin of denial. Justin immediately remembered when Patrick ran from the classroom when Justin broached the same subject. Justin would forever regret that missed opportunity.

"You don't know what all Father Kremer does for me and Larry. He is good to us."

"I don't doubt that. We're just concerned that Father Kremer may not always act in Larry's best interest."

Larry got up and said, "Mom, I think I'll let you talk. I'm going to feed Daisy."

"Wait, please. I need your help too." Tom looked up at the boy, nearly as tall as Tom.

"I don't want to talk about Father Kremer. He helps us." The boy stepped toward the door.

"Wait, son. The priests are right. We can't go on like this," Katie said. "It ain't right."

"Mom. Please. You can't do this. Please." He turned and sat back down in the wooden chair, crossed his arms, and looked away. His face was scarlet with embarrassment or perhaps anger.

"It ain't right what's going on. These priests can help."

"Thank you, Miss Hall," Justin said. "Yes, we can help. We want to help not just you and Larry but also Father Kremer."

The boy slouched as Katie Hall told how Al Kremer came to their home every Tuesday, driving from the city on his day off. He and Larry went out for several hours alone, returning in time for the priest to have supper with them. He'd pay Katie twenty-five dollars each visit, "to help raise your son," he told her.

"I don't know how to stop it," Katie said with tears welling.

Justin heard Larry sniffle before he wiped his eyes with his sleeve.

"That's why we're here," Tom said. His compassion told Justin that Tom was a gifted pastor.

∴

After more than an hour, the priests outlined the need for Katie and Larry to meet with the archbishop at the chancery to tell him their story. They agreed to all ride together the following Monday morning, two days later.

CHAPTER 43

JUSTIN HAD DONE THIS twice before. He determined this was to be the final time.

"What is so important that you had me shuffle my day's schedule, Father Zapp?" Mark raised his right eyebrow above his new black-rimmed glasses.

"The life of a boy, your Excellency." Justin felt calm and confident.

"Yes." The prelate glared at the boy.

"Your Excellency, Larry has been asked to perform immodest acts with Father Kremer," Katie began. Tom and Justin's coaching showed immediately.

"Can the boy speak for himself?" Mark asked.

"It is hard. He's embarrassed, as you might imagine," the mother said. Larry sat close to his small mother with his head bowed.

"I must know more than you are telling me. You are accusing a priest of God of perhaps committing a mortal sin with your son. This is a grave charge."

Katie recoiled in shyness. The lavish conference room in the big city, sitting in front of an archbishop, a room of highly educated clergy in black suits must have shaken her, Justin thought.

So Justin stepped in. "Your Excellency, Larry Hall has told his mother what Father Al Kremer does during his weekly visits. After Larry gets home from school, Father Kremer takes him to a private place near their home and sexually abuses him. Father Kremer returns the boy, eats supper with Larry and his mother, and then pays Miss Hall twenty-five dollars to help her pay bills before he returns to St. Thomas More. This has gone on for nearly two years."

"Larry, is what Father Zapp is saying true?" The archbishop's face was crimson.

Larry was silent, staring at the walnut conference table before him.

"It is all true, your Excellency," Katie said.

"I didn't ask you, Miss Hall. I asked your son." The prelate's authority oozed from his lips.

Larry raised his head and looked straight at the archbishop and said, "Yes. Every . . . every . . . everything that Father Zapp said is true."

"Very well. I understand your concern. I will study this and get back to you and your mother. Thank you both for making the long trip here. In the meantime, I suggest you tell Father Kremer not to visit you anymore." He collected himself, took a deep breath, stood, and walked toward the door. With his hand on the doorknob, he turned to the two priests and said, "Father Gentry and Father Zapp, can I have a word with you in my office before you take Miss Hall and Larry back to Freiburg?"

In the dark-paneled office there was a lingering scent of flavored pipe tobacco. The overhead fluorescent light stole the patrician quality of the room and made it sterile.

"You think you've finally boxed me in, boys?" He sat in his oversized leather swivel chair and pulled out his pipe from a top desk drawer. As he stuffed tobacco into the small barrel and lit it, biting the stem, he sucked in air and puffed a thick haze from his mouth and leaned back. A sweet aroma filled the room.

After moments of silence, Justin said, "No one is trying to box you in, your Excellency. I am concerned about children and I am concerned about Al Kremer's mental health."

"Well, it sure appears you're trying to trap me so I get rid of Al. You holding a grudge against him, Justin?"

"No. He is a nice man. Can be a caring pastor and we all know he is a gifted fundraiser. Those things aren't in dispute. What Tom and I know is now what you, Fred, the Schultz family, and those families at Tom More all know. None of us is trying to trap you. We're trying to do the right thing for the boys and for Kremer. That's all."

Justin had never felt so calm. It was as if a powerful force stood next to him and placed a supportive hand on his shoulder.

"Puttin' on a little weight, aren't you, Tom?" Mark said as if to unburden the heavy moment.

"Coming middle age." Tom glanced up at his superior with a modest smile, and then looked down.

Justin directed the conversation back. "Can we count on you to remove Al from pastoral duties immediately and send him away to professionals for help?"

"Let me think about what to do. I know you both are sincere, at least I think you are. But removing Al is a major event, as I've said before. Remember, right now he's raising two million for the new college administration building, and he's adding nearly three quarters of a million to his school at his parish. To pull him away now could threaten these projects."

"I understand. But he is a bigger threat to Larry Hall and others. These are people, not buildings. The psychological wounds he is inflicting will last a lifetime for these children. And who knows if another Patrick Gardner is waiting to commit suicide? "

"Enough. I get your point. I'll think it over and let both of you know. Perhaps you can return the mother and son to Freiburg now.

We all have other matters to attend to."

"With due respect, your Excellency, Al must be removed from parish work immediately and sent away for treatment. And I do plan to notify the legal authorities." Justin felt serene.

"Well, you must remember, you are morally bound to be obedient to me, your archbishop. I am not morally bound to do what you want." Mark cocked his head and lowered his brows.

"Your Excellency, you are morally bound not to scandalize one of these little ones. That, as I think we all recall, is a teaching from the Lord himself."

"Now you presume to preach to me?"

"Just, perhaps, to refresh your memory. You may also want to remember that there is a legal issue before you."

"The state attorney and police chief here and in Freiburg are my friends, all good Catholics. I'm sure they are more loyal to their archbishop than you seem to be at the moment." Mark leaned across the desk and put his pipe in his mouth, inhaling and then slowly emitting a straight gray stream from the corner of his mouth.

Justin sat back, noticing Tom's face was white as alabaster listening to the exchange.

In a quick jerk Mark stood and said, "That will be all, gentlemen. I'll let you know tomorrow my decision when I call Father Gentry at his rectory."

CHAPTER 44

D URING THE RETURN RIDE to Freiburg, Justin and Tom complemented Katie and Larry for talking with the archbishop, and Justin said he understood Katie needed the extra money she received from Father Kremer.

"It must be difficult raising a son by yourself, Miss Hall," Justin said.

"You have no idea, Father. But Larry is a good boy. He never gets in no trouble or nothing. He stays home and puts together those plastic racing cars and airplanes, don't you, son?"

Larry grunted a yes, and Justin could see from the rearview mirror he was staring out the window, expressionless. Justin knew the emotional roller coaster he must be riding.

"Can you make it without Father Kremer's money?" Tom stretched his neck to look at Katie sitting behind Justin, who was driving.

"I feel bad about that. I know it's wrong to take it. I hate doing it. But, no, I don't need it. I've been buying them U. S. savings bonds for Larry's education. Should I give it back?"

"No, Katie. You should keep it for Larry's future. But, as the archbishop said, the visits must stop," Tom said. "Can you tell him to stop coming to see you?"

"I don't want to hurt him. He'd be upset if I told him that. I don't know what to do. I know it ain't right." Her tone was different than two days before when she wanted to cooperate.

"Mother, PLEASE, don't you understand?" Larry's burst stunned the adults.

"What?" Her voice was more like a wounded dog's whimper than a caring human mother.

"Don't you see what Father Tom and Father Zapp are saying?" he yelled. "Father Kremer is sick. He hurts me! I never want to see him again and these priests and the archbishop are telling you to make sure he stays away from me!"

A long pause ensued. Finally, the shy feminine whisper came from the back seat. "I will call him long distance tonight and tell him not to come this Tuesday . . . or ever again."

"Thank you, mother." Larry exhaled.

Silence descended for the rest of the journey.

∵

The next afternoon Justin met Tom at St. Peter's Hill rectory.

"I've never seen that side of you." Tom popped a cap on a bottle of beer.

"I haven't either. Sometimes God gives us what we need when we need it, if we're paying attention."

"Yeah, I guess so." Tom took a long swig.

"You and Fred deserve credit. And you've both suffered for it."

The priests waited until after business hours for a call from Mark.

None came.

And none came the next day, or the day after.

∵

Justin flew back to Rome the following weekend, less than a week before the start of the historic council on October 11, 1962. Sitting alone in a row of empty seats near the rear of the plane, a gray haze of cigarette smoke filling the fuselage, he savored the quiet space to sort the jumble of feelings and events of the week. Images of Tom kept jumping around in his mind. The once agile, sleek athlete had slipped into a quagmire of self-induced deterioration. But an inner core seemed to remain in the young priest, solid and good. Had it not been for Tom's clear, sensitive judgment, nothing would have ever been rattled in the chancery, with Fred Klein or even with the Pope. Now the rapid decline of Tom Gentry and the non-response of Mark, following the latest meeting with victims, stirred Justin's rage, making his whole being boil. He took heavy breaths to calm as he flew over the Atlantic, watching the eastern horizon broaden with the golden light of another dawn.

When he arrived in Rome, Justin learned Mark had taken a different Pan Am flight two days earlier. Perhaps the archbishop deliberately avoided Justin in making his flight plans. Regardless, they would eventually cross paths during the Council in the tiny enclosed Vatican city-state. Then Justin would confront him again with the abuse of Larry Hall.

∵

At the opening ceremonies of the council, from his reserved seat in St. Peter's Basilica as a peritus of the pope, Justin witnessed the spectacle of the twenty-four hundred bishops processing in alphabetic order into the largest church in the world. He caught a glimpse of Mark in a cluster of Asian, Australian, African, European, North and South American prelates with surnames beginning with "O." Scattered up and down the long line were cardinals, including Beal, Calabrese, Koenig, and Richard Cushing of Boston, who nearly two years before stood behind President Kennedy on the cold inauguration day in Washington, D.C. Each face glowed with optimism at the excitement of the special moment. It had been nearly a century since the last gathering of all the bishops of the world in such a council. Then the Papal States struggled for political survival and relevance. To the consternation of many, the pope at the time, Pius IX, manipulated the bishops in attendance to enhance the papacy in a sweeping reactionary move, declaring himself and his successors to be infallible in matters of faith and morals.

From the start, John XXIII set a tone to ensure this council, the Second Vatican Council, must be different than any of the twenty previous councils. The church in 1962 was at an elevated point in her history. The faith was spreading to all points of the globe. In Europe, North and South America, and Australia, parishes, hospitals, colleges, orphanages, seminaries, monasteries, and convents flourished. Missions outside these areas gathered thousands of converts each year. Pope John's vision for this meeting, outlined in his opening speech, was a dialogue with the whole world, not a self-righteous shunning of it. Now, on this October day, all the years of preparation, research, meetings, debates, and haggling could bear the fruit the pope wanted.

That opening statement was also charged with subtle messages to the conservatives that a new era was dawning for aspects of the church that were stubbornly stale, outmoded, immobile, and contrary to the original message of Christ. Of the entire speech, two sentences pierced Justin's ears. The pope, in a calm, smooth tongue, spoke in Latin, "In the everyday exercise of our pastoral ministry, greatly to our sorrow, we sometimes have to listen to those who although consumed with zeal do not have very much judgment or balance." Justin thought of Mark's zeal to enrich his archdiocese with new buildings, new projects, and added prestige, and of how Mark missed the need to protect innocent children.

A second sentence reinforced Justin's understanding of the Successor of Peter as a leader who reflected God's care for people. "Today, the Spouse of Christ prefers to use the medicine of mercy rather than severity. She considers that she meet the needs of the present age by showing the validity of her teaching rather than by condemnations."

With these words Justin felt a rekindled urgency to be as insightful and holy as this humble, skilled, caring man. In dealing with Kremer, Justin did not want to condemn or seek revenge. But he wanted to use the "judgment and balance," much of it learned in his years of therapy, to stop the child sexual abuse with "the medicine of mercy rather than severity," as he envisioned this saintly pope might do in a similar situation. Firm, but loving, summarized the approach he would continue to take with Archbishop Mark O'Connell.

He left the opening ceremony wondering about Mark's vendetta against Tom and Fred. Once Justin's time in Rome ended, would he be the next target? He tried to convince himself it didn't matter.

Chapter 45

A FTER THE ELABORATE CEREMONY, at a reception for the American attendees, Justin found his first opportunity to talk with his immediate superior.

"Nice to see you here, Justin," the archbishop said.

He passed him near the long table with layers of enticing food: yellow, orange, and white Italian cheeses; deep purple grapes; thin slices of seasoned Italian sausages; delicate soda crackers; and warm round loaves of sliced fresh bread with brown crusted tops. The American delegation cut no corners. The ice-sculptured centerpiece was a replica of the dome of St. Peter's. A champagne fountain, in a continuous gurgle, promised to satisfy the delegates' need for refreshment.

"I am still waiting for the phone call. You promised," Justin said.

Justin stood directly in front of Mark and looked into his clear blue eyes. A low mingling of conversations surrounded them as prelates, periti, observers, journalists, and diplomats meandered into the grand hall.

"All the preparations for the council have kept me busy." He chuckled and turned sideways, appearing to move on to more welcoming Americans in the group.

"I don't think you understand the importance, your Excellency. . . ."

The conversations of the swelling crowd in the room drowned Justin's voice.

Mark walked away.

∵

The night of the opening of the council over 200,000 pilgrims filled St. Peter's Square with anticipation. In the center of the massive piazza, surrounding the one-hundred-feet-tall obelisk, brought from Egypt nearly five hundred years earlier during the post Reformation period of uncertainty, teens and young adults from Catholic Action carried torches and formed a human cross, chanting and singing, urging the Holy Father to speak from his window in the papal residence overlooking the square. The serene pope did not disappoint. Justin stood near a stone column, twice the size of an Indiana farm silo, a few hundred feet from the opened window and heard the tender words over the public address system. They seemed directed specifically at Justin and the boys in Indiana: "Dear children, dear children, I hear your voices," he began. The crowd roared approval. "My voice is an isolated one, but it echoes the voice of the whole world. Here, in effect, the whole world is represented. Now go back home and give your little children a loving gentle kiss and embrace. Tell them it is from Pope John."

Justin leaned against the stone pillar and wept for joy. He felt God more alive in that moment than any in his life. Not only did his years of scholarly preparation for this historic event seem to culminate on this night, but more importantly, he knew the pope himself was his ally in freeing Hoosier boys from the scourge of Al Kremer. Now, regardless of what had happened to Larry Hall and the dozens of other victims, all would be well, somehow. Justin knew in his heart the pope himself, if necessary, would support all the effort Justin, Tom, and Fred had made to protect God's family on earth, especially the fragile children.

Walking back to the area where hundreds of taxis and buses grouped to transport the departing pilgrims, Justin's mind stirred with specific questions about how all the good would be carried out. What strategy would he employ? What would be required of him? Mark's silence chilled and exasperated him. How could his archbishop be moved to act?

The crowd jockeying for cabs and buses seemed endless. He felt jittery and started walking the two-mile distance to his apartment. Along the way he moved into deeper thought, giving scant notice to people, noises, blaring music, lights, store windows, smells from restaurants and coffee bars, and sounds of barking dogs.

Wasn't the problem deeper and wider than Al Kremer? What kind of organization permits its leaders to be so flawed and to hurt so many innocent kids? And why the cover up? How did men like Basil Epperman and Al Kremer ever get past the filters that were supposed to be in place within seminaries to bar from ordination the twisted men who would use children for the selfish release of their sexual urges?

He wondered whether the ancient, baroque, monarchical Catholic Church, with its layers of ritual and pomp, its tiers of authority and control, its international wealth and power had strayed in so many ways from the original simple intentions of its founder. It had digressed so far that a Mark O'Connell seemed more devoted to preserving the prestige and influence of the structure of this socially potent institution than simply caring for the safety of kids.

And what of celibacy, a necessary form of self-denial that Justin knew from the start was part and parcel of his vocation to priesthood. Did Holy Mother Church, in her attempt to discipline her clergy, unwittingly cause the deviant behavior Justin had experienced and now confronted? Did it make sense to encase young candidates for the priesthood, at the height of their sexual stirrings, in isolated seminaries, away from healthy settings where families functioned day to day and young people dated and married? The sexually immature men who were eventually ordained from such cloisters often had difficulty being close to women, of feeling comfortable in mixed crowds. Justin knew some, in their confusion, desperation and loneliness took lovers, male and female. Perhaps they could cope in no other way. They probably longed to continue to serve the flock as priests, but felt compelled to satisfy their strong, normal human desires any way they could. And Justin knew more than anyone else that some priests turned to children, the worst form of sexual pathology. These deviants crushed the psyches of the innocent. Few of these victims could escape the anxiety, the confusion, the nightmares, the depression, fears, health problems, and self-hatred Justin knew so well. Each was wounded for life. Their only hope, based on Justin's fortunate experience, was the combination of a skilled therapist and Divine Grace.

He walked past a couple holding hands, giggling. They looked to be in their twenties. How natural and beautiful, Justin thought. Why has the church, especially during the last thousand years, been so afraid of sex? A powerful force, yes, definitely. But, he mused, God made sex to be enjoyed and to bring men and women close, as close as two humans can be physically, if not spiritually.

Denial of this beautiful part of life, hiding behind walls and segregating its clergy from the closeness of women, seemed more dangerous than a welcoming attitude. It's like trying to re-cap an open soda bottle once shaken; it'll eventually explode.

By the time he was in bed, he was mentally worn down and tired from the hike, but his spirits soared; his conscience was clear. He slept well, no headaches or stumbling trips to the bathroom.

CHAPTER 46

THE BLUR OF ACTIVITIES the next few days made it impossible for Justin to find Mark, let alone have a conversation with him about Larry Hall and Al Kremer.

Frustrated, Justin, on the fourth night, sat at his new IBM typewriter in his apartment to craft a letter to his prelate, saying he wanted a decision on the removal of Kremer by October 20. Perhaps in parallel providential scripts, that was also the day, unknown to Justin at the time, the Catholic president of the United States announced the blockade of Soviet ships carrying missiles to Communist Cuba, which set in motion the most dangerous ten days in human history.

Much has been written in history books about international events that followed, when the leaders of the two most powerful nations on earth threatened each other with mutual destruction. The drama that unfolded was monitored everywhere with fear and prayers, including in the tiniest nation on earth, Vatican City.

Justin Zapp, like billions around the world, imagined the worst. After the daily council sessions, he quietly retreated to the chapel behind the ancient bronze statue of St. Peter, whose polished toe millions of pilgrims through the centuries had touched in reverence. The sculpture of the first pope was on a five-foot-high pedestal in the huge basilica in front and to the right of the main altar. As he prayed for world peace in the shadow of the image, Justin knew the interior war that had waged within him for years was not yet over. But he was armed and ready to do what was necessary to engage Mark O'Connell.

By October 23, the day he was scheduled to meet the pope with his other periti to discuss progress on the documents on Catholic-Jewish relations, Justin still had no word from Mark. At the conclusion of the formal meeting, he approached the pope's secretary, Don Loris Capovilla.

"Monsignor, I have a local pastoral matter to discuss with His Holiness. Could a very brief meeting be arranged?" He felt his palms moisten with the nervous words.

The pope, sitting at a distance, looked up from the conversation with several other periti. He evidently overheard Justin's yet-to-be-refined Italian request to his secretary and gestured for Capovilla to approach. Immediately after receiving the pope's direction, the tidy man, in a flowing cassock trimmed with crimson, came to Justin.

"His Holiness will see you in the papal chamber in five minutes."

Justin nodded his agreement, looked up at the pope, and exchanged short smiles.

Once Justin was in the ornate room, trimmed in bright yellow with white walls and thick silver and gold embroidered drapes, Pope John rose from behind his massive papal desk to extend his hand to Justin. He directed him to sit in the solid chair across from him. To Justin's surprise, the pontiff, in slow movements, came around the desk and took the chair inches from Justin.

"Father, tell me what troubles you." The late afternoon October sky bled oranges, reds, and purples through the tall window behind him.

Justin gripped the arms of the high back, hand-carved chair and inhaled fully several times to calm himself.

"Your Holiness, I hesitate to involve you, given the heavy responsibilities you carry every day, especially the demands of the council."

The pope leaned toward Justin as if to ensure he caught every word. His eyes, deep in his round face, appeared to hold secrets of holiness and his own mortality. Justin wondered how long he'd be with his flock, scattered around the globe, given his slow gait and the pallid appearance.

"In my archdiocese, His Excellency Mark O'Connell will not act to remove a priest who is repeatedly abusing boys in a sexual manner." The words tumbled out. "The archbishop, who knows of the abuse from several sources, including two brave young priests, refuses to discuss it anymore, despite my pleas that the priest be removed from pastoral duties." Justin's eyes moistened and he bowed his head.

The old man leaned closer and touched Justin's forearm. His old skin was thin, nearly transparent, over his chubby hand.

In a warm tone the Pope responded in slow Italian, "Go back to Archbishop O'Connell once more. Tell him I am aware of his obligations to remove this priest immediately, address his responsibilities to the legal authorities, and tend to the pastoral needs of the children who have been harmed. If he does not act immediately, please ask Dom Capovilla for another private audience. We must love the children, Father. And we must never be a source of scandal to them or harm them in anyway. It is the worst of sins."

He removed his hand from Justin's arm and added, with a tilt of his head, "I am with you and God is with you."

Justin was speechless. With all his preoccupations with day-to-day management of the church—the enormous task of steering the council away from conservative shoals, his concern for world politics, especially peace during this tense time—how did the pope ever agree to help Justin deal with an intractable archbishop who was covering up the sexual raping and molestation of boys by a locally prominent priest in far-away Indiana? And the pope saw it so clearly, something Justin had dallied with for years.

Pope John had spent his career in the Vatican diplomatic corps, and it showed in his few simple, careful words to Justin. The pope was sending him as his emissary to the archbishop to avoid a face-to-face dressing down of Mark by the pontiff, which would surely derail Mark's career plans. With Justin as the messenger, O'Connell's road to a red hat could remain open, assuming he complied with the directives of the Holy Father.

Over the next ten years—it was commonly understood in the political church circles—the cardinal slots in several major cities would be vacant, including Chicago, Philadelphia, Baltimore, New York, and Los Angeles. Their leaders' tenures were not finished, but most had already left their marks on their flocks and the handing over of their stewardships was in sight. If Mark was to remain a candidate for a red hat for any of these cities, or within the Vatican curia, a personal, documented scolding by the pope would pose a major threat. But for the pontiff to send a firm message indirectly, without documentation, would result in a positive outcome for the children in Indiana while positioning Mark for any forthcoming vacancy in the College of Cardinals.

Smart pope, Justin thought that night as he read his breviary in his cushioned chair at his apartment window. Justin prayed for confi-dence to carry out the mission. The night sky glistened with thousands of diamonds.

CHAPTER 47

FROM THE ATTENDEES' DIRECTORY, Justin learned Mark's hotel address in Rome. Following the next day's session at St. Peter's, well after dark, Justin waited at the archbishop's hotel room door for his return from the Vatican. Finally, after an hour vigil, at 10:35, the elevator bell's dull clang sounded, and Mark, his silver-haired head down as he reached into his pocket for his room key, walked toward Justin. When he looked up at his vicar general leaning against the wall, Justin's arms crossed across his thin chest, he said, "Not now, Justin. I'm tired. Whatever's on your mind can wait until tomorrow."

Justin stood straight and moved to block the entrance, his arms still crossed. "No, your Excellency, it cannot wait. I have a single message from His Holiness."

Mark stepped back, his mouth opened wide, his face shed of color. "What? You've betrayed me to the pope? How could you?" His face shifted to a snarl. "After I've promoted you and given you everything you've ever wanted?" Now his color went from ashen to scarlet. He poked his index finger toward Justin. "I've satisfied your every whim." His voice rose and raced. "I've nurtured your scholarly career, made sure you had your tiny private space to do your self-centered little scholarly research, your education in Washington and here in Rome, and now you do this to me! Now you destroy my chances to do God's work as a leader in his church? What are you thinking? You're no better than Judas Iscariot!" He then shouted, "Now get out of my way! I'm going to bed." He reached for the door knob and Justin, his arms still crossed, shifted to block Mark. He glared at Justin.

The elevator bell clanged again and a waiter got off pushing a cart of covered food on trays toward the other end of the long golden carpeted hall. The smells of roasted lamb and mint shifted in the opposite direction toward the priests.

In a low, firm voice Justin said, "His Holiness wanted me to deliver the message that he is aware of your obligation to immediately remove Father Kremer, meet the legal reporting requirements, and care for the children harmed."

Mark snapped, "I know you meet the pope regularly. No doubt you two are real buddies by now." He spoke the words through his teeth, barely moving his lips. "You think I don't know you're also the one who sabotaged me with Calabrese? I could have been in his office by now." Now he shouted, "I know more about you than you think. You're nothing but Judas reincarnate. You're a self-righteous, self-centered S.O.B. I'm sorry I ever trusted you."

The door next to Mark's room opened and a sleepy middle-aged woman, her bleached blond hair rolled in tubal curlers and white cold cream covering her face like a death mask, stuck her head out. In soft Italian she asked the men quiet down. Justin acknowledged her request in her language.

He then whispered to Mark, "I am merely the messenger." He stepped aside for Mark to unlock his door. "Have a good evening. I will continue to pray for you."

Looking Justin in the eye, Mark said, "Go to hell."

He walked into his room and Justin started toward the elevator.

The archbishop's heavy door slammed before Justin pushed the down button.

∴

In Moscow and Washington, another confrontation, a global one, continued. Behind the scenes the humble rotund pope who had skillfully just used his papal power to influence Mark O'Connell, was also trusted sufficiently by Nikita Khrushchev, the Soviet Premier, and President Kennedy, to suggest ways for each leader to save political face and keep the planet from self-immolation. The pope's training and experience in diplomacy in Sofia, Athens, Constantinople, and Paris had equipped him for his role as behind-the-scenes messenger for both parties.

On October 29, 1962, the Soviet Union agreed to remove its missiles from Cuba and the United States pulled missiles from Turkey. War was diverted.

That afternoon in Indiana, Mark, who had interrupted his work at the council to fly home two days before, issued an official statement to every priest of the archdiocese that Al Kremer was taking an indefinite medical leave of absence. Monsignor Patrick Duffy, a seventy-nine-year-old retired priest, was assigned administrator of St. Thomas More parish.

CHAPTER 48

S EVERAL DAYS AFTER MARK'S return to Rome in early November 1962, for the final weeks of the first session of the council, Justin saw him in the open hallway outside the aula, the Council chamber, where a committee just adjourned its work for the morning. The tall windows in the yellow and white marbled hallway cast a thin noontime rectangle of late autumn light across the faces of the prelates and their periti walking in cross directions, hurrying to make phone calls or arrange their luncheons.

"Good afternoon, your Excellency," Justin said, standing with his hands in his cassock pockets.

"You happy?" Mark looked drawn, tense, and defeated.

"I have no desire to hurt you."

The massive bells of St. Peter's rang the Angelus, and, as if echoed, bells from the dozens of churches in a several mile radius did the same, creating a euphonious aura to the moment.

"Then why did you keep pushing me?" His rage from their encounter outside his hotel room had not subsided.

The broad salon quickly thinned of people as the two moved near the wall, out of the bright sunshine.

"You know what this means for his parish and for the college. It will take years to get back on course. Those buildings will probably never be built."

Justin felt lectured.

"And what of the boys he's hurt? How long will it take for them to get their lives back on course?" Justin calmed as he spoke to the now ruffled archbishop. The Angelus bells finished clanging, trailing off in echoes.

"They're just kids. They'll bounce back. You don't understand kids, do you? You were an only child in a pampered home with doting women." His voice rose, his color rising to a deep pink. "You never had to tough things out. These kids are more resilient than you're giving them credit for, reverend vicar general."

"No, they are not."

Now Mark's furrowed eyebrows reflected his fury. "You don't know what you're talking about. Don't worry your fragile mind about the boys. Just drop the whole issue, will you? You got what you wanted. The pope got what he wanted. Kremer's gone. Move on, little man."

Justin felt his indignation build, but he remained determined to appear calm. Part of him wanted so much at that moment to assail the smug superior with sharp words.

"I think the rest of the pope's message was to report all this to the legal authorities and to care for the children abused. That means, in my mind, making sure we don't have another Patrick Gardner. Remember that resilient boy?"

With "resilient boy" he felt his angry side slip out.

Three African bishops walked past them, absorbed in their own conversation in Swahili.

"He had mental problems. Don't blame that on Kremer."

"I wouldn't be so sure about that, if I were you."

"Why don't you just focus on your work for the pope and Moinet. Leave the governing of my archdiocese to me, will you? And if you talk with your buddy Freddy Klein tell him to mind his own business. He jumps ship and then throws a hand grenade on board as he swims away. Shows a lot of class."

Mark turned on his heels from Justin, the gold chain clicking against his filigree pectoral cross. From under his cassock sleeves his gold cufflinks on his white-starched dress shirt glistened as he passed through the sun spots. The ornate corridor had emptied, except for Justin who watched his superior disappear into a side hallway.

Justin and Mark, aside from cordial greetings while passing in the presence of others, had no further words the rest of the first session of the Council, which ended the first week of December.

∵

Home for Christmas in 1962, Justin planned to rest and catch up with Tom and Fred. The gray, wet December Hoosier sky reminded him of winters as a child when he awoke before the break of day to carry buckets of coal chunks from the shed to fill the parlor stove. The women who cared for him showered smiles of approval when he lifted the lid of the appropriately named "Warm Morning" black steel cylindrical container and carefully tipped the coal into its raging fire. Curiously, this memory, connected with the drab sky, left him with a sense of being secure and loved. Life was orderly and limited then, before his departure for Presentation Seminary. He never wanted to lose that memory of serenity.

The estrangement with Mark upset him, but he was at a loss to know how to repair the breach. He prayed God would soften Mark's heart. Justin wanted to be ready to reconcile when his boss was ready.

∵

"It's rumored he went some place in New Mexico that works with priests with sex problems. Probably be back at Tom More by summer," Tom Gentry said.

The two priests were in Tom's office at St. Peter's Hill rectory, the same office used by Justin years before. Justin arrived in mid-morning. The desk's surface hid under a pile of unopened mail, old newspapers, and two ash trays with mounds of butts surrounded with empty beer bottles.

"It doesn't work that way." From his own years of therapy Justin knew any deep psychological change would take time. He questioned whether the deviant attraction to boys was curable. Justin sat across the desk from the obese priest and noticed a half dozen or so books on the mostly empty shelves behind him.

"I don't know anything about it. I just know Fred called after we got O'Connell's letter a few weeks ago and we're glad Al's gone. How'd you ever get the boss to pull him?"

"God works through men like you and Fred. You two are here on the ground, living with the mess Kremer caused. And you've both paid for taking action."

Justin's thoughts wandered back to the days and nights he had spent in this room exploring obscure texts of the early Christian Fathers with relish. Ambrose, Augustine, Eusebius, Basil the Great, Tertullian, John Chrysostom, and his patron Justin the Martyr.

"Not taking any credit yourself?" Tom brought him back.

The parlor clocked chimed ten times.

"Yeah, we all worked together. But the work you and Fred did was essential. You both took chances and were bold." Justin's body relaxed in the upholstered chair and added, "We do have friends in high places, remember?" Unlike the last time they met, this conversation with Tom was free of tension. A frightening, destructive storm had passed.

"Thanks," Tom said. "And look where it landed us. So, really, you can level with me. We've all been bruised by this mess. I don't think this is the end of things. The kids are messed up in ways we don't know. God, think of Patrick. What a wasted life. And I bet you there are more Patricks hiding, alone and ready to break, and more Kremers doing dark deeds in our quiet rectories."

"Maybe." Justin sensed Tom to be passionate about an issue that Justin felt would unfold well, even if he didn't know the specifics about how it would all happen. Perhaps a little of the trust in Providence of the serene pontiff had rubbed off. "But we can't fix something we don't know about. Probably the best we can do is stay alert."

"You don't have to worry about me. I connect well with kids. If something's happening here, I think I'd know it."

"And let O'Connell know?" Justin leaned toward Tom.

"Well, no, not by myself. I'd tell you first because I trust you. The big guy, well, let's just say I'd let you be my buffer."

Tom grinned at Justin. His cheeks were like twin softballs. His eyes bloodshot. He seemed to have swelled even more since Justin saw him in October.

"I don't want to know about it. But I'll do what I need to do if you report something. I'll act. No. I should say we'll act together."

Justin left St. Peter's Hill knowing his alliance with Tom was solid, but he was concerned for his colleague's physical and mental health.

∵

The next day in the city Justin lunched with Fred at the Tee Pee. Gentle snow fell over the parking lot as he got out of his rented cream-colored Fairlane 500. Fred waved through the diner's partially steamed window.

Settled at a booth, Fred, whose face seemed tight with gray tones, did not hesitate to speak of his bitterness.

"It's sick. You can't tell me Kremer won't do it again. The guy's nuts and he's going to screw more boys. Guaranteed. O'Connell wants the construction on the college building to start this year, and Kremer's the only one who can make that happen. Same with the Tom More addition."

The men paused as a small-boned woman in her fifties, with a brief light pink apron over a calf-length white dress asked for their orders. She wore an oval Miraculous Medal on a silver chain that divided her small breasts. With a jerk she removed a sharp yellow pencil from the wedge between her ear and a tight line of graying hair. Nudged close to the table, she stood ready to jot on the pale green pad. Her plastic name tag pinned to her wide lapel said "Belva." She didn't offer Justin, in his Roman collar and black suit, any special courtesies.

Once she retreated to the kitchen, Fred said, "I think O'Connell finally got the message. He doesn't want any of this to interfere with getting a red hat." He adjusted the wide paper napkin in his lap.

"We don't know all the motives. But Kremer's gone and the kids are safer." Justin felt a wave of unease wash over him listening to Fred's cynicism. In a red plaid cotton shirt and beige slacks, Fred's baby face had lined.

Justin tried to steer the conversation. "And how's school?"

"I love school. Physics is where I want to be. I'm through with all the crap at the chancery. Got a fellowship to finish my doctorate. The whole church stinks. I want no more of it."

So much for guiding the topic away from Fred's bitterness. Justin switched tactics and decided to engage him with directness. "So, you won't reconsider?" As soon as the words left his mouth, Justin knew his timing was off.

"Why? Didn't you hear me? O'Connell is out for a red hat. He doesn't care about anything else. My staying in the priesthood means I'm just another one of his puppets. The entire church is a mess, based on selfish interests of the hierarchy. More power, more prestige, more money."

Belva brought coffee in white porcelain cups and saucers with tiny matching cruets of cream. The round beige paper tops on the cream read "Hoosier Dairy," framed by a map of Indiana.

"I can't deny what you're saying. But what isn't a mess? You think university life's pure? Government? Business? It's just life. Messy, ugly at times. But also good and beautiful. This council is going to change everything for the better; I know it. And there's hope that policies about priests abusing kids will be written. We'll never be perfect. But better. If you leave, your talents can't help with the reforms we need, don't you see? You were brave to do what you did with those parents and the archbishop. Brave. Without you and Tom we could have a lot more boys hanging themselves."

Fred stirred the cream into his coffee and kept his head down. A family with five boys, from early teens down to a toddler, scooted into the large booth next to the priests.

"I'm asking you to reconsider. Don't you understand? You're the kind of guy we need right now. You've got guts to do the right thing."

Fred didn't look up as he slurped his hot drink.

In another plea, Justin said, "Pray over it. Get professional help if you need it. God started something good in you when you were ordained. God'll give you what you need to be a good priest."

Suddenly Justin reminded himself of the first time he sat with Father Hugo Peters: the priest probably made profound comments, but they washed over Justin with no effect. He wondered if his words flowed over Fred in a similar way.

So Justin shut up.

After several moments of silence, Fred said, "Sounds dandy. But I think I'm too far gone. I don't think I can go back and face all that."

They ate the meal while talking of the weather, Indiana's Governor Matt Welsh's tax hike, and Fred's plans to spend the holiday with his parents in Terre Haute.

Justin left the restaurant feeling hollow. He knew Fred was a good man, capable of being an excellent priest, but he feared Fred had shut out the Spirit, leaving him to sort his own way in the world with a weakened faith. And faith is what Justin relied on to carry him through his torturous dark days and nights. Its power sustained him in therapy, transformed him from being a reclusive, passive, childlike man into a determined, yet still at times frightened, focused man. Therapy alone didn't do this. Therapy, he realized, was the means God used to lift him over the chasm of fear and despair. Grace building on nature, Aquinas said. He longed to get through to Fred the primacy of faith but felt powerless to make it happen.

Walking from the diner, Justin noticed *Time* magazine on the table of a man eating a bowl of chili. The pope's picture on the cover carried the label, "Man of the Year."

CHAPTER 49

A S 1963 BEGAN, RUMORS swirled within the Vatican of Mark
O'Connell's appointment to the College of Cardinals. But dozens of bishops and archbishops across the globe awoke each morning to see a cardinal in their shaving mirrors. Because Mark was respected by the Secretary of State, Cardinal Calabrese, who had assured his elevation to the episcopacy four years earlier, and because Mark had performed well at the first session of the council, acting as a mediator for the first approved document on reforming the liturgy, people gave him short odds to get a red hat, even though there were no vacancies at that moment.

He had widened his circle of contacts both in the Vatican Curia as well as among the American cardinals. When Justin was asked by council observers which diocese in the United States he claimed, he received envious responses. From an outsider's perspective, Justin's archbishop was the ideal.

A *Look* magazine correspondent, in a casual remark to Justin, said, "Archbishop O'Connell is balanced, genuinely pastoral, and a remarkable communicator. I anticipate he will shortly be a cardinal who will hold an important post."

Justin, in charity, offered no counter opinion.

By early spring, Mark juggled several responsibilities, his way of deftly campaigning for the hat. He found a new man in Indiana to shake money trees, hoping to top off the fundraising goals for the administration building at the college and the Tom More additions, and he made sure key men in Rome knew of the progress. He also worked to raise dollars for the St. John Vianney Shrine project, giving him more high marks with conservative Curia members. The archbishop's vision of a pilgrimage destination for priests throughout the world, honoring the humble French curate who died over a hundred years before, was about to be real. Placing the shrine in Indiana, whose Catholic beginnings traced to French missionaries in the early nineteenth century, promised to enhance the prestige of the Hoosier archdiocese and wouldn't tarnish its prelate's either.

In late March, back at the chancery, Mark wrote Justin that a child psychiatrist at the state medical center would provide services to any of Al Kremer's victims who sought help. The letter read in part:

> Not only will he assess each case, but he will make home visits to those in rural areas to give the therapy needed. He specializes in work with children who have been sexually abused and has written extensively in this field. The archdiocese will pay all expenses and will compensate any family whose victimized child may need special help in school or with medical needs.
>
> It is important to know, also, that the Indiana attorney general's office, at my request, is currently conducting an investigation into the allegations against Father Kremer.

Justin speculated the letter's content was intended more for the pope and his inner circle than Justin. He also presumed those higher-ups had received the exact letter. Regardless, the needs of the children were being addressed. The letter also gave Justin hope the archbishop's attitude toward him might be thawing.

An occasion to accelerate Mark's not-so-subtle lobbying effort intensified with a request from the secretary of state to meet after Easter on April 14 of that year to plan relief efforts to the Congo. Justin, curiously, received an invitation to the same meeting. He questioned the request because he had nothing to do with the secretary of state's office, focusing his attention and time instead on his research specialty.

But Mark's presence made sense. As chairman of the Catholic Relief Services, a position he discreetly maneuvered to obtain, he handed out money, food, and medical supplies to desperate dioceses in poor countries in South America, Africa, and Asia. CRS was set up in 1904 by America's bishops and the organization had a stellar reputation internationally. Now its chairman, Mark, was gathering multiple IOU's among the hierarchy in poor nations, whose Catholic populations were swelling. But Justin noticed Mark also seemed to honestly understand the necessity of emergency assistance in these places, including, perhaps, the newly independent African nation of the Congo, caught in a devastating civil war since 1960.

Walking into the cardinal's conference room in the Vatican, Justin eyed Mark, the first occasion to exchange more than casual greetings since the tense conversation nearly five months before. Justin received a cold stare and limp handshake. Mark had aged, his face sagging, hair thinning, and neck and girth puffed.

He sat in a cold silence across from Justin at the end of the long conference table, awaiting the entrance of the cardinal and his staff. The room's overhead lights added little to the natural light that beamed into the large chamber from the tall, wide windows on opposite sides of the room, open and screenless, letting in the cool spring Roman air. From his chair, Justin noticed a gray, white-spotted pigeon perched on the pale copper gutter high on the stone building next door, cocking its head as if ready to eavesdrop on the meeting about to get underway.

In a flash the octogenarian cardinal walked in with his small retinue, all dressed in floor length black cassocks and starched white Roman collars. The cardinal, of course, beamed in crimson. The two Indiana clerics, dressed in black suits, rose in respect.

Monsignor Carlo Santini, without introductions, began reading from a stack of papers, "The Congo was a colony of the Belgium government beginning in 1885. As African nations accelerated their struggles for independence in the mid-1950s, the Belgium Congo, as it was known, followed suit."

The pigeon must have found the introductory remarks unremarkable and flew away. Justin, ever the student, scribbled notes in his spiral notebook.

"In 1957, Belgium granted permission for local governing units to be established and hold elections for their posts. But the Congolese were not satisfied with these expanded liberties, nor the thirty-year plan for full freedom from colonial rule that had been proposed by the whites." Justin felt like he did sitting in a classroom with a boring professor back at Presentation Seminary. Monsignor Santini possessed a similar monotone and held a distanced facial expression with every word. He was a tall, bald, middle-aged Italian with deep olive complexion and a heavy shaven beard.

"Some of Congo's tribal leaders banded together and demanded full independence shortly after the 1957 Belgium scheme for local elections. Independence eventually was granted in an official handing over of power by the Belgium king in Stanleyville on June 14, 1960."

A cross breeze ruffled Justin's notebook and the large map of the country that another assistant had unrolled on the table a few feet from Mark and Justin. Justin stretched to help steady the map. Mark didn't move.

"Within months, the new nation's tribal factions were at odds and a three year civil war ensued. Cities and villages were destroyed and the infant nation's infrastructure left in shambles. The United Nations intervened with one of its first-ever peace-keeping forces to restore calm." The monsignor closed his folder and waited for the cardinal's move.

"As I have read reports of these conflicts in the Congo," the cardinal began, "I have feared the new country would be the place where the super powers, the United States and the Soviet Union, might stage a proxy war. Both nations have interests in this large nation rich with gold, diamonds, and other valuable minerals." The cardinal looked at the Hoosier clerics as he spoke. His face, round and ballooned from perhaps too much pasta and good wine through the years, spoke with benevolence and honesty. Justin kept waiting to figure out what role the secretary of state envisioned for him in this political crisis in a faraway land. He glanced at Mark, who focused on the cardinal with intense interest, like a school boy wanting to please his teacher.

"By early this year," Calabrese continued, "after the United Nations contained the rebellion of one of the breakaway provinces, the country's leaders asked me for emergency aid for the victims. Because, since the 1400s, the country was an active missionary land, the Catholic population represents half of the country's seventeen million people. Now I am eager to respond to the requests. That's where you two come in."

Justin still waited for all the pieces to come together. How did he become one of the "you two?"

"Yes, your Eminence, Catholic Relief Services can help. I understand the UN reports over a quarter million refugees and about 100,000 dead?" Mark seemed eager to impress with quick numbers.

Justin recalled regularly reading the *New York Times* headlines and seeing pictures of suffering Congolese children and women, murdered soldiers, and burning homes and businesses. The library at the Immaculate Conception received the daily *Times* a week late.

He also recalled reading details of the death of UN Secretary General Dag Hammarskjold in a mysterious plane crash while on a peace mission to the Congo a year and a half before. But his knowledge of the entire situation was cursory at best.

His mind strayed. The cardinal, who had close ties with the Kennedy family and perhaps top officials in the U.S. State Department, might have had a hand in the assignment of an American like Mark to lead the CRS several years before. Was the cardinal's unspoken agenda to have Mark (and himself?) serving American interests in winning the public opinion battles over the Soviets among Congolese tribal leaders?

"And so I want to have you both go to the Congo in late May or early June to meet with local church leaders and the government officials to coordinate our relief with them and the UN."

Justin was still confused about his place in all this. But before questioning the cardinal he waited to hear Mark.

After clearing his throat, the archbishop began. "Your Eminence, I am most pleased you have called on the American church to help in this important effort." He looked squarely at the cardinal. His demea-nor was sophisticated, smooth, and nearly regal. He went on to state he would be ready to fly to Africa when the cardinal thought the time opportune.

When he finished, Justin let several moments of silence pass before addressing Calabrese. He took a breath and asked, "Perhaps you might explain my role in this mission, since I am in Rome as the pope's peritus and not as a diplomat?" Justin looked up to see that the pigeon had returned. Maybe it was as eager as Justin for an answer.

The cardinal smiled and said, "The Holy Father and I see great potential in you and your archbishop. No, you are not a diplomat now, but God may have plans that exceed the work you are now doing for His Holiness."

Justin reacted with surprise that must have been evident to the two prelates at the table. He leaned back in his chair to collect himself, placing his palms on the polished wooden table and looking at his lap. He wanted no part of the hierarchy beyond his work with Father Moinet for the pope. Returning to the quiet life of a scholar in Indiana would suit him fine.

"So," the cardinal continued, "my staff will make the necessary arrangements for the trip. You both will need immunizations, which our medical staff will provide. Monsignor Santini will accompany you and will continue to brief you over the next few weeks."

CHAPTER 50

I T WAS A COOL April evening, the Thursday after Easter. Justin noticed on his way back to his quarters the streets around St. Peter's Square swelled with pilgrims. Honking and screeching as they wove in front of each other and spewing diesel and other noxious fumes from their behinds, cabs and buses jockeyed for positions to carry the tired, curious tourists to and from hotels, restaurants, and train stations. Several omnipresent Roman cats scurried behind overflowing garbage cans.

His apartment phone rang as he walked in.

"I'd like you to join me for supper tonight." The sound of Mark's voice startled Justin. Mark had been aloof toward Justin at the meeting just an hour before. But it was the first indication of a possible rapprochement. Justin agreed to dine with him.

Justin, in his prayerful moments, had reflected on the hatred he felt from Mark in the wake of the last major confrontation. But he also knew his superior to be capable of tenderness, recalling his brotherly concern while Justin was hospitalized in Cincinnati nearly five years before. Regardless, Justin wanted to reconcile if Mark indicated a desire to do so.

Justin lingered in his room during the interim between the phone call and the time to leave for the scheduled supper at eight thirty. He took the city bus to the Trastevere neighborhood. From the bus stop he walked, in deep reflection, the five blocks to the restaurant, appreciating Rome's sights and smells, its chaos, congestion, noise, amalgamation of rich history, contemporary style, and self-indulgent impulses all mixed with the highest of Catholic ideals in curious and mysterious ways. Truth, self-sacrifice, justice, hope, and faith mingled with whores, boozers, murderers, cheats, thieves, and assorted racketeers.

For St. Peter's Basilica to be planted in the middle of this pagan hedonism seemed as dramatic as the statement that Jesus Christ himself made in being born into our human cesspool. Somehow, with all our weakness and evil acts, we are, at our essence, something of God. And that something is the only thing that gives us hope.

Justin didn't know how much longer his work for the pope, who was rumored to be dying, would keep him here. Once Good Pope John passed on to God, Justin might not be needed by his successor. The comment by the cardinal at the end of the meeting confounded Justin and left his future vague. Now, walking the streets of the Eternal City, Justin felt impelled to appreciate the gift of living here at this time in history to play a small part in the crafting of the schemata on the church's relationship with Jewish people. And what a unique privilege, too, to know this special, holy pope, Yves Moinet, and Cardinal Calabrese, each men of great faith who had shown their love for Christ's church and lived to help guide her toward a new era of possibilities.

He also reflected on what he was about to do: dine with Mark in their first meeting since their rancorous encounter. Justin took no pleasure in taking his superior to task. But he felt a deep peace with his actions. Kremer was gone and professional help was enlisted for his multiple victims, and the authorities were investigating. His prayer was for Mark to set the disciplinary standards to deal with sick priests who sexually abuse children and, most importantly, to provide professional help to each victim. Legal responsibilities also need to be addressed. Was Kremer a felon? What did the law require about reporting sexual abuse of minors?

He felt new opportunities unfolding with this serious pastoral issue in his home archdiocese at the same time the amazing council's work on behalf of the universal church continued.

"I am pleased we could meet," Mark said after they placed their orders with a middle-aged waiter dressed in a tuxedo. Mark had chosen one of the most elite restaurants in the city. The price of one meal here could feed Giovanni for a month. The large crystal chandeliers, trimmed in gold, emitted a subtle, soft light that merged with the haze of cigarette smoke in the crowded room. A string quartet played Mozart in the far corner behind the archbishop, lifting the heavy moment with smooth, brisk melodies.

From the start Mark's tone and demeanor gave no hint of past tensions, a change from the limp handshake and cold silence in the cardinal's office. The shift confused Justin, who remained circumspect. He remained quiet and let Mark lead the conversation with comments on the Italian spring weather, the pilgrim crowds, and his concern for the health of the pope. As he continued his monologue, there was no reason for Justin to believe the meeting's intent was anything other than the repair of their fractured relationship.

Once the food arrived and the waiter paused to ensure all was satisfactory, Mark leaned across the table, with its embroidered white cloth, graced with ivory-colored china trimmed in gold, sterling silver utensils, and crystal wine and water glasses, and said to Justin, "You're looking well. Put on a few pounds and even sporting a spring Roman tan."

"The break from the council helps me catch up on a backlog of work. Not so stressful right now, but it'll gather steam as we head into the next session in the fall," Justin said. He offered nothing else until he gathered more clues from Mark.

The conversation remained superficial as they ate their expensive steaks and delicate pastas and salads. Justin estimated superficial was several shades better than hostile. Perhaps this was progress. By mid-meal the prelate had finished one bottle of Orvieto wine and had ordered a second. Justin eschewed the wine and the last course, the rich Italian cream puff.

With a cup of dense coffee in his hand, his dessert plate scraped clean, the archbishop turned serious. "I want to give you a heads up." He took a small sip of the drink. Justin braced for a new twist on some church gossip.

"You've impressed the pope and Calabrese. You're tough and honest and smart. You're no longer the wimp who sat on the knob back at St. Peter's Hill, lost in your books." His eyes held a suspicious shine, telling of the wine's influence.

Where was he going? Was this an introduction to a harsh rebuke? Justin's stomach, filled with heavy food, swished and sloshed.

"I received word today, in a meeting after we left the cardinal, they're looking at you as a replacement for me as archbishop."

The cardinal's hint earlier in the day was more substantial than Justin knew.

"What?"

"Calabrese says he has a place for me here. Wants me to head up the new Congregation for the Clergy to oversee guidelines for diocesan priestly life."

Justin forced himself to sit forward, to collect himself, to respond with politeness. "A red hat. Congratulations, your Eminence." He nodded his head and tucked in his lips in acknowledgement of his superior's victory, but his insides erupted with the implications for himself.

Mark smiled and took another sip of coffee then caught the eye of the waiter and asked for his favorite grappa. "We'll toast each other!"

When the liqueur arrived, Justin raised his minerale gasata and offered a toast to the soon-to-be cardinal. Mark responded with an acknowledgement of Justin's anticipated elevation to the episcopacy, clinking his tiny grappa glass against Justin's crystal water glass.

CHAPTER 51

THE CONGO, THE LARGEST country on the world's second largest continent, was highlighted in yellow, with the dark line of the equator running across its northern third. Monsignor Santini's second briefing proved as dry as the first. The same conference room windows were open again, but the pigeon wasn't around.

"The southern provinces were hit hardest," he said. He stood over the same map, rolled out across the long conference table, and used a rubber-pointed thin dowel to locate the areas of conflict. "We plan to land in Elizabethville's airport where we hope the diocese will eventually arrange for the trucks to unload the food and supplies to be distributed through each parish." He spoke as if the entire operation was to be carried out with the military precision and forethought of D-Day.

"And no one from the Vatican has been on the ground up to this point?" Mark asked.

"No. We want to work with our air and sea shipping contacts and our network of churches in the country once we are there."

Justin listened. As outlined, it seemed his role was to tag along, essentially to broaden his knowledge of the world and the operations of CRS. He wondered if he was being groomed not just to replace Mark as head of the archdiocese, but also head of CRS. The thought did not sit well with him. God was chuckling at Justin's plans for himself.

∴

Paolo Giovacchino invited Justin to learn bocce on a narrow sand court in the shaded well-worn piazza in front of the church familiar to Justin and his beggar friend. The Giovacchinos lived several streets beyond the piazza, making it a convenient meeting spot for Justin and Paolo. It was late April, the sun soft on the budding trees and spring grass surrounding the court.

"You'll learn quickly," Paolo said. He seemed eager to ease Justin's anxiety about the priest's limited athletic aptitude.

"I need coaching on form and strategy," Justin said, using a near scholarly frame of reference.

The sandy spot was well maintained by the local men who used the game to socialize on warm evenings, competing against each other in strategically landing a four-inch solid ball nearest to a target ball lying in the level sand pit. Paolo scheduled the lesson for Justin several hours prior to the neighborhood men's arrival in late afternoon.

In imitation of his Roman friend, Justin arched the ball in the air and it landed where he aimed. He tried to model the grace in Paolo's form, his legs positioned apart, his tossing arm straightened as he pulled the ball behind him, moved it underhand, and released it at a precise angle.

"Aha! You did it!" Paolo clapped and fisted the air at Justin's success on his first try.

Justin felt relief and a smidgen of smugness at placing the ball in a winning position; it was helping to distract him from the unofficial news of his episcopal appointment, the Congo mission, and what both presaged.

After several more practice runs, Paolo suggested a competitive round. Justin glanced at the bench behind Paolo and saw Giovanni, scooting on his tail to center his seating. He shoved his crutches under himself and grinned when his eyes met Justin's.

"Giovanni!" Justin shouted. He walked from the sand pit.

"Your burden has lifted?" His toothless smile warmed Justin. Several children ran and screamed in play beyond the beggar's bench.

"Yes, one seems to have lifted. Perhaps another is on the horizon."

"So, my prayers are working?"

"Prayers always work. Just not always the way we want."

A mother pushed a stroller past them, humming a lullaby. Giovanni caught sight of the young woman and raised his eyebrow in flirtatious approval.

Moving his eyes back to the priest, he said, "It will all be well. Don't worry, Father."

Justin nodded approval and said, "I'm about to win my first bocce game, can you pray for my victory?"

Giovanni laughed and said, "I'll pray you lose so you'll be toughened for the next cross you bear!" His toothless laugh seemed hyperbolic from booze.

Paolo beat Justin by a wide margin. Giovanni stayed at his seat and beamed approval until the old regulars moved onto the playing area and Paolo bid Justin farewell.

As he left, Justin walked to the one-legged beggar, shaking his hand in a transfer of several bills so Paolo would not notice.

∴

Before he began his walk back to his apartment building, Justin spent an hour in silence in the darkened church, trying to sort through the changes anticipated from the meetings with the two prelates. He knew enough from his years of therapy to be on guard when one of his superiors asked him to perform a certain "duty." Suspicion of their motives and designs to control him seemed integral to his psychological make-up now. He had wrestled with himself, his demons, and his past long enough to pay immediate attention when the signs erupted: insomnia, abdominal issues, and the pounding throbs across his forehead. He didn't want to be a bishop and he had zero attraction to anything close to administration. He was a simple pastor and a theologian. But, in cooperation with God's will, if the pope himself wanted Justin to abandon what he thought was his personal vocation, he knew he must consider it. The pope, and, yes, Cardinal Calabrese, were sincere, dedicated men. Unlike Mark, there was no reason to think they wanted Justin to do anything against his own conscience. His clear mind distinguished a resistant, occasionally manipulative, Mark O'Connell from the kindly pope and cardinal.

The sun had set and the only lights in the cavernous church were the red sanctuary lamp and the soft spot light above the large crucifix over an ornate altar at the back wall. The side door behind him opened, but he did not turn around. Feet shuffled closer to him. He looked to the aisle to watch a frail, bent woman in a tattered shawl, lace scarf, and floor-length brown dress pass him. She knelt at the communion rail, made the sign of the cross in slow motion, and bowed her head. He heard her whispers in Italian, but couldn't make out the words. Then she was silent for a long period.

He wondered what crosses she had born in her long life and speculated her faith had perhaps sustained her through World Wars, the Depression, and who knows what other personal heartaches.

Refocusing on himself, he reflected how God had worked in convoluted ways over the last five years to bring him to this juncture in his service to the church. Despite periods of worry and seeming failure, he had received the graces needed in every situation and to eventually see Kremer's abuses stopped.

If God wanted him to be the next archbishop in Indiana, then he'd be in a position to make sure no priest ever abused another child there. And, in another convoluted unfolding of events, Mark could do the same for the world-wide church as head of the office dealing with norms for all diocesan priests. God would give them both what they needed when they needed it. All would be well.

He walked to his Roman home in an unexpected gentle April rain, his sport shirt and cotton slacks dripping and clinging to his thin body. He laughed at the simple child-like experience of cocking back his head and drinking raindrops.

CHAPTER 52

THE PAPAL INNER CIRCLE said little about the pope's stomach cancer. His public appearances were infrequent since the first of the year. The impressive encyclical Pacem in Terris, on international peace, was released in early April to rave reviews, perhaps in response to what he experienced the previous October during the Cuban Missile Crisis working behind the scenes to avert the annihilation of humankind with nuclear weapons.

"We pray for his recovery," Mark had written to all parishes in his Easter letter. Justin, who received it in Rome ten days after it was read from every pulpit, and several days after the lavish meal with his archbishop, wondered what might happen if the pope died before making the final decisions on Mark's and his own anticipated appointments.

Regardless, the trip to Africa remained on schedule. During the balance of April and all of May, Justin caught up on his research for Father Moinet and got the required vaccinations in anticipation of the journey to the tropics. He also read several books on the history of the Congo and the newspaper and magazine reports dating back several years. This research, along with the verbal and written briefings by Santini, prepared him for what he may encounter in his meetings in Stanleyville.

The last week of May, Mark landed in Rome for his final preparations with Santini and the cardinal. After Mark spent a day getting over jet-lag, Justin agreed to meet him for lunch near the cardinal's office just outside the Vatican walls.

Justin had hope, after the elaborate supper they shared weeks before, that their relationship had begun to heal, but he would wait to size up the mood of his superior before letting down his guard in any way.

A major test of the possible reconciliation came with a letter to Justin from Tom Gentry on Mark's jet-lag day. Justin waited until he was in his apartment to read it, assuming it was a routine update on Tom's life.

May 23, 1963
Ascension Thursday

Dear Justin,

At the CYO convention last week two eighth grade boys from St. Procopius, my home parish as a boy, told me they'd been molested by their assistant pastor, Marvin Buckler. You may have remembered Marv from some of the lectures you gave the priests' assemblies when you were stationed here at St. Peter's Hill. I investigated, talking with each set of parents. They are at their wits end.

You and I agreed I'd tell you if any other kid is getting used sexually by one of our own. Sorry to give you this troubling news on the eve of your trip with the archbishop to Africa. Not sure the exact date of your departure. Had I not experienced the mess with the suicide of Patrick I may never have fully understood how damaging abuse is to kids. Maybe some quick action on this can happen before you both leave, at least to pull Marv from the parish until the whole thing is fully investigated. Hope so. The parents and boys are willing to meet you and the archbishop to give the facts. I doubt the boss trusts my word alone on this.

Marv sounds like a sick man. This has all gone on under the radar for several years according to the boys.

Look forward to your response. Have a safe trip.

Yours in Christ, Tom

Justin put the letter on his orderly desk and shoved his hands over his face. He knew Marvin Buckler from the priests' gatherings within the tight clerical circles. He seemed alert, friendly, and curious during Justin's lectures and discussions. He was in his early forties, the decade between Justin's age and Tom's. Polite, engaging, he was a skilled musician who had written a number of published church hymns and was in a position to craft the new liturgical music anticipated for the vernacular mass that was approved during the just-ended session of the council.

The tragic news raised the specter of many more priests in the archdiocese being sexual predators. And, beyond the archdiocese, how many more Basil Eppermans, Al Kremers, and Marvin Bucklers were there in other American dioceses or in places beyond the nation's borders?

That evening the Giovacchinos had Justin for a farewell supper before his trip.

Maria prepared handmade eggplant parmesan, one of Justin's favorites.

After the meal, Justin, Paolo, and Maria sat on the balcony, Paolo smoking a cigar, Maria knitting, and Justin finishing off a small bowl of lemon gelato.

"Excited about the trip?" Maria asked. Her eyes focused on her handiwork.

"It'll be educational." Justin licked the spoon's last taste of creamy dessert and smiled.

"I don't think I'd want to go to a country with so much trouble. I lived through the war here in Italy as a boy. It's not pretty," Paolo said.

"Most of the fighting seems to be finished," Justin said. "We're going to see what we can do to help the people with food and housing and the basics."

Children playing soccer in the street below erupted in shouts then calmed.

"We'll pray for your safety," Maria added. "And I'll pray for whatever else is bothering you today."

Justin lowered his eyebrows in confusion. "What do you mean?"

"A mother knows when her child is troubled. And I use this skill with you." She looked up and grinned at him.

A woman walked onto the balcony two apartments away and moved the cotton rope line along its pulley and began to take down dried clothes. She folded each item before she placed them in a wicker basket.

"How so?" Justin felt uneasy, suddenly wondering if his usual manner of concealing the tensions of his ecclesial life from the Giovacchinos may have all along failed with Maria.

"You seem like you have something on your mind. Off and on I have suspected there is a worry you have about church issues that you carry like a heavy sack of flour."

Paolo blew a line of smoke above himself and said, "I live with this, Father. Can't get away with anything."

"It's nice she notices us so closely."

"Whatever it is today, I'll say a prayer the Virgin will help you," Maria said. "My parents died in the war. We can't assume life will give us time to complete our plans. Death has her own schedule." She resumed her knitting.

"I need the prayers, but I'm not sure what you mean by completing our plans." He set the bowl on the tile floor next to his chair.

"I just know today is all I have. All my big plans and hopes for my family may never happen. Just look at what happened to Giuseppe on the bike."

"You are a wise woman." Justin smiled at her as she focused on the yarn and needle in her lap, which, loop by loop, took the shape of a sweater.

CHAPTER 53

A T THE CARDINAL'S OFFICE the next morning, before the final meeting with Mark and Monsignor Santini, Justin took a risk of having the positive tone of the trip disrupted by showing Mark Tom's letter.

Holding the thin aerogram in both hands the archbishop shook his head midway through the message.

"What a mess. This could disrupt everything," he said. His face was scarlet and his sky blue eyes squinted with anger.

After several minutes of thought, during which Justin stood in silence, Mark said, "We've got to contain this before we go. I'll wire Pat Duffy at Tom More and tell him to go to Procopius and let Marv know he must take a leave until I can fully investigate the matter after I get back from Africa. I'm not getting in knee deep this time. I'll end it now."

"Are you both ready to start?" The dull monsignor stood at the conference room door.

"Give us a minute," Mark said.

"Look, you wire Gentry and tell him we're on this. Does anyone else know?"

"I don't know who knows. But what difference does it make? If you're pulling Marvin immediately until you investigate, what more can be expected? I think the pope and his men would have to say you're being responsible," Justin said. He felt in some ways another person was saying this, as if a strong, decisive stranger occupied his body.

"Think so? Well, okay then, I won't worry about leaks."

"More important than leaks or the pope are the kids, remember them?"

"Don't get smart. Yeah, I'll have Duffy alert the child psychiatrist just for the record. When I get back, and if the allegations are true, I'll call the psychiatrist and get him connected with the parents and call our attorney to deal with the legal end."

The monsignor returned to the doorway and gave the two of them an impatient look.

"We'll discuss more later," Mark said to Justin. He smiled at the monsignor and walked into the conference room. Justin followed.

When the hour long meeting ended, Mark and Justin remained in the room and refined their plans to have Patrick Duffy and Tom Gentry deal with this new allegation.

Justin, in his compline prayer that night, felt grateful for what transpired that day. How far Mark had come. His quick action offered promise he could address this issue on an international scale in the post he was about to assume.

Justin sat before his open window looking into the Roman sky and whispered a prayer of gratitude. An owl in the distance hooted a soft hoot.

∴

The next day a letter arrived from Fred Klein. Seeing the return address, Justin anticipated news that Fred knew about Marvin. But Fred surprised him.

May 25, 1963
St. Gregory VII

Dear Justin,

Rumor mill has it you are moving back to be the new archbishop and O'Connell will get his red hat in Rome. This is a good news/bad news rumor. I like you as archbishop, but am not sure about O'Connell inside the Vatican. But if it is true you'll be the new archbishop, I may be reconsidering whether to return to the priesthood. It would be an honor to work with you as my superior. You are honest, brave and, I sense, a deeply spiritual man who only cares about doing what is right.

I know you probably cannot confirm these rumors now. But I just wanted you to know I hope the one about you is true.

Have a safe trip (Tom told me you are going to Africa with O'Connell for CRS).

Sincerely in Christ,
Fred

Justin felt perhaps the last conversation with Fred at the Tee Pee may have had a better result than he knew at the time. In all the confusion and twisted logic of the Kremer case, some good things may, in the long run, happen to benefit many.

∴

Nine days later, on June 3, 1963, Justin and Mark sat in the waiting area at the Rome airport hangar where the private planes were loaded.

Mark's plan to handle the crisis with Buckler was executed with precision. Marvin was moved to an all-adult apartment building downtown near the chancery and told not to be near any children until the archbishop had returned and a full investigation was complete. He was to report to Pat Duffy daily. The psychiatrist was notified and Tom given the duty of collecting testimonies from the new victims in preparation for their meeting with Mark upon his return.

"We've worked well on this," Mark said.

"And we've got a chance to root out other abusers if we can set up guidelines in the archdiocese."

"More than that."

"What more?"

"Did you forget where I'll be by year's end?"

The noise of a plane taking off interrupted their conversation.

"Yes, the Vatican."

"We have the pope on our side and I'll be directing the new office to lay out guidelines for all diocesan priests the world over."

"And?"

"Well, if this evil is as widespread in other diocese as we've seen just in our own, then I'll have to deal with it everywhere."

Justin felt a wave of peace fill him. Mark's comments could not have been more reassuring. Was this the same man who bludgeoned him each time Justin insisted Kremer be stopped? Was this the same man who told Justin to go to hell when threatened with losing his position of power in the hierarchy? Now, in a reflective tone, Mark O'Connell suggested universal standards to ensure sick priests never abuse children.

A small gathering of wealthy travelers—men in tailored suits and sleek Italian loafers, women in stylish dresses with well-coifed hair, stylish hats, bejeweled fingers and necks, and handcrafted leather purses—mingled in anticipation of the announcement of their private flights.

Once the two clergymen paused in conversation, Justin looked up to see a familiar face walk into the room. The sight of Dr. Goldberg sent a jar through his body. Part of him wanted his therapist not to notice him in his black suit and Roman collar in the small waiting area. Despite the years of work with him, despite the most intimate feelings, thoughts, and experiences of his life shared with him, despite the power of their relationship to confront Justin's deepest fears and longings, and despite the truth that this man transformed his entrenched fear into acts of defiance and courage, Justin wanted to hide from him.

Dr. Goldberg scanned the room for an empty seat, eyeing Justin immediately. Justin stood to greet him, part of him anticipating a verbal scolding for ending the therapy in defiance months before.

But the therapy never ended with that final shunning of all the Jewish therapist had suggested. It continued within Justin as his life unfolded with news from Tom of Larry Hall's abuse, the final push against Justin's dark side, leading to the real transformation of his deepest self.

"Nice to see you again." His voice held the same familiar warmth. His eyes connecting with Justin's and his handshake firm.

Justin introduced him to Mark, a man Dr. Goldberg had grown to know well without ever having a face-to-face encounter. The doctor gave no hint of his role in Justin's life. For all Mark knew, he was a Jewish friend who had collaborated with his vicar general in developing the material on Catholic-Jewish relations for the council.

To clear the air, more for his own benefit than to accommodate Dr. Goldberg, Justin said, "Things have gone as you suggested. All is well."

"I am happy for you. You are a good man."

The clerk announced a flight to Milan, and Dr. Goldberg waved the clerics goodbye.

Justin and Mark's private flight boarded next. They walked with Monsignor Santini across the tarmac and climbed the shaking, slim metal steps to enter the narrow door of the small six passenger plane.

·.·

The propeller engine aircraft carrying the pilot and the three person papal entourage on its mission of mercy was over the Sahara Desert of North Africa when Pope John XXIII took his last breath. The young Italian pilot, in radio contact with Rome, got the news of the death of "Good Pope John" an hour into the flight.

Shortly before midnight on that same day, June 3, 1963, the papal plane, caught in a severe tropical storm above the thick Congolese jungle, mysteriously lost power and crashed. According to press reports the sole survivor was Archbishop Mark O'Connell.

POSTSCRIPT

BEGINNING IN EARLY 2002, an explosion of reports of sexual abuse of children by Roman Catholic priests spanning decades erupted in the North American Catholic Church, spreading throughout Europe, South and Central America, Asia, and Australia, costing the church billions of dollars in settlements, destroying its credibility as the living body of Christ in the world, and, most tragically, revealing thousands of innocent victims.

ACKNOWLEDGMENTS

For her patience, constancy, and love, I wish to thank my wife, Debbie. Special appreciation goes to Wade Hall, Sena Jeter Naslund, Louella Bryant, Crystal Wilkinson, Rachel Harper, Roy Hoffman, Joseph E. Wayne, Jr., and Philomena Y. Wayne for giving me foundation. The remarkable editorial skills of Fleur-de-Lis Press managing editor Ellyn Lichvar guided the finishing of this novel; I owe her immeasurable gratitude. The wisdom, skill, care, and guidance of Julie Brickman, Philip F. Deaver, and Leslie Daniels were essential in shaping this work.

Note on the Author

Jim Wayne, a practicing psychotherapist, received his Master of Fine Arts in fiction at Spalding University's low-residency program. He lives with his wife, Debbie, in Louisville, Kentucky, in a district he represents in the Kentucky House of Representatives.

Fleur-de-Lis Press is named to celebrate the life

of Flora Lee Sims Jeter

(1901–1990)